THERESA VERBOORT
Illustrated by Amy Blumenstein Collen
A
Sapling
Grows

A Sapling Grows

THERESA VERBOORT

A SAPLING GROWS

Copyright © 2023 Theresa Verboort
Author Credits: Illustrated by Amy Blumenstein Collen

Book design by DesignWise Art

All rights reserved. No part of this book may be used or reproduced by any means, graphic, electronic, or mechanical, including photocopying, recording, taping or by any information storage retrieval system without the written permission of the author except in the case of brief quotations embodied in critical articles and reviews.

Certain characters in this work are based on historical figures, and certain events portrayed did take place. However, this is a work of fiction. All of the other characters, names, and events as well as all places, incidents, organizations, and dialogue in this novel are either the products of the author's imagination or are used fictitiously.

Books by Theresa Verboort may be ordered through booksellers or by contacting:

Theresa Verboort
www.theresavwrites.com

Because of the dynamic nature of the Internet, any web addresses or links contained in this book may have changed since publication and may no longer be valid. The views expressed in this work are solely those of the author and do not necessarily reflect the views of the publisher, and the publisher hereby disclaims any responsibility for them.

Any people or things depicted in stock imagery provided by iStock Photo or Pixabay, or resourced a research images for the depiction of illustrations are used for illustrative purposes only. Certain stock imagery ©iStock Photos / © Getty Images.

ISBN: 979-8-9885397-0-4 (sc)
ISBN: 979-8-9885397-1-1 (e)

*To my hard working parents
who raised six rambunctious kids
in difficult circumstances*

CONTENTS

1

—— CHAPTER ——

Leaving Home, 1984

I bulldoze my way to the top of the ridge and stop, breathing heavily and sweating through my sweatshirt in spite of the late September chill. Kali pulls up beside me and squats down to rest. At eleven years of age she's almost as strong as I am. I look back at the string of people following behind me. Paul, my boyfriend, is heading up the line, riding one of the mules, since his leg is still weak from being broken, with the sheriff and his forensics team following, leading three more mules.

We're heading in to the site where my parents and older brother are buried, and the bodies of our dear friend, Vietnam Don and our mortal enemy, Bryce, repose. The sheriff has received permission from the Forest Service to remove the bodies. We can't use any motorized vehicles in the wilderness, however, including helicopters, without approval from the top of the political chain, hence the mules.

After a brief rest, we head on down to the old "farm," where my family grew cannabis to pay for our supplies. Paul will stay there to help the sheriff and his men exhume our family's remains and take them all back out to be autopsied. I'm glad I won't be a part of that process.

The team will camp there overnight while Kali and I continue on to our cabin. We'll have to camp along the way but I'm anxious to get back to our animals that we had to leave behind.

Once we get to the clearing, I studiously avoid looking at the still figures of Bryce and Don. Kali can't resist heading over to "Wolf," Don's big, loyal black dog, who is still standing guard over Don's body, and has started a mourning howl at the sight of us. Paul hauls out some dog food that he's brought and feeds the poor creature, while Kali runs and refills his water can from the creek. I finally can't resist trying to comfort poor Wolf, and Kali and I both spend some time petting him and sweet-talking to him. I'm hoping he will let the workers remove Don's body without taking off someone's arm.

But Kali and I have to move on to our wilderness cabin. We rest a bit and have a bite to eat, while the men set up their campsite. We have our sleeping bags and supplies that we need for our journey. It's getting late, with only an hour or so of daylight to get us on our way, so we hoist the backpacks over our shoulders and prepare to leave.

Paul gives me a kiss and a warm hug, a worried frown on his face. "I'd really like to come with you. Are you sure you'll be all right?"

"We've managed to survive out here all these years. I think we can manage another couple of days. Besides, I have my shotgun, so I feel pretty safe."

"If I didn't have to return with the sheriff and his group I'd come with you anyway. I'll get the truck, meet you back here in a couple of days and help you herd the animals on out. Be careful. I love you, Judith."

I smile, give him another hug. "I love you too. We'll see you in three days."

With that, we trudge on to our destination.

Kali and I hike on into the wilderness, tired though we be. Kali is stoic, just placing one foot in front of the other. We clamber along the rocky path for an hour or so, until it levels off for a short distance. I'm watching the sky. The light is fading, so I look for a good place for us to bed down for the night. We find a small clearing, and I decide that we've gone as far as we can go. We lay out a tarp and, zipping our sleeping bags together, spread them out over it. I don't bother building a fire. Digging into our backpacks. I pull out jerky and protein bars and a couple of apples. We dine on those with water from our canteens. I try to keep up a running commentary on what we'll need to do when we get back to the cabin.

"First we'll have to feed and water the animals. And milk Mabel. Then we'll tackle the packing and decide what we need to take. We'll spend the night there and then leave bright and early the next morning." Silent Kali gives tired nods of her head. Finished with our repast, we step away from our campsite to relieve ourselves. Then, slipping off our shoes, we crawl into our sleeping bags, throwing our jackets over the top of us. I keep my shotgun close by my side. Together we (I) say a short prayer and Kali promptly falls asleep.

I lie there a while, thinking about the gun battle that left Don and Bryce both dead. Poor "Vietnam Don." We really had grown to love him, despite his rough ways. Memories of his gruff, practical assistance, as he nursed me back from my injuries from the bear attack, hurt my heart. And I know that Kali is mourning the loss of Pepper, our little black and white mutt who was our companion for so many years. I can't think about the last time I saw him, with his bloody injuries, without tears forming. Also, I'm not happy that they're going to dig up my parents' and brother's remains, but they have to do autopsies on them and I can't stop them. Plus, it's illegal to bury bodies in the National Forest.

My mind flashes back to that terrible night when Bryce and his gang gunned down our parents and David. I'll never be free of that scene. And Kali has never spoken a word since. As for Bryce, I feel only emptiness where hatred for my family's killer once obsessed my mind. I'm glad he's dead. I know it's not Christian, but I can't help how I feel. But there's no satisfaction in it. Soon, exhaustion takes over, and the next thing I know, it's morning.

The next day, leaving at dawn, it takes us about eight more hours to reach the cabin in late afternoon. We pause, and, looking down from the top of the hill, I realize how small the area actually is and how beautiful. The meadow glows warmly in the late October mellow light, and the pond in the center reflects the sky. The clearing is ringed by brush and conifers, interspersed here and there by a bright yellow patch of a big leaf maple and the brilliant orange/red of the vine maple. I can barely make out our cabin, hidden in the trees. The moss-covered roof provides good camouflage.

There's a cold chill in the air, and I shiver in my jacket.

Kali turns impatiently and gestures down the hill. She's anxious to see our animals. I'm anxious too, as they've never been left behind for so long. We start down towards the cabin at a trot.

Now it's time to get to work, and take leave of our wilderness home. Once we're packed we'll hike out with the animals to join Paul after he brings a truck in to the trailhead.

First things first. We drop our backpacks on the porch and head up to the cave to tend the goats and other animals. The goats are bleating piteously as we approach, and the dogs are barking wildly. As we open the pen, Sandy, Paul's dog, and our faithful guard dog, Fret, leap out, jumping at us and licking our faces, barking and crying for our attention. It takes us all of ten or fifteen minutes to calm them down. Kali's ecstatic to see her pets, and runs from one to the other, hugging them. The cacophony of bleats and barks and whines is almost deafening for a while.

"Kali, let's feed them all and then I'll have to milk Mabel. She must be hurting. Then we'll check on the cabin and start packing, okay?"

She nods, and we fork hay into the goats' trough, checking on the water. They need a refill, so Kali runs to the cabin for a bucket, pumps it full, and brings it back, still running. I go into the storeroom and bring out some dried meat for the dogs, who attack it greedily.

I take the bucket and milk our one remaining nanny. There's not a lot of milk, and I figure her kid has been helping herself while we were gone. I give a generous portion of it to our five semi-feral cats. I'll have to figure out how to cage them to take them out with us. The Forest Service won't want us to leave them here. They're definitely not native to the wilderness.

We then check on our much-loved donkey, Amigo, who loudly brays his delight at the sight of Kali. Kali hugs him, and pets him, and throws him some hay from our meagre supply that we've foraged for the animals. Then she hauls another bucket of water from the pump for Amigo. The animals all fed and watered, we go on to the cabin.

It seems so strange to enter our mossy little home. It's almost disorienting after spending two nights at Paul's parents' house. It looks small and shabby and rough. Its logs have aged to a natural grey, blending in with the landscape. I realize how rustic it must look to a stranger. It feels cold and damp and deserted and smells musty when we enter. I decide to light the fire in the cookstove one last time. Soon the cheery flame is warming the chilled space.

I look around and try to think of all that we can take out, and what we must leave behind. This is the only home I've known since I was eight years old, when Mama and Daddy brought David and me, along with Gramma, to live in the wilderness. Now, here I am, starting a whole new life at twenty-one. As for Kali, she was born in this cabin.

I take a few moments to sit in Gramma's willow rocker that Dad made for her, and just rest. I remember the times she sat here, knitting or reading to us or cuddling Kali. It's so comforting. I wish I could take it with me. I think about our early days here, when we were all together, hiding out from the world. It was exciting to explore our wilderness, and learn how to hunt and fish and work together. Knowing that we weren't supposed to be living here in the wilderness gave it a delicious edge of danger. David and I loved it here and thrived, running wild. Mom and Dad and Gramma all seemed happy too. Dad's PTSD almost disappeared, and Gramma was in her element, foraging in the forest.

Abruptly, I shake my head free from reminiscing. We have much to do. Now we must leave, and can take only as much as we can carry. Kali is quiet, sitting on David's cot. I wish I knew what she was thinking.

I lean forward in the chair. "Well, Kali, what do you think we should take out with us? As many of our clothes as we can? That won't amount to much. We can't take the food we've stored away. We'll have to leave it here. Maybe we'll wanta come back for a visit, so it'll be nice to have. I'll take our family photo album, and Mamma's Bible, and I don't know what else. Maybe some of our books. What d'you want to keep?"

Kali shrugs. Then she hops up, runs into the bedroom and brings out her doll and the stuffed owl I made her. I smile. "That's a good start. Let's see how much we can get into Daddy's old duffel bag."

Together, we dig the duffel bag out from under the bed, and start sorting out what to take. I collect a gold locket that belonged to my mother from a little box in her dresser drawer. I open it and my eyes mist over at the tiny picture of her and Dad when they were first married. She was so beautiful, with long, black hair and dark brown eyes, and he looks so handsome, with his crew cut and hazel eyes. I got the oval shape of my face and cheek bones from my mother, but my hair and eye coloring from my father. Kali is darker, like mama. I will never stop missing them, and David and Gramma. I put the locket around my neck, and pick up the little photo album. There aren't many photos in it but they're all precious to me. They're snapshots of us all when we were young, and the only pictures of David and Gramma that I have. I put it in the bag.

As I rummage through the small dresser that was my mother's, I find a packet of papers. My and David's birth certificates and a few other business papers are in it. These also go with the album. I may need them later. There aren't many items of clothing that I need to take. I'm sure we'll be getting new stuff in the future, as soon as I find a job. I pack the buckskin vest and blue-checked cotton shirt that I made, and a couple of my mother's blouses, underwear, and two worn pairs of jeans. As I sort through the shelves that hold my clothes, I come across a stack of six notebooks that I had filled with my journaling long ago. I have to take those.

I add Kali's sparse wardrobe to that, including the buckskin tunic I made her, and the hats and mittens that Gramma made us, pajamas. Soon the duffel bag is nearly full. I look around. Just about everything, other than the dishes, cookware and stove, was handmade by my family. There are some of Kali's projects here too. There's the quilt she made, with a little help from me, to cover her cot. I have to take that. I decide to take a couple of her drawings and the last two workbooks she's finished. Her future schooling will need to continue from what she's already learned.

I'll have to dispose of all the food that can spoil, but there's not much of that. We'll have to take some with us to eat along the way. We'll be camping out at least one night.

I check through all the kitchen shelves to be sure I haven't missed anything that needs to be taken or thrown out. As I feel around on the very top shelf, I notice a small tea tin, wedged in behind a chunk of two by four that braced the shelf in the back corner. In all the years we'd lived there, I hadn't noticed it. But then, I just never got around to cleaning that top shelf. I pull it down and pry off the lid. There, in a neatly banded roll, is a stash of money. I had no idea that was there. But then, the two of us had no use for money out here all these years. It hadn't occurred to me to wonder where my parents might have put Dad's profits from the pot sales. I'm shocked as I count out $2500 in 50-dollar bills. I'm flooded with gratitude. Now I have a nest egg to help us begin our new life. I roll it back up and shove it down into the bottom of my back pack.

I sit down at the rustic table my father made and think a bit. "Kali, let's stoke up the stove and make a good dinner. There's a little flour left, so I'll mix up some biscuits. We can take what we don't eat with us in the morning. And I'll make a stew so we can have that to eat along the trail. We'll be ready to pack out tomorrow."

She nods, smiling, and we set about preparing the food. Kali runs out to the cave to get dried meat and mushrooms, and some canned greens that we had preserved. While the stew bubbles, we continue sorting through our belongings. We pile the things we're taking out on David's cot. I sort through the rain gear we have stored on the porch, decide we'll take our ponchos, in case it rains while we're traveling, and leave the rest—rain pants and coats and boots, in the house. The ground is damp but we can walk faster in our moccasins, minus the rain boots. I figure they'll just deteriorate if left out in the open. Maybe we'll need them again someday.

I look around our parent's room. It's a bare little space, and I think about the time Kali was born in this very bed, when I was ten. After our parents were murdered, we shared this room too. Again, I have to wipe the tears from my eyes and swallow the lump in my throat. There's no time for sentiment.

I go into Gramma's little lean-to room and look around. There isn't much here that I need to take. I pick up her family Bible, and a thick, gray cardigan she had knitted and cherished, just to have something of hers. I look through her shelves and her trunk, but she didn't have much. I find a small handwoven basket that holds her treasures—some bits of jewelry, hair combs, some shells and feathers. Also, there's a picture of my grandfather on the bedside table. I can't leave that behind. There's a thin sheaf of papers in the bottom of the trunk, beneath what's left of her clothes. It's tied with string, so it must have been something important. I decide to take that also, and look at it later.

We eat a good, hot meal, then pack the leftovers in lidded two-quart sized lard cans to reheat on the trail. We wash up the dishes for the last time. I want to leave the place clean. I wonder if the Forest Service will leave it as it is, or tear it down? Maybe they could use it for something. I know that if it's left to the elements it will eventually be taken over by the forest and its creatures.

One more check on the animals and we settle in for our last night here. After we wash up, we crawl into our parent's bed and fall immediately asleep.

In the morning, we're up at dawn and dress hastily. After a cold breakfast of what's left of the goat's milk from the night before, and peanut butter with hardtack that we'd brought with us, we wash our glasses, throw on our jackets, and are ready to roll.

I hustle out to milk the goat, and feed the cats and dogs again. Then I pause. Before we go, there's one more thing I have to do. I turn to Kali. "Do you want to come with me to say goodbye to Gramma?"

She nods, hangs her head, her face suddenly sad.

We trudge up the hill behind the house, the dogs trailing behind. The little cross looks forlorn and lonely as we approach. We both sit down under "our" tree, and just let the peace and loneliness sink in. Breathing in the familiar scent of the forest around us, I replay scenes of our remarkable Grandmother in my head; showing me how to pick mushrooms, how to recognize various plants and herbs and explaining their uses, the time we went out in the snow and slid down the hill over and over for Kali's amusement. I remember how she comforted us after our parents and David were killed, and kept us going through the long, bleak winter. She taught me so much. I miss her terribly. We sit for half an hour or so, with the cold and the damp chilling us. I feel desolate, as if her spirit isn't here anymore. She has moved on, as she wanted us to do. I stand up. Kali joins me at the grave. Holding her hand, I softly say our goodbyes. "We're going, now, Gramma. We will never forget you. We'll visit you when we can. We love you. Goodbye for now." Kali flutters her hand in a sad farewell, and we move on down the hill to our new life.

I put dried venison and fruit from the storeroom in our backpacks, along with a few eating utensils, and our fire starter, and tie our sleeping bags on top. Then Kali manages to gather the cats into an old wooden fruit box I found in the storeroom. They'll let Kali approach, while they shy away from me. Her special animal communication skills far exceed mine. Sometimes I wonder if she has some mysterious way of "mind-melding" with them. She gets down on all fours and looks them in the face, making mewling sounds, which she has added to her bird call repertoire. They let her pick them up. Once they're in the box, however, it's a different matter. It takes us half an hour or more, madly scrambling after the cats, laughing, shrieking, recapturing them, trapping them in the box, and finally, covering it with an old sheet, which we tie down tightly. I'm grateful that they'll let her handle them. They claw at the cracks between the slats and raise a rumpus, but finally quiet down. I'll have to tie the heavy box to Amigo's back somehow, along with the duffel bag. I pack three metal bowls to feed them and for watering the animals on our journey out.

I'm thinking, how will we water and feed the cats? If we let them out of the box they'll scatter into the woods. I return to the house and find an old sheet. All of them are old and starting to fall apart. I rip five long, narrow strips of cloth off of the sheet and fold up the rest. We'll use these to leash the cats when we get to our camping spot. Then we pile everything onto Amigo and the goats, using up all the rope we have left.

We shrug into our backpacks, slinging the ponchos over them in case we need them. Then I pick up the loaded shotgun, (all the extra shells are in my backpack and jacket pockets) and, closing the cabin door firmly, say a silent, tearful farewell to our little home. Will we be able to handle civilization after spending most of our lives here in the wild? A shiver of fear runs through me. This is the only world I've known for thirteen years. Will I be able to make it on the outside? I'll have to, for Kali's sake if not for my own. I'm not sure where Paul and I are headed. Maybe, eventually, marriage?

I lean my head against the door, and vow that we will come back someday and spend a night here. I don't know what Kali's feeling. She seems a little downcast, but she's still so young, so enthralled with our new world. She probably won't miss it. Life is an exciting new adventure to her. She makes an impatient jerk with her thumb, wanting to be on our way.

Slowly, we move out through the clearing and up the rocky path back to the outer world, careful not to trip on the slippery slope. At the top of the hill I pause and turn for one last look. Rays of the rising sun caress the valley. The peace and serenity of it fills my heart. I'll have to keep it there. Then we turn and move out at a steady pace.

Our little caravan, including us, the dogs, Fret and Sandy, one nanny and two yearlings and a kid, along with Amigo and the cats, manages to make it back to the "farm" site after ten hours of steady travel, with just a short break for lunch and a couple of brief rest stops. It's nearly dark when we get there.

2

CHAPTER

Kali Speaks

The clearing is in deep shadow when we arrive. It's a bittersweet "homecoming." This is where our parents and big brother were gunned down, that fatal fall night in 1979. But it's also where we had fun times camping and singing around the campfire. I loved exploring the woods around the area. And this is where we met Paul. And where we caught the killers. As we look around we can see the disturbed ground from which the officers exhumed our family's bodies. I feel a shiver of cold pain run through me at the sight. Where will I mourn them in the future? I'm glad it's done and they're gone. I didn't want to see that. They will have hauled them back to Gold Beach, along with Don's and Bryce's bodies. They also dug up the cannabis and, apparently, burned it. Good riddance! I can still smell the stench of it.

But the place has been cleared out. Leaves are drifting down over the site, renewing the earth of the place. In a year or two it'll all be grown over and no one will ever know what happened here.

I picture Don, our dear old friend, who shot the killer, Bryce. I was glad to see Bryce gone, but Don was a huge loss to Kali and me. He was our protector and friend, bringing us occasional supplies that made our lives easier. He was like family to us.

I find a packet hanging from a tree, containing a small pop-up tent that Paul has left us, along with some granola bars and bottled water, plus a note from him. It makes me smile. *Judith, I'll be back tomorrow with a truck at the trailhead. We're packing out the remains today. I'll get the truck and meet you on the trail. Get a good night's sleep and know that I'm thinking about you. I love you. Paul.*

We hustle to set up camp again. I'm uneasy staying here. I feel like this place is haunted, or at least filled with pain. But it's the best campsite on our way out, with the little creek running through and a wide, flat area for our tent. There's food for the animals too. I quickly milk Mabel, release the goats and Amigo to forage, and feed the dogs and the cats. This is a difficult procedure, as the cats are mad to get out of the box. They've been yowling off and on most of the way. We pull back one corner of the cover just far enough to let them out one at a time, and they scramble to get out. Kali captures them and holds them in the folded remains of the sheet that I brought while I rig a harness out of the strips that I had torn off of it, with the cat wriggling and fighting the whole way. Then I tie the other end of the strip to a nearby sapling, and we let the spitting cat go. We go through this procedure five times, until we have them all safely out of the box, and give them two bowls of the goat's milk, along with some of the dried venison, and a bowl of water.

The cats aren't happy about being confined, but I don't know what else to do. I wish I could have left them to forage for themselves, but knew we couldn't. The Forest Service is firmly against that sort of thing. Plus, cats don't live long in the wild, and they decimate the bird population. I'm more of a dog person, myself. I like cats but they're a nuisance at times. They seem sneaky and secretive to me.

But Kali loves all animals. She talks cat talk to them and pets them and calms them down, then leaves them a fresh bowl of water and a little more of our venison supply.

We heat up the can of stew over the campfire, and have a hot dinner. We give the leftovers to the dogs, along with some of our remaining dried meat. Paul should be here tomorrow, so I think we have enough food to last until he gets here.

We sit by the fire that Kali built in the firepit, to warm us and our food, and keep up our spirits. Finally, I set up the tent, placing the sleeping bags inside. Kali stays close by my side. There's been too much death here. The picture of my parents and David being murdered by those four thugs is forever seared in my brain. But knowing that the men who did it are either dead or in jail does ease the pain a little bit. And I no longer have to fear them.

Back by the fire, the night sounds are reassuring. The babble of the creek, the creaking of the tree branches rubbing together in the breeze, an occasional voice of an owl, are all normal "home" sounds to me. I talk to Kali about the good times our family had here, and try to help her remember the life we had before tragedy struck. "Remember when David whittled a horse for you, out of that piece of cedar? And when Daddy carried you on his shoulders to the swimming hole, and we all went swimming? And the time it snowed and we made snow angels?" I find myself softly singing one of the songs my mother taught us. Kali leans against me. I put my arm around her as I croon "Puff the Magic Dragon," and her eyes come to half-mast.

Soon, I can feel myself lagging, and douse the fire before we crawl into our sleeping bags. The silence of the forest closes in, as the dogs settle down with the goats and Amigo. It will be a cold night, but the tent is snug, and it doesn't take us long to drop off.

The next morning, I milk Mabel and feed the animals again. Three of the cats have chewed through their leashes and taken off. I am furious. Those cats have been nothing but a pain from the start, and I'd be tempted to leave them if it wasn't for Kali. However, after I put out the bowls of milk they come running out of the brush and lap it up. While they're feeding, Kali manages to capture them one by one and gets them, spitting and struggling, back into the box, where I have placed the last of the jerky. Having fed and watered the animals, I decide to pack up and head on out towards the trailhead to meet Paul. It's time to get out of here. We breakfast on granola bars and water, as we lead our menagerie out on the narrow, steep, rock-strewn game trail. After a couple of hours, the trail widens and becomes more packed dirt than rocks. The trampling of the sheriff's men has made it wider and easier to follow. That's a relief.

More hours go by and we're over halfway to the trailhead when we run into Paul. I'm so happy to see him, my pulse is racing. Judging from Kali's reaction, grinning ear to ear and waving her arms, she's happy too. Sandy, Paul's dog, dashes ahead and jumps up on him, whining and yapping, and demanding attention, which he lavishes on her with hugs and jabbering until he gets her calmed down. After that, it's my turn for a big hug and a kiss.

He grins down at me. "You just couldn't wait to see me, could you?" He gives Kali a hug too. "I'm so glad to see you two. I was worried that you might be bear meat. Or maybe I should have been worried about the bears." He turns serious. "It's good that you came to meet me. It'll save us time getting back. We have to leave off the animals, and the sheriff's department still has questions for us. They're doing autopsies on the remains now."

He sees the pained look on my face. He puts his arm around me. "I'm really sorry, Judith. I know it's painful for you, but they have to do the autopsies to gather evidence. And there's so much happening that needs our attention. And I know that Mom's anxious to get you girls settled."

"You're right. It's just hard to think about, that's all." I shake my head, straighten up. "Yes, we need to get going." I give him a quick kiss, ignoring my impulse to make it longer, and grab Amigo's rope. "Let's see if you can keep up." And I head on up the trail at full speed. Kali giggles and trots after me, with Paul trailing in the rear. His leg is still weak and he's using a walking stick so it isn't easy for him to keep up. I'm glad we shortened his hike by meeting him. The trail continues steeply, with boulders and brush on one side and sheer drop-off on the other. But we're used to this and Kali's like a mountain goat. She has no trouble keeping up, although Amigo brays his objections a couple of times. However, he's a good packer, and is sure footed on rough terrain.

We make it to the truck in just about four hours, with several rest stops. Somehow, Paul has procured a big farm truck, with a tailgate that lets down and a ramp so the animals can hop in. Once the animals and our bags are secured in the back we're on our way.

Paul explains that he has arranged for a local goat farmer living outside of town to take Amigo and our goats and Fret, who would not be happy in town. He's a herd dog and needs to stay with his herd. I explain this to Kali and try to reassure her that we'll visit the animals often. I'll miss them too. They've been our companions for so long, it's hard to think of not seeing them every day.

Kali shakes her head vigorously, signing emphatically that she wants to stay with the animals.

"Kali, it's not possible right now. Someday we'll have a place of our own and we'll be able to keep them. But now we're guests of Paul's parents, and can't impose on them. That's all there is to it."

Kali subsides into sullen silence.

We pull into the farmyard and Paul introduces me to the lady who runs the place with her husband. She looks to be about thirty, and her name is Cheryl. Slender and tall, she's wearing jeans and a sweatshirt with work boots, her brown hair tied back in a pony tail. I feel comfortable with her immediately. I tell her how grateful I am on behalf of our menagerie.

She smiles kindly. "I'm sure we can fit them into our herd here. They look healthy and I'll have the vet check them the next time he's out. We've known Paul most of our lives and we're happy to do him a favor. Your donkey'll be an added bonus as a guardian for the herd. And your dog, of course."

I thank her for that and we lead the goats and Amigo into the nearby fenced area. Fret follows them. They look right at home. I introduce Cheryl to each animal and she seems quite pleased to have them.

I'm shocked as Kali throws a full-blown tantrum when it's time to leave. She grabs Amigo and hangs on for dear life. Tears slide down her face and she howls, "Naah, naa, noo, no, no," at the top of her lungs. She is so startled that she stops abruptly. Paul and I are stunned and we both stare in astonishment. She spoke! I'm so happy that I burst into tears and grab her and hug her tightly, whirling her around and around.

"Oh Kali, you said a word. I can't believe it. You said a word. If you can say "no" you can say anything."

She stares at me and a big grin slowly crosses her face. "No! No, no, no, no," she shouts. She grabs on to Amigo again.

"Kali, we have to go. The animals'll be safe here and you can visit them whenever you want. They'll have friends to play with here. They'll love it and they'll be safe, you'll see. Paul's family doesn't have any place to keep'em. And you know that Fret'll take care of his herd. Really, they'll love it here."

She bows her head and glowers mutinously at the ground. Then she straightens up and, with tears streaming down her face, hugs each animal in turn, patting them lovingly.

Sheryl is observing this whole operation. She steps up and pats Kali's shoulder. "Kali, I promise you, your animals will be happy here. We'll take good care of'em and your goats'll have lots of friends. Your donkey too. And Fret'll be looking after'em also. You can come see'em whenever you want. Okay?"

Slowly, Kali nods her head and, letting go of our kid, whom we've named "Spider," after the spidery shaped black blotch on her forehead, she plods back to the truck. I thank Cheryl profusely, and get in the cab with Kali. I ask Paul to put Sandy into the cab with us, and Kali hugs her as we take off.

I put my arm around Kali and croon "No, no, no, no." I can see the trace of a smile on her face.

"No," she says. "No, no, no, no ..." Together we make a chorus of it and Paul joins in and we're all soon laughing.

The cats have to be left at an animal shelter, unfortunately. Kali's unhappy about that too, and hangs on to their crate for dear life. But we have to leave them. Paul's family already has a cat. Again, there are tears and "No-no-no-no." But I put my foot down firmly. We have to go. I promise to get her a cat as soon as we have our own place. Apparently, she's worn down, so, finally, she meekly gets back into the truck with us. But tears are streaming down her face. I chatter about all the things we're going to do and she gradually seems to cheer up a bit. When I mention that she can take a nice hot bath before bed, she perks up. She nods, wipes her face and hugs Sandy tightly to her for the rest of the ride.

3

— CHAPTER —

Where to Begin?

We end up back at Paul's parents' house with just Sandy in tow. Kali and I will miss our animals but, for now, this is the best solution.

The house is a low, rambling one-story log structure, resting on a hill outside of town, overlooking the Rogue River. Behind it we see a wall of forest, I think it's beautiful.

We haul our duffel bag and jackets and camping gear into our new home, amid lots of chatter and confusion. Paul's mother greets us with hugs, and flutters about, helping us haul our things.

She urges us to wash up and heads for the kitchen, where she's prepared a lovely dinner for us—spaghetti and meatballs. It's Kali's first experience with spaghetti and it's fun watching her figure out how to eat it. She loves it and ingests an enormous helping along with two slices of garlic bread and salad.

It's so strange to have someone fussing over us. I've always taken care of everything. It's kind of nice to just relax and let someone else do it, but I feel guilty. Kali and I jump up to help clear the table and do the dishes when we're done. However, Sharon has an automatic dishwasher, so the job is done quickly. She shows me how to load it and turn it on. I grin at her. "I can get used to this very easily."

She chuckles. "Yeah, it didn't take me any time at all."

Kali wanders into the living room and sits disconsolately by the window, her arms around Sandy. She's Kali's devoted companion when Paul's not around.

As we follow her in, Sharon looks at her moping there. "Why is Kali so sad?"

"She had to leave all her animal friends behind at the farm and the animal shelter," I tell her. "They've been her only friends all her life, besides me and Don. It's really hard on her."

"Well then, we have to do something. Why don't you and Paul take her back to the shelter tomorrow to get one or two of her cats? Maybe that would cheer her up."

"I'm afraid it would be a terrible nuisance. The cats are pretty feral, not housebroken at all. They're outdoor cats."

"Well, we have plenty of outdoors here. Why don't you bring two of 'em home and they can keep each other company outside and Kali can continue to have them in her life? They'll keep the mice at bay."

"That's really generous of you. Are you sure you won't mind?"

"Absolutely not. I want her to be happy. She's had enough trouble in her life."

I thank Sharon profusely and go to tell Kali. Her face lights up and she nods vigorously and hugs me. "Okay, Kali, we'll get them in the morning. But we can only bring home two, you understand?"

She vigorously nods her head in agreement, and happily heads to our room to unpack her things. I'm relieved for her. I really want her to be happy in our new life.

The next day we go to the shelter and she retrieves two females, a black one and a tiger stripe. It's expensive to get them back, as they've already been "fixed." At least we won't have to worry about what to do with kittens. I fork over $95 of our precious stash. It goes too fast, I'm afraid. What will I do when it's gone?

The cats are really wary but Kali finally coaxes them to calm down and go with her.

When we get back to the house, Kali opens the door and they shoot out like their tails are on fire.

"Well, Kali, you'll have your hands full until you can get'em used to living here," I tell her. *Good luck finding them*, I think.

She grins and sprints after them. Gradually, over time, she gets them used to the new surroundings and they let her feed them on the patio every morning. But she's the only one who can approach them. I'm just praying that a coyote or other predator doesn't get them. They don't like Sandy, so they steer clear of her, and Sharon's cat, Inky, pretty much stays inside.

We have a lot to get through in the next few months. But after a couple of weeks, I want to do something that we've never done before. We need to go to the beach and see the ocean. Paul takes us down there on Saturday, along with Sandy, and we're both completely enthralled. The vastness of the ocean, the roar of the surf, is mesmerizing and scary at the same time. Kali and I take off our shoes and feel the sand between our toes. It feels wonderful. Hand in hand, we run out into the water about calf deep. Suddenly I feel dizzy as the wave sucks out the sand under our toes. It's a disorienting feeling. Also, the water is freezing. We both squeal and quickly retreat back to the sand where Paul is standing, a big grin on his face. Meanwhile, Sandy is running up and down the beach, having a great time.

"Wanna go for a swim? No? That's what I figured. What do you think, ladies? Do you like the beach?"

"I love it." I turn to Kali. "What d'you think, Kali?"

She whirls and dances on the sand, with a huge smile on her face, nodding her head. "She loves it too," I tell Paul.

He chuckles. "I thought you would. How'd you like to build a sandcastle, Kali? I brought some buckets and shovels. This may be the last sunny day here until spring."

She nods vigorously, grinning ear to ear.

"You two go ahead," I say. "I'm gonna sit right here and watch the waves." I plop down on the sand and dig in my toes. The sun shines down on the long rollers as they make a dark blue line, then rear up, becoming a translucent jade green, before crashing into a long row of white foam. I am transfixed. The roar of the sea, the rhythm of the waves is hypnotic. I look up and down the beach. I only see two lone people, walking in the distance. I'm surprised that it's so deserted.

Paul and Kali get the shovels and buckets out of the truck. Together, they spend the afternoon building a huge sand castle. Sandy checks out what they're doing between spurts of running on the sand.

Finally, pushed into action by the cold breeze, I can't resist joining in. When we're done, we all gather around and admire it. It has a moat, and turrets, and a wall all around. I take Paul's hand. "It's grand, isn't it? Thanks for thinking of it. It's been fun for Kali and me. Shall we hike down the beach a bit?"

We walk down the beach as Kali collects stones and shells along the way. Paul takes my hand in his big, warm paw and it feels like home. I want to stop time for a while and just "be."

Paul leans over and asks, "So, Judith, how are you feeling? Are you happy to be back with the rest of the human race? Are you glad you came out of the Kalmiopsis?"

I lean my head on his shoulder. "I'm happy but often confused and scared. I have so much to learn, to get used to. Every day brings new experiences and challenges. I have to get used to traffic, and people, and learning a whole new way of life. But I love being with you and your family." I stop and look into his eyes. "I love you. But I don't want to be a burden on your family. I need to figure out how I fit into this world and how to take care of myself and Kali."

He puts his arms around me. "We can work it out together, Judith. I'm in this for the long haul. I promise to be with you every step of the way. We'll handle it one step at a time. And when you're ready, I want you to be my wife. But I won't pressure you about that."

My eyes tear up. "I'm so glad I have you. I want that too, I think. But I have to figure out who and what I am under my skin, and where I want to go from here." I reach around his neck and kiss him, and he kisses me back enthusiastically. We stand there a moment, arms around each other. He's the only man I've ever kissed, and I really enjoy the sensations it arouses in me. At the same time, I feel confused. Is this something special between Paul and me, or does it always feel this way with anyone? Finally, I realize I'm freezing. The cold ocean breeze has kicked up. The sun is low on the horizon.

"Thank you for bringing me to the sea at last. I love it. Let's grab a blanket from the car and watch the sun go down, then I probably should be helping your mother get dinner on the table. She's teaching me so much about cooking. And about what you like." I grin. "I think she's trying to train me to be your wife."

He chuckles. "That's fine with me. I'm looking forward to that. Let's sit on that log over there and watch the sunset, then we'll pack it in."

By the time we head back, Kali has her pockets bulging with shells and stones. As darkness descends, we head home to dinner, tired but happy to have seen the ocean at last.

Sharon takes us shopping the next Monday to acquire new wardrobes. "You girls need more clothes if you're going to fit in around here. And I *love* to shop."

Since there is almost nowhere to shop for clothes in Gold Beach, we drive seventy miles to Coos Bay. It's a beautiful drive up the coast, through the small town of Port Orford, then the hamlet of Langlois, then, Bandon, nestled along the mouth of the Coquille River, and on through forested hills, and I enjoy it very much. Kali is wide eyed all the way, her head turning back and forth as the scenery changes.

Coos Bay seems like a metropolis to me. There are all kinds of vehicles whizzing through, buildings everywhere. It's a hilly town, and busy. Once there, we start at JC Penney, downtown. I'm almost overwhelmed by so much merchandise in one place. There are shelves full of clothes of all colors and sizes, and racks of more clothes and every kind of apparel one could think of. My mind is whirling. Kali looks around with her jaw dropping, her eyes huge, and grabs my sleeve. She's shaking with excitement.

I don't know where to begin. But Sharon suggests that we start with the basics, underwear and socks, and move up from there. "Judith, you probably can use new bras, can't you? And panties? And Kali too. She could use a couple of "training" bras, don't you think?"

I'd never heard of "training bras." What are they supposed to train you to do? It hadn't occurred to me that Kali might need such a thing. But then I realize that she's starting to bud out into young womanhood. It startles me. I'm embarrassed that I hadn't noticed before. So, the next thing I know, we're trying on bras in the changing booth. Then we go on to panties, choosing comfortable, practical cotton ones. Having made those selections, we continue to socks, again picking out serviceable cotton ones.

From there, keeping in mind the cash I had found in the cupboard, Kali and I move on to jeans, swim suits, sweaters and blouses and a new dress each. Having explained to the clerk what we are doing, she becomes our ally, as excited as we are. Sharon and the clerk bring us items that they think are needed and Kali and I continue trying on everything.

"Oh, Judith, I think this windbreaker would be really useful for you, don't you? It's water proof and has a hood. It'll be good to have in the rainy months. And one for Kali too, I should imagine."

We try them on and decide that yes, we need those too. Our old ones are really worn out. I am so grateful to Sharon for her input. It's hard to remember when I actually spent money for anything. Not since I was about thirteen, I think, on one of our visits to town. Dad would give me some money to buy ice cream and gifts for Mamma, Gramma and Kali. I always loved that. I'd spend hours in the variety store, picking out just the right gifts for them. A lump forms in my throat at the memory, and I quickly concentrate on our purchases.

Sharon and Polly, the clerk, show us what women and girls our ages are wearing these days. Polly trots back and forth bringing us things to try on. She really gets into the process and starts making suggestions of her own.

"You'll find that young women are really liking this brand of jeans these days." And, "This blue sweater would look lovely on you."

Kali seems ecstatic over all our purchases and grins delightedly as she shows off each item. I let her pick what she likes. She falls in love with a red, ruffled polyester dress with a swingy skirt that looks adorable on her. She tries it on and hugs herself as she looks in the mirror and twirls. This we have to have. It's the first time she has ever had a chance to pick out her own clothes, ready-made at that. And we never wore skirts in the woods. Her girly side is really coming out. She's preening like a banty rooster. We find a pretty pair of Mary Janes to go with the dress, and dress socks. Kali trots back and forth in the new shoes, enjoying the sound of them clicking on the floor. I realize that Kali, at eleven, is really smart in forest and survival skills, and in taking care of herself, but is still a little girl in many ways. There are so many new experiences for her to absorb. I'll have to trust Sharon to help us both learn new ways of doing things and behaving.

Sharon has a great time helping us choose items that are both pretty and practical, shaking her head or nodding approval with each choice. I try on a pair of high heels with my dress. As I teeter around on the miserable things, I decide they're the worst fashion invention ever foisted upon women. I settle for a pretty pair of black slip-on shoes with a low wedge. That will have to do.

Sharon hovers. "You'll probably want these panty hose to wear with those shoes, Judith. They'll look lovely with that dress." So, I'm introduced to panty hose. I'll try them on when I get home. Kali and I both pick out a pair of tennis shoes for every day. I look at the ones with a racy rounded check mark on the side, but they're too expensive, so I settle for a cheaper pair instead.

My dress is a soft, form fitting, long sleeved, turquoise knit with a round neck and a narrow chain belt. Its simple style suits me and I haven't had anything this colorful in a long time. In fact, I can't remember the last time I wore a dress. I only buy what I think we will need to fit into society. I don't want us to look different from the other women and girls I see shopping in the store. I'm relieved that many of them are wearing jeans and tee shirts. I'm especially concerned that Kali be well dressed. She'll have enough trouble because of her mutism, although I am hopeful that she's made a breakthrough on that. However, I have to watch my spending. Our nest egg is rapidly being depleted. We climb back into the clothes we wore into the place. It will take us a while to adjust to wearing store-bought shoes, I'm afraid.

Sharon treats us to a wonderful lunch at a café in town. It's the first time Kali has eaten at a restaurant. And I can barely remember eating out once when I was a child. Exactly what is the procedure here? My nerves twanging, I hide my insecurity as we follow Sharon's lead and sit down in a booth. Kali's eyes grow big as she points to the many choices on the menu. Together, with Sharon's input, we decide on hamburgers and French fries and sodas. Kali's delighted with it all, smiling happily between bites, and gobbles it down with gusto. I discover that I love it too. The sweet soda tingles on my tongue, the ice cream creamy in contrast.

We take our haul home at the end of the day, dragging bag after bag into the house and collapsing on the sofa.

Sharon opts for the rocker and plops down. "This has been the most fun and exciting thing I've done in ages. I'm glad I left dinner in the crock pot. I'm worn out."

"Kali and I'll help you as soon as we catch our breath. I can't thank you enough for all your help, Sharon. We couldn't have done it without you."

After a few minutes of rest, Kali and I take our bags into our room and head for the kitchen.

Paul comes in from work and I feel a thrill of satisfaction at how well he's walking. At Sharon's urging, Paul went to a local doctor to have his leg checked. The doctor sent him to Coos Bay to see an orthopedist. The orthopedist said it looked pretty good, and was healing well, but he wanted him to see a therapist for the next couple of weeks to learn exercises to strengthen it. Consequently, he's been driving to Coos Bay twice a week, but seems to be walking much better now, and the cane is a thing of the past. I am really relieved that my "doctoring" of Paul's broken leg has worked out so well.

The image of him, helpless, in our cabin pops into my head when I think about it. It was a busy and crazy few weeks before he was on his feet, taking care of himself. I was so drawn to his long, muscular body and thought he was the handsomest man I'd ever seen. Of course, I didn't have many to compare him to. I loved caring for him. I know Kali enjoyed it too. We both fell in love with our patient. But I think Kali has accepted that Paul will be more of a "big brother" figure to her now and in the future.

Time flies by as we try to become accustomed to the world that has evolved while we were secluded in the wilderness. It gradually dawns on me how much I have to learn. There are new kinds of phones, (you just punch the numbers) that you can just pick up and carry with you, and machines that do various household chores—the vacuum cleaner, the electric mixer, the automatic washer and drier, the microwave, a big boxy affair that sits on the kitchen counter, and gas cooking range. I am very cautious around that stove. The way it "poofs" into fire with the turn of a knob startles me every time. Sharon shows me how to sort the laundry and set the washing machine. So much easier than the old washboard.

Besides all the new gadgets and machines we have to learn about, there are personal hygiene items. I'm thrilled with the new sanitary pads that are on the market. Then there are the hand lotions and creams that keep our skin soft. My hands are rough and calloused from our rugged life, as are Kali's. The lotion feels really good on them and they're starting to soften up. The first time Sharon introduces me to lipstick, I am astonished at the difference it makes as I look in the mirror. I like the feel of it on my lips. However, it wears off so quickly that I wonder if it's worth the bother. I rarely use it. But Sharon introduces me to lip balm, and I use it regularly, as it feels good on my lips and lasts longer.

And Kali, poor Kali, is learning about a whole new world. The little things delight her— peanut butter and jelly on sliced bread, for example. I had forgotten how much I liked them when I was a child.

Hot dogs, hamburgers, French fries, bananas, oranges—everyday things to most people, were all new discoveries for her.

Kali is enthralled with television. She watches it whenever she's free from her studies to do so. I find her watching "Sesame Street," as well as cartoons, and whatever comes up that appeals to her, such as "Wild Kingdom." Shortly after the "No" event, as I think of it, I walk in one day while she's watching Sesame Street. She turns to me and points at the screen. "Elmo," she says.

I gasp! "Say it again, Kali. Can you say any other characters? Kermit, or Miss Piggy, or Oscar?"

"Elmo, Oscar," she says. That's as far as she'll go, but it's enough to bolster my hopes for her. She also seems to have fallen in love with Mr. Rogers, and I encourage her to watch that. I try to monitor her, but I'm hoping she picks up more words from watching television, and learns more about how modern society works. One day, as I pass by our room, I hear her humming Mr. Rogers' theme song. Occasionally a word pops out with the tune. "Day ... would ... be mine ..." This is an exciting discovery for me. Perhaps she'll return to the world of voice through music. I make a mental note to myself to see that she gets music lessons in the future.

I'm fascinated by the TV myself, and am learning a lot from watching it. I remember TV from my childhood but it was in black and white. This one is in color. I'm studying the new fashions and hair styles. Some I like, some appear silly to me. Women seem to spend too many hours of their lives fussing with their hair, curling it and expanding it. And the makeup floors me. I am not interested in putting goop on my eyelashes and face. I figure people will just have to adjust to the real me.

I try to catch the news so I can see what's happening in the world. I learn that a movie star, Ronald Reagan, is the president. I thought that was strange. There's a program that features the popular music of the day, with dancers writhing around. The dancing looks formless to me but fun. Kali and I try imitating the moves and have a great time dancing around the living room. Some of the music I find grating and indecipherable. It just sounds like shouting against a background of loud racket with a driving beat. A group called "The Rolling Stones" is hard to understand, but we enjoy dancing to the beat. There's a singer who has long, beautiful legs and shows them off as she jumps and gyrates to "Proud Mary," which also makes me want to dance. And there's a skinny, boy who dances wildly in jerky movements and sometimes makes squeaking sounds while he sings. He also seems to fool with his crotch a lot. I wonder if he has an itch. Then, there's the young blond woman who dresses very skimpily and struts, dances and rolls around on the stage when she sings. It makes me wonder if this is how women these days want to be seen. Not my style. Will I ever be able to fit into this culture today? There are so many things I have never done. I've never been to a dance, or been to a ball game or a movie. In fact, until our Coos Bay adventure, I'd almost never eaten in a restaurant. It's overwhelming.

And then, there's the problem of the close proximity to Paul. He's staying at his parent's house too, while he recuperates. I find it hard to be so close to him. I feel my pulse jump when he comes in from work. He gives me that happy grin and asks what's new with me today. I tell him all about what I've discovered that day. I find myself wanting to be with him all the time. I love the way he looks at me with his slow grin, and his beautiful brown eyes crinkling. It makes me shiver inside.

However, I don't feel like I'm completely ready for a deep personal relationship yet. It makes me hold back. There are too many things I have to learn before I become comfortable in my own skin, let alone the intimacy of love. And I don't want to be dependent on anyone. I just don't know how to absorb all of these feelings. Fortunately, he's been going down to the Forest Service office and doing desk work for the time being, so he's out of the house for eight hours each day. He's patient with me and doesn't push me for more than I feel I can give.

I keep myself busy doing whatever household chores I can find, and even go out and chop wood for the fireplace occasionally. It feels good to be doing hard physical labor again and I actually enjoy it. It helps me relieve a lot of pent up energy. Then, before I know it, I've stacked up a huge pile of firewood, ready to go.

One day, while I'm dusting in the living room, Sharon comes in from the kitchen and catches me looking at a photo album from the book shelf. I'm enthralled. There are dozens of pictures of Paul. Paul as an adorable infant, Paul as an equally adorable toddler, Paul as a young boy, wearing his little league outfit, Paul as a teenager. He's obviously had most of his life caught on film. I glance up as Sharon looks over my shoulder at the pictures. "Sharon, what was Paul like, growing up?

Her eyes look dreamy, as she talks about her only child. "He was a beautiful baby, and the light of my life from the start. He was so smart, and quick. He was inquisitive and could get himself into trouble. Once, when he was about six or seven, I found him out in the shed, hammering boards together. It was a mess. I asked him what he was building, and he said, "A dog house for Rusty." Rusty was our dog at the time, and he thought he needed a better house. He had used some boards that Doug planned for something else, and sawed some of them in half. Doug was really upset, but I thought it was very creative.

"He was very athletic in school. Played football and baseball and basketball. And got pretty much straight A's. He ran around with his nerdy friends. They didn't date much. Instead, they went out in groups—beach parties, dances. All in all, he was a busy boy."

"I wish I had known him then."

"I think you'd have been friends."

"I think so too. It's fun to see him as a child. Kali and I don't have many pictures of our younger years."

"That's a shame. We'll have to start taking a lot of them now. Kali'll be grown up before you know it."

Sharon, a retired school teacher, is home schooling Kali. I show her what I've done in the past to communicate with Kali, and she learns some of our hand signals. But mostly she talks to Kali and is beginning to draw a few more words out of her—"book, add, subtract." She has ordered some standardized tests to find out what Kali's grade level should be. Kali surprises us all by coming out at fifth grade level. Sharon decides to work with her to help her complete the fifth-grade level so she can start sixth grade next year.

I'm really happy about that. I tell her, "I think that's a great idea and I'm so happy to have your help. I did my best to teach her from the study materials my parents purchased before they died. It wasn't easy, since she wouldn't speak. Did I mention that I heard her singing parts of Mr. Rogers' song in our room the other day?"

Sharon's eyes light up. "We could try singing sentences to her. We'll use simple tunes like "Old MacDonald" to ask her questions. Maybe that'll get her more accustomed to using language."

Kali laughs the first time we do it, but then joins in the game, singing simple, one-word replies. Sharon and I are both thrilled with our breakthrough. Kali's vocabulary is small but she's expanding it every day.

Sharon is a quilter. There are beautiful quilts on the beds and a couple of hangings on the walls. She uses a fancy electric machine. I'm hoping that someday she'll teach me how to use it. She's shown me how to thread it and make the needle go up and down with the knee pedal. Maybe I'll do some sewing in the future.

Meanwhile, Paul manages to take us a couple of times a week to see our animals. They're always happy to see us, and come running when Kali calls. She's always so excited to be with them, hugging, petting, running around the field. I vow to myself to someday have a place where we can keep them with us.

4

CHAPTER

Kali Makes a Friend

Bart and Gimpy, the remaining members of the group that killed our parents, were arraigned, told the charges against them, pleaded "not guilty," and held on $800,000 bail each. It's a huge relief to me, as I'm sure they can't come up with the amount they need to get out. Paul and I attend the arraignment proceedings, as do several rough looking men and women. They're all dressed in jeans and sweatshirts or tee-shirts. The three hulking men have beards and long, stringy hair. The four women are bulky and a couple of them have bleached yellow hair. There's one very old, shriveled, gray haired lady with thick granny glasses. She seems to be the leader of the pack. They glower at the judge and at me, giving me a strong feeling of foreboding.

As we're leaving, I see a man taking our picture from the side. Startled, I grab Paul's arm. "What's that guy doing? He took our picture."

"It's just a local photographer from the newspaper. He's harmless."

I duck my head until we're in the car. I don't want my picture taken by some stranger.

Paul and Kali and I will have to be witnesses at the trials of the men. I dread it but it will be a while before we have to go through that.

As I had promised Don, I look up his mother and brother to tell them what happened. Paul takes me to their home. They live in a modest ranch style house on the edge of town. Don's brother, Eric, looks like him, even without a beard. His mother is a sweet, white haired, tiny lady, wearing a flowered house dress and apron. She bustles about, bringing us coffee and cookies, her hands fluttering over the arrangements, before we settle down in the living room. They're very sad but, I think, in their hearts, they knew he would come to a sorry end, living on the run in the wilderness.

They want to know all about our friendship and whatever details I can give them about Don's life and death in the Kalmiopsis.

"Don helped us so much, bringing us supplies that we needed. He tended my wounds when the bear attacked me. He was a good friend. When the raiders who killed our parents kidnapped Kali, I went in to rescue her. I was just about ready to shoot Bryce, their leader, myself, when Don leapt out of the brush and did it for me. I know he did it to keep me from doing it, but Bryce managed to shoot Don before he fell." I pause, my eyes moist, I clear my throat. "Don was a hero. His last thoughts were of you. He asked me to tell you what happened. His last words were to, 'Tell my mother.'"

Eric looks stoically down at the floor, swipes his hand across his face, while his mother wipes her eyes and blows her nose. Finally, she tells me, "I'll always be proud of my son. I'm so happy that he had you and your sister to visit. I'm sure he enjoyed your company. He was always a caring man. If it hadn't of been for the war, he would of had a nice family and led a good life. Thank you for tellin' us about him."

Eric glances up and says gruffly, "Yeah, thanks for tellin' us. We'll see to it that he gets a honorable burial."

"I worry about his dog, Wolf. He was Don's full-time companion. He was never without him. Wolf was still by his side when we went back in to fetch Don's body. He's at the animal shelter in case you want to see him."

They look at each other. "Mom, I think we need to bring Wolf home. It'll be like havin' a piece of Don here, don't you think?"

Tears well up in her eyes. "Oh yes. We must rescue him. Don would have wanted us to."

It's a difficult meeting, and I feel relieved and drained when we leave. We will be invited to Don's funeral.

The following Sunday, Sharon invites us to go to church with them. I'm surprised and feel awkward. She emphasizes that we certainly are not obligated to go but are welcome if we wish. I finally decide that it will be good for Kali to mingle with other people. Maybe we'll meet someone her age for her to befriend.

I put on my new slip, and then take the panty hose out of the package. Hmmm. They're long and delicate looking. What's the best way to approach them? I check the package for directions. Not helpful. I sit on the bed and pull the "panty" part over my feet. Slowly, I drag them up around my knees. They stretch and stretch and, struggling, I try to pull the footed parts onto my feet. My big toes go right through the sheer fabric, sending runs all the way up to my knees. Frustrated, I yank them off and fire them across the room. *Who invented these things? I'll just wear my shoes without socks.* So, we put on our new shoes and new dresses (which get a whistle and appreciative comments from Paul), and go with the family.

I feel so awkward, as I follow Sharon's movements. They dip their hands in a dish of water at the entrance of the church and cross themselves. I mimic their movements, as does Kali. We all sit together in a pew. The last time I was at a church service was when I was eight, in Pastor Robert's garage. It feels strange to be around so many people. The church is pretty, with statues of Mary and Joseph in front on each side of an altar, and a cross with the Christ figure on it hanging over that. There are flowers in tall vases in front of the altar. Kali and I watch as the procedure unfolds.

A priest enters, preceded by a boy and a girl wearing white garments. He is dressed in beautiful robes. Interesting! This is so different from the services I remember in Pastor Roberts' garage. The service takes place in front of us and I watch with awe and interest, as does Kali.

There's an atmosphere of quiet reverence in the air. People stand up and kneel down or sit on some silent cue. Sometimes the priest says something and the congregation replies in unison. It's all calm and prayerful and there's occasional bursts of music led by a man with a guitar and his lady companion. There's a long sermon, followed by more prayers until, finally, everybody gets up and goes up to the front to take a wafer and drink some wine. Sharon whispers that we can stay where we are, or go up for a blessing, folding our arms across our chests to show that we aren't Catholic. We opt to stay put. After that, a few more prayers, announcements and a song, we're free to go.

We walk out with the others and soon Sharon is introducing us to the priest, who shakes our hands warmly, then to other people who are milling around. I'm delighted to see Cheryl and her husband, Aaron, there. We have a chat and Cheryl reassures Kali that the animals are doing well. Soon, they have to leave to tend to chores. Everyone seems friendly and welcoming. We meet a younger couple who have several children, Al and Gerry Holcomb. One of the children, Lucy, Sharon tells me, is Kali's age. Sharon introduces her to red haired, freckle faced Lucy, and whispers in Lucy's ear. Lucy's eyes grow big, and she smiles as she says hello to Kali. Kali looks at her wide eyed, and grabs my hand. I feel a mother/sister's anxiety as I pray that these two can be friends.

"Kali doesn't talk much, and she's shy," I explain. "But she's smart and a good listener. She may be in your class at school next year. I hope you'll be friends."

Lucy looks serious for a moment. Then, smiling, "I'd like to be your friend, Kali. Maybe we can play together sometime."

I feel my throat catch. Kali nods, shy as a mouse, half hiding behind me. I quickly chime in. "We'd love to have you come over to play some day. We'll give you a call next Saturday and maybe you can come over." I look at her mother, who has kind eyes. She smiles.

"I'm sure she'd like that. Call us any time, Judith. Sharon has our number. We'll arrange something."

I'm filled with gratitude. "We'll be sure to do that, thank you. Kali doesn't have any friends here yet and I'm sure she'd love it."

After a few more minutes of chatting, people start drifting to their cars and driving off. I feel very happy as we leave.

Over the next three or four weekends I realize how kind Lucy is for such a young girl. She learns quickly how to communicate with Kali, and I notice that Kali is starting to speak more words to her. They play together outside, running through the woods. I realize that Kali is actually learning how to play. She's never had a friend her age before. I'm thrilled and so delighted that Kali has made a friend.

They come in for lunch, giggling, hand in hand. Kali has introduced Lucy to her cats, and they've played hide and seek in the woods behind the house. Lucy is awed by Kali's ability to talk to the birds.

"Did you know that Kali can do bird calls? We sat in the brush and Kali called to the birds, and they practically landed on us. Kali even had one perch on her hand. I wish I could do that."

I smile at that. "If you had grown up in the forest I'll bet you could. Kali didn't have any other kids to talk to. So, she talked to the animals in her way. We're working on getting her to talk to people."

"Oh, I'd like that. Don't you want to talk to me, Kali?"

Kali nods her head. "Lucy. We t–talk."

A chill goes up the back of my neck. Excited, I chime in, "Way to go, Kali. You can do it. Lucy, thank you for encouraging her. She'll be chatting away when you both start sixth grade next year."

I feed them peanut butter and jam sandwiches and sliced apples and milk, and, after they watch some cartoons on TV, they run off outside again.

5

The Funeral

The process has taken six weeks, but we finally receive our family's cremains, in individual containers. When we actually have them in hand, I look at the pitiful little plastic containers sitting on the table and finally, the enormity of it all hits me. Tears run down my cheeks and I can't seem to get a hold of myself. It's as if an overloaded cloud of pain has burst and I simply sit there and weep. Copiously! This is what's left of my parents and David. Gone forever. Kali puts her arms around me and we cling to each other. Once again, I am gripped with fear for us both. Will I be able to adjust to our new life? Will I be able to make a living and get Kali the help she needs? I feel so overwhelmed by all that's happened to us, and the uncertain future. It's as if the crushing weight of our tragic events is suffocating me.

Gradually, I finally manage to regain control. Kali is weeping too so I have to get hold of myself. I must persevere for Kali's sake, if not my own.

I become aware of Paul's arms around us both, Sharon is hovering anxiously beside him, tears in her eyes, with Doug helplessly looking on, his own eyes glistening.

I wipe my face and blow my nose on the tissues Sharon has brought, and help Kali mop up her face. It begins to sink in that I'm not alone in all of this. Paul and Sharon and Douglas are all gathered around us. Paul takes my hand and Sharon sniffles, and hugs us both before she hustles into the kitchen to make a round of tea for the adults (milk for Kali).

Kali makes a face at the cow's milk. It tastes very different from the goat's milk she's used to. But she politely sips at it. I gratefully accept my tea, add sugar and milk, and the warmth of it soothes me, helps me focus.

Sharon sits across from me and takes my hand. "Judith, we want you to know that you're not alone anymore. We'll do whatever we can to help you find your way here. You're safe with us."

I nod, squeeze her hand. "You don't know how much that means to both of us. It's been years since we've had family around us. I'm so grateful."

We sit around the dining room table and make plans for our family's funeral. We could have a military funeral, and bury Dad free in a veteran's cemetery, but I refuse to do that. The military ruined my father's life. And I want to keep our family together. We will have a small memorial service at the town cemetery, and bury the three pots together in one grave. Sharon offers to make the arrangements, and to have the Baptist minister say a few words.

"I have some money," I say. "I have about nineteen hundred dollars left after our shopping spree. We can use it to pay for the burial plot and the minister."

Sharon and Douglas look at each other. Sharon takes my hand, her eyes full of concern. "I hate to have you use up your savings, Judith. Perhaps we could cover the costs and you can repay us when you're established and have some income?"

"Thank you so much. I appreciate all you've done for us, but I need to do this. My folks had that money stored away for the future, and I feel like I need to use it for them."

She pats my hand. "All right, Judith. I'll call the cemetery manager today and make the arrangements. Is there anything else we can do?"

"I can't think of anything. We don't have any family left, and they've been dead a long time. It's best to keep it simple. I really appreciate your help."

Sharon's eyes glisten, and I can see she is moved. "If you let us, we'll be your family for as long as you need us, won't we Doug?" She looks up at her husband.

"Um, sure!" he blusters hastily. "We enjoy having you girls here. You're going to be fine. We'll be eternally grateful to you for saving our son."

I feel tears gathering again, and, with great effort, swallow the emotional turmoil in my chest. "I … I feel so fortunate to have your help. All these years I was afraid to come out of the wilderness because I didn't know what I'd do. I had no one to turn to for help, and I was afraid Kali would be taken away from me. I really want you to know how thankful I am. And we'll try not to be a nuisance while we're here."

Sharon laughs and gives me a hug. "I'm not at all worried about that. You can stay as long as you need to. I really enjoy having girls in the house. And you've been so helpful with the housekeeping and all. It's nice to have female allies around too."

"I'm really indebted to you all. The world has changed so much since I was a little girl. I know I have a lot of catching up to do. It'll take time to get our new life together."

"We're happy to give you that time, Judith. Before you can plan for your future, you have an enormous number of new things to take in and I'm sure you'll want to finish your schooling too. Let's just take it one step at a time, one day at a time. We'll get you on your way to a new life, together, if you're willing."

And so, we find ourselves standing in the local cemetery on a cold, rainy October Friday, as the minister says a few prayers over the remains of our family. It's a short ceremony and the minister steps forward, shakes Sharon and Doug's hands. He turns to me, taking my hand and trying to give me some comforting words, which barely register. I thank him and he leaves.

The cemetery sits on a bare, grassy hillside, no landscaping. Bouquets of plastic flowers are scattered around on various graves. Shivering in the cold wind, I wrap my coat around me. I can see all the way down to the highway, and beyond that, the beach, and the rhythm of the waves washing in comforts me. It's a good place to rest forever. I don't cry. I've used up all my tears. Memories of my family flow through my mind. We stand around the gravesite for a while, and I notice a stranger off to the side taking pictures. I'm wondering if this is standard procedure for all funerals here. Paul sees him too, puts his arm around me, and glowers at the man until he turns and slouches off.

I bid farewell to our loved ones in my mind as I keep my arm around Kali. I picture Mamma, Daddy, and David each in my head, and release them to the universe. They will always be in my heart but I have to move on with my life.

There's a small, temporary marker to show who is buried there. We can't afford a headstone yet, but I vow to earn enough money to pay for one someday. After a few more minutes, we all return to the house together.

Kali and I remain close for the rest of the day and, leaving the others behind, go for a walk in the woods behind the house. There are walking paths hacked through the brush by Paul's family, as they own about fifteen acres. Once we're in the trees, Kali and I both relax and walk in companionable silence as we listen to the forest talk, and the occasional call of the birds. It brings us comfort and soothes our souls. We return to the house, and I'm feeling calm and accepting of our circumstances. Kali sets the table for dinner as I help Sharon in the kitchen. Paul gives me a hug before we sit down. "Are you okay, Judith?"

I nod and give him a smile. "Yes, I feel like my family is finally properly buried and at peace. It's been a good day."

The Saturday after that the doorbell rings while we're finishing our breakfast. Sharon, brows raised, looks at Doug. "Who could that be?"

"Well, I'll get it and find out," and he gets up and heads for the door.

We hear a brief conversation at the door before Doug comes back into the kitchen, a slight frown on his face. "Judith, there's a reporter here from the local paper. He wants to interview you."

My mind whirls. *Whatever do they want?* "Why me? D'you think I should talk to him?"

"That's up to you. He found out about you and Kali from the police reports and thinks it would make an interesting story." He grinned. "Who knows, you might become famous."

"I've no desire to be famous. I don't want to be some freak. I have way too much to do to bother with that. What do you think I should do?" I look at Sharon and Paul.

Finally, Paul reaches for my hand across the table and speaks up. "This is a small town. The story's bound to come out sooner or later. You may as well tell them your version of it so it doesn't get all twisted up and inflated into what it's not. You may be the subject of conversation for a while but then it'll blow over. Why don't you give it a try? I'll come with you. If you feel uncomfortable at any time, I'll boot'em out."

I let that sink in, waffling back and forth in my mind, then slowly stand up and head into the living room with Kali in tow and the others trailing after.

6

CHAPTER

Wild Girls

The reporter from the Gold Beach paper is a balding, portly, middle aged man wearing too tight gray sports jacket and black slacks, plaid shirt with clashing flowery tie, and thick, horn-rimmed glasses. He's accompanied by the camera man I recognize from the cemetery.

The reporter smiles broadly, revealing crooked yellow teeth, and holds out his hand. "Miss Johnson? I'm Dave Eland, from the *Curry County News.* This is our photographer, Jim Hogarth. I'd really love to get your story for our next edition. Do you mind if I ask you some questions?"

I hesitate. "I'm not sure why you want to do that, but I guess it'd be okay." I perch on the edge of the easy chair, while he sits on the couch. Paul and his parents hover nearby, while Kali leans against me. I put my arm around her.

"I read the police report on some of your exploits in the Kalmiopsis. I believe it'll be fascinating to our readers. Would you tell me how long you lived there and how you ended up there?"

I explain how my family went into the wilderness because of Pastor Roberts preaching about the "end times" coming. Our parents wanted to protect us and we lived there all those years undetected.

The cameraman clicks a few pictures of us all. I shift in my seat. "Does he have to do that?"

"I hope you don't mind if we publish a picture or two with your story. It makes it much more interesting to our readers."

"I'm not sure I want our picture in the papers. And you'll have to ask my friends how they feel about it."

He looks at them questioningly. "How about it, folks? Is it all right with you?"

They exchange glances and, finally, Paul says, "This is Judith and Kali's story. It's their decision."

Dave looks at me. "Okay?"

I think about it a moment. "I guess it will be all right."

"Great! So, how did it happen that you ended up living all alone so far from people?"

I explain that my father was growing *cannabis* for "medicinal" purposes, and that pot raiders killed my parents and brother. I described how Kali and I escaped and rejoined our grandmother at our cabin in the wilderness, where she finally passed away from a heart attack.

"How was it that you stayed there by yourselves for so long?"

I lean forward, resting my elbow on the arm of the chair. "We were used to living there, and we had no family on the outside. And I had to protect Kali." I didn't feel like explaining to him that I was afraid to leave because I had nowhere to go, and was afraid of the killers, and didn't know what would happen to us if we were found out.

He looks at Kali. "Would you like to add anything, young lady?"

I interrupt. "Kali doesn't speak to strangers."

He coughs, turns red. "Oh, I didn't mean ... um," pause. "Well, tell me, how was it that you ran into the infamous "Vietnam Don?" And he helped you?"

"Don was my father's friend, and he found us and helped us sustain our lives there. He took care of me when I was injured by a bear." I can feel myself welling up and, turning in my seat, cough to cover my emotions. Swallowing hard, I continue, "He brought us supplies and kept an eye on us. He was a wonderful friend and a hero. He killed Bryce in a firefight in the end, but Bryce shot him too. He deserves a hero's burial."

"So how did you manage to survive, all alone in the wilderness like that? And tell me about the bear injury."

I pause to think, again shifting in my seat. "We had our cabin, and raised vegetables and fruit and had our goats and chickens. So, we had eggs and milk and goat cheese. We foraged from the forests around us. There are many wild foods that my grandmother taught us to use. Also, I brought down game when I could for meat. We managed very well." I tighten my arm around Kali, who has been leaning against me quietly. "But it was a lonely life, and we only saw Don occasionally."

I went on to explain how the bear attacked us and how I shot it and was injured in the process. "The bear practically landed on top of me and managed to rake my arm as it fell. Don found us and rescued us, tending to my wounds and getting us back to our cabin."

"That's some story. Our readers'll eat it up. I understand that you may have been suspected of being the mysterious "Kalmiopsis Packrat." Do you care to comment on that?"

I clench my fist, squirm in my seat. They don't need to know how I scavenged off of backpackers and rafters, trading my wild foods for items we needed. Could I be arrested for stealing? Even though I considered it "trading?" I'm starting to perspire.

"I don't know what you're talking about."

"And how did you come into contact with the Ranger?"

I tell how we rescued Paul after he broke his leg while looking for pot growers in the Kalmiopsis. Also, that I can't reveal the details of how we rescued Kali from the kidnappers because the trial hasn't taken place yet. The reporter seems impressed. His eyebrows pop up.

"Wow. So, in the end, you all managed to rescue your sister and bring the suspects into custody. That's amazing! What are your plans for the future?'

"Ah, I hope to finish my education, and get a job and take care of Kali. That's all."

"What about marriage?"

I gulp. Of all the nerve! It's none of his business. "I don't have any plans at this time," I say as coldly as I can. He's gone too far. I stand up to let him know that I'm done. Kali senses my resistance and stands up with me, frowning at the man.

"Would you like to say anything else to our readers?"

I pause. "Only that we're trying to adjust to our new life. We need our peace and privacy for that."

"I appreciate that. You've had an extraordinary life and I'm sure our readers'll be fascinated by your story. Do you mind if we do a follow-up on your progress in the future?"

"I'll think about it. We really don't want a lot of attention."

He turns to Sharon and Paul. "How do you folks feel about what your guests have done? Will they be staying with you long?"

Sharon rears back, surprised and seems a little offended. "These girls are heroes. They saved our son's life, and they can stay here as long as they want. We love having them— and helping them adjust to their new lives."

Dave stands up. "Well, thank you all. I appreciate you taking the time to answer my questions. This is a great story and I'm sure our readers will love it."

I keep cool. "Thank you."

I have misgivings as the men leave. Was this a mistake? I hope not, for Kali's sake as well as my own.

The following week, Sharon brings in the paper and shows me the spread. There we are, Kali and me, on the front page. Big headlines— "Wild Girls Come out of the Woods." I am furious. I slam down the paper. "We aren't 'wild girls,' I almost shout. "That's terrible. What will people think of us? They'll assume we're freaks."

Sharon puts her hand on my shoulder. "I'm so sorry, Judith. That's a terrible headline. I'm going to call the paper and give'em a piece of my mind."

"What should I do? I don't want people thinking that we're weird or crazy or something. This is terrible."

"Read the rest of the article, dear, and you'll see that it's very complimentary. They told your story pretty much as you told it to them. I just think the headline was meant to get attention."

I take a deep breath and read the article. She was right. They told it straight. I calm down a bit. But I still am upset about the headline.

The day after the paper comes out, the *Coos Bay Argus* calls me. They want to come down for an interview too. I think about it. Maybe I could undo the damage the local paper has done by calling us "wild girls." So, I agree.

The Coos Bay newspaper story also ends up on the front page. Their headline reads, "Survivors Come Out of the Wilderness." Well, at least they didn't call us "wild."

I figure that will be the end of that. Boy, am I wrong. Two days later the doorbell rings and when I look out, there's a van parked out front and several people milling about. Puzzled, I open the door and am confronted by flashing cameras and a microphone stuck in my face. "Ms. Johnson, Channel KNOK from Eugene here. We were wondering if we could have an interview with you?"

I back into the house and slam the door. What in the world is going on?

Sharon and Kali come in to investigate the uproar. I'm backed against the door. "What's happening? I never saw anything like it."

Sharon peeks out of the window. "Oh my God! It's the TV news people. It looks like they want to interview you. It seems that you've become famous after all. What do you want to do, Judith? Should I ask 'em to leave?"

"Oh yes. Please. They scare me. I don't know if I want to be on TV."

Sharon steps outside. Soon she's back. "They say they just want a few minutes of your time to ask a few questions for the evening news broadcast. What do you think? Shall I still ask them to leave."

I look at Kali. "What d'you think, Kali? D'you want to be on the evening news on TV?"

She shrugs, then nods, smiling. I think about it. Will this be the end of it? It makes me so nervous. What will happen? On the other hand, I can't think of what it can hurt. Paul thought it would blow over in a few days. Maybe this'll be the end of it. Maybe our story could be a warning to others who might be concerned about "the end times." Finally, I reluctantly agree to a short interview.

Sharon lets the reporter and camera crew in. Before I know it, I'm sitting on the sofa with Kali, answering questions. They're pretty much the same questions that the previous reporter asked. I give a condensed version of our story and avoid questions that might jeopardize the coming trial. They ask Sharon about our relationship and how we happened to be there and she calmly tells them that we're friends and we'll be staying there for the time being.

Then, I stand up. "I'm afraid I have to go. Thank you for your interest, but I have nothing more to say."

"Thank you so much for your time, Ms. Johnson. We'll be in touch. I hope you like our report. Here's my card if you think of anything you need to ask me or want to comment on further."

I take the card, and Sharon ushers them out. She closes the door behind them. I ask, "What do you think, Sharon? Did I do the right thing?"

"We'll see when we watch the broadcast."

When we watch the evening news I'm apprehensive and excited. They finally get around to telling our story, and it's pretty straightforward. They had cut out a lot of what I said, and I think I look very uncomfortable and stiff. Kali's delighted to see herself on TV. She claps her hands and grins widely. I think she came across as very cute. All-in-all, I think it was fair. And there was nothing said about "wild girls." So, I figure that's that and it will all be over and forgotten.

Again, I am wrong.

$$7$$

CHAPTER

Fame

Three days after the TV broadcast, when I pick up the mail from the mailbox, I see an envelope addressed to me. Curious, I open it right then and there. It's a crude, misspelled message written in a childish scrawl. "Do not tok at triel. You will be sory!" A jolt goes through my body. Somebody's threatening me. Angry, I rip it up and stuff it in my jeans pocket. How dare they? Haven't we suffered enough? I decide to ignore it.

The next day I call the education department to find out what I need to do to get my GED. I'm told to come in to the office and they will give me forms to fill out, arrange to test me, and see how to proceed from there. Sharon drives me, with Kali in tow, down to the continuing education office in the administration building, and we walk in to take care of it.

The lady at the desk, Nora Peterson, we discover, looks up as we come in. She's wearing big gold rimmed glasses on her thin nose, and has her graying brown hair pulled back in a tight ponytail. Her bright green sweater adds color to the otherwise dull office. Her eyes widen, and she jumps up and extends her well-manicured hand. "You're the girl from the Kalmiopsis. I saw you on TV last night. It's a pleasure to meet you. You're a celebrity around here."

I am acutely uncomfortable and can feel my face flush as we shake hands over the top of her desk. Is this going to be happening a lot? "Um, it's nice to meet you."

"Well now, Ms. Johnson, let's see if we can help you get that GED and on with your life. I found your story fascinating and tragic. You were very brave to live through that as you did. My hat's off to you." She sits back down and looks at the papers I've handed her.

"I see you have no official schooling after third grade, is that right?"

"Yes, I was homeschooled by my parents for several years after that."

"Very well. We'll have to test you to see where you need further schooling and which credits you need to earn. We have to work through the community college in Coos Bay. Can you come back for the tests on Wednesday?"

I gulp as my pulse jumps. Am I ready for this? I look at Sharon. She nods. "Yes, I can."

"What time?"

"Testing is done from nine to four. After that, it will be a few days before we get back to you."

"Okay. I'll be here. Thanks."

"You're very welcome. And good luck. If you have any questions, please feel free to call me."

As we leave, Sharon decides we need some groceries and pulls into the Supermarket parking lot. As we walk into the store I notice people staring at us and whispering to each other. I feel like exhibit number one. I duck my head and concentrate on what we're doing. I haven't shopped in a supermarket since I was about twelve. I try to ignore the attention as we make our selections, and concentrate on discovering what's new in groceries. I notice a large number of prepared foods and cake mixes on the shelves. And the freezer cases have everything from fruit to vegetables to breads and meat, and frozen desserts. The cereal aisle has endless choices. It's sensory overload. Kali just stares and points excitedly at things that catch her attention. At the meat case she is enthralled by all the different offerings, pointing excitedly at various items. She points to some whole fish on display. "Fish." I'm pleased that she says the word. In the bakery section she makes happy tummy gestures. I tell her we'll bake something at home. She nods and wanders around, looking at everything.

Sharon wants to show me how to make Hungarian goulash, so we pick up meat at the meat counter, and then the pasta and produce we need. She also picks up basics for baking, some spices, toiletries, and bread, eggs and milk, fresh fruit and salad greens. By now the cart is nearly full. We head for the checkout counter. The chubby clerk behind the counter looks up and her eyes go big as she blurts, "Omygosh! Ain't you the Kalmiopsis girls? I saw you on TV last night. Wow! What an adventure!"

Sharon speaks up matter-of-factly. "Marcy, this is Judith, and Kali. They're staying with us for a while. You'll get used to seeing them."

"For sure. It's fun to have celebrities in town. We don't get many of those."

I remain silent until we're back in the car. "I didn't realize that this would be a big deal, Sharon. I'm sorry if it causes disruption in your lives."

She looks at me and smiles. "We'll survive. It's not a problem for us, as much as it may be for you." She pats my knee. "But, I'm sure it'll all cool down soon and everyone will forget all about it. Don't worry."

Later that day I trot down to the mailbox to get the mail for Sharon. The mailbox is at the base of the hill, as are others near the road. I grab the handful of envelopes and ads, head back up the hill, and deposit the stack on Sharon's desk in the kitchen.

That evening, as I'm peeling potatoes for dinner, Sharon picks up the stack and shuffles through it. "Judith, there's a letter for you," she says. She hesitates. "It looks weird. Who could have sent it?"

Surprised, I wipe my hands and take the envelope. Concerned, I study it. There isn't a return address on the envelope, and my name is crudely printed, along with the address. Afraid that it's another threat, I open it and stare at the lined notebook paper that comes out. In crude block letters I read, *"If you no wat's good 4 yu, yull keep yor mouth shut at triel."* "Shut" is underlined heavily.

My gut churns and I feel a surge of anger throughout my body. Who are these people to threaten me? I look at Sharon. "It looks like I'm being warned not to testify at the trials for Gimpy and Bart. It's the second message I've been sent."

Sharon looks at it, frowning. "What do you mean, the second message? Did you get another one?"

"Yes, but I tore it up. I didn't take it seriously."

"You should have. It could be from one of their families. They all have very bad reputations around here. The Leland tribe have lived out in the bush for generations and are a nasty bunch. I think the sheriff's even afraid of going on their property. Gimpy's family lives closer to town but they're not much better. And we don't know what kind of connections Bryce had. I think we should turn this over to the police."

"Do you really think this is serious? It looks like a child wrote it."

Still frowning, Sharon shakes her head. "Those people don't go in much for schooling. The school authorities have had several run-ins with both families because of truancy. I'm sure this has come from one of them. We have to take it seriously."

We take the note in to the sheriff's office. A deputy looks at it and assures us that they will handle the situation. I'm not sure what that means. But I'm still left on edge. The trial's a couple of months away. But I have other things to worry about— getting a job, getting my GED, helping Kali, adjusting to our new way of life, and so, do my best to put it out of my mind.

On Wednesday I go back to the education office to take my placement tests. It takes all day, and I'm nervous. My hands are shaking when I start, but I plow through them as best I can. I'm glad

I've done all that reading while we were living in the Kalmiopsis. I feel like I did well on everything but the math and science portions. I never really mastered mathematics past the basics, on my own in the wilderness. Resigned, I decide that there's nothing to do but wait for the results.

That evening, before I go to bed, I pad down the hall bare footed to get a glass of water in the kitchen. I overhear Doug and Sharon talking. I stop and listen. Doug says, "You know I appreciate what they did for Paul, but how long do you think we'll have them staying here?"

"As long as it takes. I love having them here. I'm enjoying coaching Kali immensely, and Judith and I have bonded, I think. She's a wonderful girl. And I want to help them get established."

"I'm happy to help'em, but you know you'll get too fond of'em and it'll be really hard on you when they move out. Remember how miserable you were when that exchange student had to go back home? They can't take the place of the babies you lost, Sharon. I don't want you to be hurt. They're not your kids."

"Don't you think I know that?" she snaps. "But it's clear that Paul's in love with Judith, and she with him. I want to bring her up to speed with society. It's got to be really confusing for her. I want her and Paul to be happy. And I adore Kali. She's really sweet and brave and struggling. They have no family, Doug, we're all they have. I won't abandon them. I'm sure they'll be going out on their own before we know it. Besides, after that threatening note, I feel like we need to protect them."

I turn and sneak back to my room. I'm wondering if Doug thinks we're a burden? Are we in the way? And what about the babies Sharon lost? I wonder if they were girls? Are we taking their place in her mind? I'm glad that she likes us, but don't want to be a burden or a worry to Doug. And what about that threat? Are we placing them in danger? I've got to plan for our futures, so we can take care of ourselves. And I don't want to marry Paul just because it's an easy solution.

The next morning, I retrieve my shotgun from the gun rack in the utility room, and hide it in my closet. I want to be ready in case there's trouble.

That Thursday, I'm cleaning up in the kitchen when the phone rings. I answer it, as Sharon's working with Kali in the dining room.

A deep voice asks, "Miss Johnson?"

"Yes."

"You don't know me. My name is Virgil Maddock, and I was a friend of your grandmother's. I saw your story on TV the other night and wanted to get in touch with you. I'm the property manager of your grandmother's estate. We've been managing her house rental all these years. I was so sorry to learn that she has passed, and also your mother. Please accept my condolences."

Stunned, I think, could this be true? Grandma never mentioned him, that I can recall. "Thank you."

"I want you to know that, since your mother is also um, gone, the property is now yours. Could you come to Klamath Falls? Your grandmother was a great friend of mine, and I've hoped all these years that she'd come back and move back into her house. Since it's now yours, there's paperwork we need to do and also, a bank account that's now yours."

My mind goes into overdrive. I haven't even thought about Gramma's house in years. I feel a jolt of adrenaline shoot through my body. This could mean independence for me and Kali. I won't have to be a burden to Paul's family. I can take care of us myself. Maybe that publicity was a good thing after all.

I manage to chirp, "Thank you so much. I had no idea." (Pause). "Come to think of it, I have some papers of Gramma's. I'd forgotten about them. I'll see if I can arrange to come to Klamath Falls right away. How can I get in touch with you?"

He gives me his phone number and address of his office, and advises me to bring my birth certificate and any relevant papers. I thank him again and hang up. I stand there, trembling, relief and excitement washing over me. This opens up all kinds of possibilities.

I rush to our bedroom and begin searching for the bundle of Gramma's papers. I might have known that she'd provide for our futures.

I find the papers in the bottom drawer of the bureau. How could I have forgotten them? Well, I have been pretty busy ... I plop down on my bed.

Sure enough, there, in a folder on top of the stack, is her last will and testament, witnessed by Virgil Maddock himself. Relief leaves me feeling weak. I haven't realized how worried I was over our financial situation. Hands shaking, I scan the document. Yes, she has left everything to my mother, and if she has predeceased us, to David and me. With a pain in my heart, I realize that leaves just me. She must have made this out just before we went into the Wilderness. Tears slide down my cheeks. Poor Gramma. Did she suspect that she wouldn't come out of the Kalmiopsis alive? No, I'm sure she thought that we'd come out some day, in spite of the end of world predictions of my parents' pastor. Why else would she keep her house? She never really bought into Robert's prophecies. She just didn't want Mama to be alone.

I try to picture my grandmother's house. It's been about fifteen years since I saw it last. I can barely remember it— a ranch style small house on a few acres of property. I hope it's still in good shape. Maybe Kali and I could live there, or we could sell it and buy a home here in Gold Beach. Or I could use the money to go to school and get a diploma so I can support us both. So many opportunities for our future.

I must get to Klamath Falls as soon as possible.

I approach Sharon about the problem. Kali's eyes go wide, and she bounces in her chair. Her face lights up with excitement.

Sharon rears back in surprise and exclaims, "Judith, that's wonderful news. I'll be glad to drive you there. This'll be exciting and fun. I haven't been to Klamath Falls in years, and it's in such a lovely setting. Call the man back and set up an appointment, then I'll arrange for us to go. We'll have to stay overnight, I imagine. Maybe

Doug can come too. I'm sure he could take a couple of days off. Business is slow this time of year."

I'm surprised by her enthusiasm. I thank her profusely and head back to the phone. I call Mr. Maddock back and we decide to meet at his office the following week on Monday afternoon. I'm so elated when I hang up, I could jump for joy. The TV interview was a blessing after all. *Thank you, Gramma,* I breathe, *even now you're with us.* My eyes mist up. I'd give anything to have her here, guiding me and sharing her wisdom as she did in the Kalmiopsis. I picture her foraging with me for wild edibles and herbs. I remember how she had a fresh, earthy scent, and how warm and comforting she was for both us girls after we were orphaned. I think about her lonely grave at our old homesite and long to spend some time there, communing with her in my quiet place.

I straighten up, mop my face, and go to explain what's happening to Kali.

That evening I tell Paul about the new development. He's very happy for me. "Wow! That's great, Judith. Now you'll have a nest egg to help you start your new life. I wish I could come with you and Mom, but I'm still trying to get caught up at work." He grabs me in a bear hug and we just lean on each other for a while. As his arms tighten around me, I feel a surge of heat from my knees to my hairline. My heart speeds up and I'm thinking I would just like to stay here like this forever. But we're not alone, and we have things to do. Finally, I take a reluctant step back.

"I'd better help your mother get dinner on," I gulp. "You must be starving. Your Dad went fishing this morning and caught a beautiful salmon. That's what we're having for dinner."

He smiles and kisses me lightly. "Sounds fantastic. I'll go wash up."

8

Grandma's Legacy

We leave at dawn that Monday morning for the long drive to Klamath Falls. We head up the coast to Bandon, then through the inland town of Coquille, and from there on past Myrtle Point. The drive through the mountains is beautiful, in spite of the rain, and Kali's head keeps swiveling back and forth as we see new territory. She's never been this far from our valley in the Kalmiopsis. She grabs my sleeve frequently to point out various animals—deer, cows, once a coyote.

I ask Sharon and Doug if they've always lived on the coast. Soon I learn that they were both born there in Coos Bay and Brookings respectively, and had met when going to Oregon State. They tell me how they found each other in a geology class one day. They started dating and married right out of college. Then Doug got a job with an engineering firm in Gold Beach while Sharon went to work teaching at the grade school. I really enjoy learning more about them as the time flies by.

We reach the I-5 corridor and stop in Grants Pass for a break and quick lunch. Then it's on to Medford. When we get there, old, childhood memories start stirring in me, flashes of life in this region with my family. I was eight when we left, but I remember the farms and forested hills. I remember going to school through third grade with my friends. I still miss them. I try to concentrate on the road we're taking from Medford on through to the Klamath basin. I fill Doug and Sharon in on how I spent my childhood in the Medford and Roseburg areas. We are really getting to know each other.

We follow Klamath Lake for several miles until we reach our motel, a modest, one story place with a covered swimming pool. We have two units next to each other. This is another first for Kali and me—a night in a motel. She's so excited that she's practically vibrating. We check in and take our luggage to our rooms. Ours looks a little worn, with faded bedspreads and a few dings in the doors, but clean. Kali throws herself on the bed with a big smile, bounces a couple of times, then we both check out the bathroom. I note that it's clean and everything seems to work. There are towels and soaps and shampoo. After we inspect the room we all head in to Klamath Falls. Sharon and Doug and I discuss what to do next. We stop at the Chamber of Commerce and get a city map. It's almost time to meet Mr. Maddock. His office isn't hard to find. I'm on pins and needles about the whole process, but try to keep a calm face in spite of inner jitters.

Mr. Maddock's office is in a low-slung strip mall with a number of other businesses. It looks very plain, with gray walls and furnished with filing cabinets and a couple of large desks. The smell of stale cigarette smoke fills the air. There are a couple of scenic paintings on the walls. A dark-haired young woman sits at the front desk and barely glances up as we walk in, smiles and says, "Hi, can I help you? Oh, you must be Judith?" Then turns and hollers through the open office door to Maddock, "They're here," before putting her face back into her typewriter and clacking away.

The desk Maddock's sitting at is covered with papers, and a couple of photos. He stands up and walks around his desk and I realize that he has Klamath Indian blood, even before we introduce ourselves. His dark skin, high, broad cheekbones, straight nose, mop of black hair, tied in a pony tail at the back, and dark, almond shaped eyes give him away. Also, he looks vaguely familiar. The tribal blood must be how he and Gramma were acquainted.

Maddock has a wide grin, and greets us warmly with handshakes all around. He's dressed comfortably in jeans, cowboy boots and a white shirt with string tie. He puts his hands on his hips and studies Kali and me. "Yes, I can see a little of your grandmother in you girls. Especially you, Judith, in your cheekbones and nose and mouth. It's a pleasure to meet Esther's granddaughters. I think of her often. I was shocked when I saw you on TV and heard your story. Your grandma was a very special lady, as I'm sure you know."

I ask, "Did you know her well?"

He chuckled. "Ever since I was a kid. She and your grandpa were neighbors of ours and I sometimes helped your grandpa around the place." A faint memory of seeing him at Gramma's house stirs in my mind.

"Your grandma was a fine person, and would always insist on feeding me when I was working over there. She made the best beef stew and venison steak and sourdough bread. I loved listening to her stories and your grandpa's stories. They loved to tell about the Modoc wars, and history of our people. They always were there at any of our tribal gatherings."

At once I feel comfortable with this man. It's so good to talk to someone who knew my family. I feel like I can trust him.

We all sit down around his desk and he starts explaining his arrangement with Gramma and what I have inherited. It turns out that I own Gramma's land and house, and that I have about $27,000 in a bank account that was set up for the profits from the rent on the house. Kali's name isn't on anything because she was born after we moved into the Kalmiopsis. Everything will have to go through probate, which will take some time, but after that it's all mine, free and clear. I am so elated. I ask if we can see the house.

"There're people currently living there, but I can ask permission to tour it with you. I'll call and see if we can run you out there."

He makes the call, and it turns out that the lady of the house is home, and gives us permission to come out the following day at ten o'clock. He hangs up, clasps his hands on the desk. "I'd like to take you over to the bank to introduce you to them over there. We'll need to make copies of your birth certificate. I have the original of her will, which she put in my safekeeping. She didn't trust lawyers. So, we can take it all over there now and get you acquainted with the manager if you'd like."

We agree, and, after he copied my birth certificate and Grandma's will, we proceed to the bank.

The bank people are very pleasant. However, I won't be able to access my grandmother's money until I can bring them a death certificate or other proof of death. We're informed that we may be able to get this through the Social Security administration, or, perhaps, the sheriff's office in Gold Beach.

This is discouraging to me. I'll have to contact the sheriff's office when I get back to town. I feel confused and frustrated. It seems overwhelming.

We end up back at Maddock's office and I am still trying to take it all in. "Mr. Maddock..." I begin.

"Please, Judith, call me Virgil."

"Okay, Virgil. Thank you so much. I appreciate what you've done over the years. But I'm anxious to see the house. We'll meet you back here in the morning. "

We say our goodbyes and are out the door. Sharon says, "Let's get some dinner and then head back to the motel. I'm sure you have a lot to think about, Judith. We can talk about it over dinner if you'd like."

"Good idea. I'm hungry. How about you, Kali?" I put my arm around her shoulders. She nods vigorously. "Yes."

I feel a little thrill. She spoke the word. She really is making progress. I give her a little squeeze, and feel my mood lighten as a spark of hope passes through my brain.

We find a nearby café in a little strip mall and pop in. The décor is kitschy (Sharon tells me) and comfortable, with old fashioned booths and a counter with stools, and a juke box (something else that's new to me) along one wall. Kali finds this fascinating, and, after we order our food (chicken pot pie for me and, of course, hamburger and fries for Kali), she slides out of the booth and checks it out. I follow her and try to figure out how it works. Doug comes up and shows us the list of songs to be played, and inserts fifty cents into the machine. Soon the sounds of "Rock Around the Clock" fill the air. Kali grins and starts dancing and giggling. I am so delighted to see her joy that I start in moving too. Doug is laughing and soon we're all jiving around the floor. When the music stops, Doug plugs more quarters in and soon the sounds of a group called "The Beatles" fills the air with "Yellow Submarine." Again, Kali is ecstatic, whirling in time to the music. It's so good to see her just having fun and enjoying herself. The few other customers in the place are laughing and smiling.

Soon, our food comes and we manage to get Kali to sit down to eat. She digs in with gusto. Hamburgers and fries have become her favorite food of all time.

Back at the motel, we agree with Doug and Sharon to meet at the pool for a swim. We jump into our swimsuits, the first time we've used them. Mine is a green one-piece and Kali's is a red, two-piece. She looks so cute in it. We grab towels from the bathroom and are on our way. The outside air is frigid so we run the few yards to the pool. Kali can't wait to dive into the warm water and soon we're both immersed and splashing around. I do find the smell, like bleach, nasty, stinging my nose and my eyes. Kali sniffs, makes a face, and just dives on down and pops up across from me. I dive under and catch her and push her up out of the water. She squeals and plops back under and tries to return the favor, but I'm too heavy for her. We have a great time chasing each other around the pool, creating minor tidal waves sloshing against the sides. I feel my tension dissolve and my spirits soar. Sharon and Doug soon appear in their swimwear and take a short dip. We have the pool to ourselves.

Sharon floats up to me and watches Kali paddling back and forth. "You girls swim so well. Did you swim a lot where you were living?"

"Well, we had a favorite swimming hole where we'd go in the summer and fall. The rest of the year it was pretty chilly. Whenever we needed a break from our routine we'd head out there. We both enjoyed it, but Kali just loved it."

That's so nice. You're both really athletic. Once she's in school she can get involved in sports. And I'll bet you'd enjoy running, Judith. There are a lot of runners in Gold Beach. It's a good way to meet people too."

"Hmmm! That might be fun. I don't want to get soft from lack of exercise. Thanks for the suggestion."

After our swim we say our "good nights" and head for our room. The cold air grabs us and we're shivering as we take turns jumping into the hot shower. I have to actually drag Kali out so I can have mine. "No, no," she squeals. I laugh and grab her and bodily yank her out of the shower, grabbing a towel and wrapping it tightly around her until she stops resisting.

"My turn," I yell, and jump in ahead of her. The warm water feels wonderful and I'm glad to get rid of the chlorine smell. I scrub my hair too. It was nice that they supply shampoo. I never thought to bring any. Done with our showers, we towel our hair dry. I wash our swim suits in the sink and hang them over the tub to dry.

Once we're in our jammies and ready for bed, we say our prayers (or rather, I say them and Kali nods as she hears the Lord's Prayer, says "Amen,") and douse the lights. Snuggled in the strange bed, I ponder the events of the day. *Somehow, I have to get a death certificate for Gramma, and get my hands on our funds.* I punch my pillow and wad it up under my head. It's too flat. Should have brought my own.

We've learned a lot, since we came out of the woods, but I know I have a long way to go. I have to learn how to do my bookkeeping, keep track of our funds, and write checks, and navigate in the civilized world. I have to get my GED and find a job so I can support us. I'll have to get a driver's license. I want to be able to take care of myself and Kali, even if I marry Paul. Thinking about Paul, I feel a surge of longing to be with him, which turns into worry. What shall I do about him? I believe I love him, but I'm not sure what that means. I've never had any experience with boyfriends, or courting. I have to be sure that marriage is what I want, for both our sakes. It's too much to think about.

Restless, I roll over on my side and calm myself by going back in my mind to our quiet place, under the tree overlooking Gramma's grave. I picture the tree, and the little cross that we placed there, and tell Gramma all that's happened and all my worries. Gradually, my mind calms down as the peace of the forest fills it. I can almost feel my grandmother's presence around me as, gradually, I drift off to sleep.

The next day, after breakfast, we head out to see Gramma's house. As we approach, I'm hit by the memories of time spent here with my grandparents. This little ranch style house had been home to us before our father came back from Vietnam. I have a vague memory of the rooms, especially the kitchen where Gramma cooked up her special dishes. I remember the perfume of wild huckleberry cobbler wafting through the house, and fresh baked bread. The house usually was redolent with the scents emanating from that little space.

The outside of the house looks neglected and run down. Apparently, the tenants over the years haven't cared for it. It definitely needs scraping and a coat of paint. The roof is covered with moss and tree duff. There are a couple of old car bodies sitting in the weed strewn yard. I'm concerned about what we'll find inside.

Sharon looks at Maddock, frowning. "It looks like it needs a lot of attention. Isn't that your responsibility?"

His brow furrows, and he gets a sheepish look on his face. "I haven't been out here in a while. They've been good tenants, paying their bills on time, and haven't complained about anything. I guess it does need some fixing up."

"That would be my guess," Sharon snaps. I'm pleased to see that she's unhappy with Virgil for my sake. Looking around, I'm upset too. This was my grandparents' place. It deserved better.

The tenant meets us at the door. She's neither welcoming nor cold, maybe a little wary—brown hair in braids, wearing jeans and a clean sweatshirt, with Nikes on her feet. Her attitude isn't unfriendly, but she seems uncomfortable, flapping her hands nervously. She ushers us in to the living room. Yes, I remember that fireplace and those built-in bookshelves. But the fireplace is grimy, and the bookshelves crammed with papers and assorted knick-knacks, and what looks like small car parts. The floor needs new carpeting, for sure, and is filthy.

We proceed through the rest of the house, and I am aghast at how beat-up and dirty it looks. The kitchen stove is covered in grease, and the place smells like overripe garbage. The walls have dents and are smeared with dirt in places. The toilets and tub are brown inside. It seems the tenants are oblivious to the mess they live in.

I half-heartedly thank the woman as we leave. I'm wondering what I'll do with the place. It's not really Gramma's anymore. It's been too long. She'd have been outraged if she saw the mess.

We end up back at Maddock's office and I am feeling disoriented and sad, and missing my grandmother. I'd give anything to have her standing by my side, supporting me.

"Virgil, after seeing what they've done to the place, I think I'll probably sell it. I can use the money for a fresh start for Kali and me. Can you handle that?"

His eyebrows go up. "I'm sorry you don't want to keep it. It could be fixed up to be a nice home for you and Kali. I know it's a shock to see the current condition, but it comes with five acres of land. It'll only go up in value. Maybe you should think about it?"

I hesitate, glancing at Sharon and Doug. *Could I really bring it back to a decent condition?* "I'll think about it. I have to get the death certificate for my Gramma before I can do anything. But I don't feel my grandparent's presence there anymore. I don't think I'll keep it." I'm fighting back tears as I speak.

"Sure. It's your decision. Just let me know. We'll proceed as soon as we get the go-ahead."

I stand up. "I will. I'll call you as soon as I get the death certificate.

"We shake hands and take our leave.

9

— CHAPTER —

First Date

We go back to the motel, pack up our things, and are soon on our way back home. I'm eager to get back to Gold Beach to find out how to get a death certificate for my Grandmother, and to see Paul.

The trip back is uneventful, and we arrive home well after dark. We bring in our bags and Kali runs off to check on her cats. Paul meets us at the door with hugs and wants to know all the details. We put away our luggage, gather in the kitchen for late snack and discuss what happened.

"What do you want to do, Judith?"

"I don't know yet, Paul. I have to think about it. But I think I'll probably sell the property and use the money to buy us a home somewhere else, maybe here in Gold Beach."

"You have a lot of decisions to make. But it's late and you must be tired."

Sharon stands up, puts her plate in the sink. "Yes, we need to get to bed. We'll talk more in the morning."

Paul and I linger for a while as the others head for their rooms. He reaches out and takes my hand. "I really missed you while you were gone."

"I missed you too." I lean my head on his shoulder. "I wish you could have seen Gramma's house. It's a mess, Paul. It'll take an awfully lot of work to bring it back. And money. It made me sad to see it."

"You don't have to decide tonight. It won't go anywhere. Meanwhile, you should get some sleep." He stands up and pulls me up with him, puts his arms around me. "Sleep well, sweet dreams." We cling to each other for a while, then share a lingering kiss. I hate to say good-night. But finally, realizing that this could go on for a long time, I break away.

"Good night, Paul. I love you."

He gives me a light kiss on my forehead. "Night, Judith. You know I'm crazy about you. I'm really glad you're back. Sleep well.

We head for our rooms and, after washing my face and brushing my teeth, I fall into bed.

The next morning, I call the Sheriff's office. The receptionist actually puts me through to the Sheriff himself.

"This is Blake."

"Um, hello, Sheriff. This is Judith Johnson. I have an important question for you."

"Oh, sure, I remember you. What can I do for you?"

How should I word this? "Well," taking a deep breath, "we buried my grandmother in the Kalmiopsis Wilderness when she passed, and I was wondering what I need to do to get a death certificate?"

"Hmmm. That'll take some time. We would need to take a team in to exhume the body and bring it out. You know, it's against the

Forest Service rules to bury someone in the wilderness. Then, you would get a death certificate. Do you want me to proceed with it?"

I pause. This is so not what I want to do. "I'm afraid we'll have to. I need that certificate to claim my inheritance. I hate to disturb her grave, but if it's the only way, I guess we'll have to do it. I could lead you to the gravesite."

"Okay, I'll start making arrangements. I'll let you know when we can go in. We'll probably have to hike in and camp on the way, with the team. That's going to cost some money. I'll look into it."

"It'll probably take three or four days. It's a long hike."

"I'll let you know. The passes are closed right now so we'll have to wait for spring. I have to get a permit from the Forest Service also. Give me your number and I'll get back to you."

I give him our number, thank him profusely, and we hang up. I'm shaking. The thought of digging up Gramma makes my stomach churn.

I'm in a glum mood when Paul comes in from work that night. After I bring him up to date, he places his hands on my shoulders, facing me. "What you need is to go out on the town with me. Whad'ya say, Judith? Would you like to come out on a real date with me tonight? We'll go out to dinner and then check out the "night life" here in town. It'll be fun."

My pulse leaps, and I hug him. "I'd love to do that. I've never been on a date." I start to turn away, then, "What should I wear? Do I need to put on my dress? Or just a nice pair of slacks? What do you think?"

He grins. "Just slacks and a sweater should be fine. There isn't any place very fancy here in town."

I hasten to my room and change out of my jeans. This is so exciting. I put on my black slacks with a bright red sweater, and slip into my dressy shoes. I look in the mirror. What should I do about my hair? I'm so excited that I can't do a thing with it. It's grown way past my shoulders. Finally, I just draw the thick, brunette mass of it back into a ponytail. I guess it's okay. Then I brighten my lips with the lipstick Sharon gave me and stand back. I like the effect. I place my mother's locket around my neck and head into the kitchen to get Sharon's opinion.

She pauses in her potato peeling and inspects me. "I hear you're going out tonight. What a great idea, Judith. You look very pretty. That color's really good on you. We'll keep Kali entertained. You two go and have a good time."

And so, filled with anxiety and anticipation, we head out on our first real date. Paul takes me to the nicest restaurant in town, a place back off the main drag. The interior is dim and clean with tables looking out over the beach. I think I'm about as nervous as I was when facing a charging bear. The elegant (to me) hostess, wearing shiny white blouse and black slacks, seats us, hands us menus. I study the menu, puzzle over the many offerings (what's "chicken cordon bleu?"), and then ask him what he plans to order.

"They make a really good steak here. That's usually what I have."

"Then, that's what I'll have too." I'm relieved to have that decided. I look around. The walls have dark wood wainscoting and are painted white above that. There are some nice, pastoral paintings on the walls, white table cloths and napkins on the tables. I'm wondering what I'm supposed to do with two forks, and decide to just follow Paul's lead. The place is fancier than any other restaurant I've been in. If it weren't for Paul, I'd be really uncomfortable.

Paul leans forward and takes my hand. "I've been waiting for the chance to do this. It's so nice to have you all to myself. Things have been going so fast since we arrived back in town, what with one thing after another. And at home there's always someone else around."

I'm happy too. "I don't think we've had any time alone since we left the Kalmiopsis. It's wonderful."

We chat about our recent events and what they mean to us. "I'm so glad I won't have to worry about finances for a while, once I get that death certificate."

"I'll come with you when you go in for the exhumation. I don't want you to go through that alone."

"Oh, I'd really love having you there. I'm filled with dread of the whole thing."

We're interrupted by a waiter, who brings us water and asks if we want anything to drink. Paul leans towards me and asks if I would like a glass of wine. I hesitate. I don't much care for wine. I tried it at Paul's house and didn't really like the taste of it or how it made me feel kind of dizzy. "I'll just have, water, thanks."

Paul orders a glass of pinot and the waiter disappears.

As dinner progresses, I gradually relax and enjoy the wonderful steaks they bring. Paul tells me about his work week, finally getting back out in the field. "It feels so good to get out of the office. I spent the last couple of days burning piles of debris we've cleared out of a natural area that we're restoring." I enjoy listening to him talk enthusiastically about his work. And I tell him about my efforts to get my GED.

I take a sip or two of his wine. I don't like it, but it feels warm going down. I'm thinking that married life would be like this— relaxing and sharing the events of the day, making plans for the future.

I can't remember the last time I ate beef steak. Probably before my family entered the Kalmiopsis. It tastes quite different from venison. But I really enjoy it. And the salad and the baked potato.

We pass on the dessert, as we're both stuffed.

We leave hand in hand, then hop into the car and head down to the waterfront area by the river. There, we head into a pub with a river view in hopes of finding music and, perhaps meeting some of Paul's friends. As we enter I hear a loud voice yell, "Hey, Paul, over here."

We head over to a group of people sitting around a large table. The music is blaring from speakers on the wall, and it seems like everyone is talking at once. The table's littered with the remains of their food and glasses of various liquids. As we come up to the table, everyone stops talking at once and stares at me.

I'm apprehensive until Paul puts his arm around me, making me feel safe, and grins at the group. "Yep, this is Judith, the Kalmiopsis lady. You'd better get used to seeing her with me." He turns to me,

"Judith, this group of reprobates are all friends of mine. Unfortunately, they have no manners so instead of talking they just stare at people."

He faces the group, points. "This guy here is Jack Clark, who pretends to manage the office. The poor girl he's with is Grace Clemmons, who hangs around with him in spite of having to work with him too."

I try to memorize the names to go with the faces. Jack—red hair and freckles and medium height, Grace—blond hair and bright red lipstick in sweatshirt and jeans. They both wave happily and tell me "Hi."

I smile tentatively. I think he's joking but I'm waiting to make sure. Aren't they insulted by his comments? They laugh and reach over to shake my hand. I guess this is just the way these people talk to one another.

"And that hulking oaf is Robert Manning." He stands up to shake my hand, dark brown hair, broad shoulders, and at least six feet four, strong features. "He works with me keeping an eye on the wilderness. His unfortunate date is Beth Coons." She's the petite one with brown hair and a green sweater with, of course, jeans. She gives me a warm smile and waves.

I smile as they all protest in mock outrage. Yes, this is how they talk to each other. They know that Paul is just joking. Still, I'm wondering how I can get used to how people interact here in the "outside." When the noise subsides, Jack grins at us and orders us to sit down and have a beer. He yells at the waiter, "Hey barkeep, how about another round!"

The waiter ambles over. "So, what'll you have?" He looks at Paul and me.

Paul says he'll have a Coors and looks at me enquiringly. "What would you like, Judith?"

I hesitate. I tried beer at Paul's parent's house one evening and didn't like it at all. "Is there something other than beer?"

"Would you like to try a mixed drink?"

Feeling adventurous, I tell him, "Okay, you order one for me." He looks at the waiter. "Let's try a Margarita."

He takes my hand. "I think you'll like that, Judith. It's sweet and smooth."

The chatter resumes and Beth leans over and yells in my ear, "Paul's told me so much about you. It's great to meet you at last. So how are you adjusting to life on the outside?"

Soon, we're involved in a lively discussion, mostly with me answering a lot of questions. I finally work up the courage to fire back some of my own. "So, how long have you known Paul?" "What do you like to do for fun?" "I hear that there are groups of runners here. Do you belong to one?"

I'm having a great time getting to know Paul's friends and watching the interaction among them. I've never had a chance to see Paul like this, enjoying his friends' company. They kid each other continuously and there's lots of laughing and insults hurled back and forth. It's my first experience being in a group like this and it's fun to watch, but a bit overwhelming. The fast repartee makes my head whirl. My drink arrives and I taste it tentatively. It's actually yummy. I make myself sip slowly, but it doesn't take long for the effect to hit me. It makes me feel a little dizzy, and I find myself laughing a lot with the rest of them. The noise level keeps going up and I'm starting to feel hemmed in and woozy.

Beth grabs my hand and says, "I need to go to the ladies' room. Want to come with me?"

Gratefully, I follow her into the cool and quiet of the women's room and am happy for the sudden respite and a chance to relieve myself.

Mission accomplished, Beth leans against the wall and eyes me as I wash my hands. "You're really a beautiful girl, Judith. And Paul is absolutely crazy about you. You're lucky. He's a great guy. We were all really worried when he disappeared. We joined the search parties but just couldn't find him. And ever since he was so hurt by his ex-fiancé, we've all been hoping he'd find someone. I hope you feel the same way about him. I'd hate to see him get hurt again."

Surprised, I pause and look at her in the mirror. "I would never want to hurt Paul. I love him. But I'm just getting my feet under me and getting used to this new life. I can't rush into anything until I know what I want and what I'm going to do. I hope you understand."

"Yeah, I can see that you have your hands full since you were isolated for so long. If there's anything I can do to help you adjust, I hope you'll call me." She pulls a pen and card out of her purse and writes on the back. "This's my home phone number. My work phone's on the other side. Any time you need to ask me anything or just want to meet for a coffee and chat or something feel free to call."

I feel tears come into my eyes and blink them away. "I ... I'd like that. I haven't had a chance to make women friends, other than Paul's mother. It'd be great to have someone to talk with who's near my own age. Thanks."

She smiles widely. "Well, now you have a girlfriend. Welcome to society." She snaps her purse shut. "Let's rejoin the party. It should be winding down soon. Tomorrow's a work day."

I slip the card into my pocket and we rejoin the rest of the group. I sip water and feel comforted to have made a new friend. Paul looks at me. "Have you had enough of this racket?"

I nod gratefully, and we stand up, say our good nights, and head out the door.

When we get to the car, we decide to drive down to the beach and go for a walk to clear our heads. However, when we get there and park, we're suddenly engulfed by the drumming of rain hitting the roof. We roll down the windows an inch and listen. I love the sound, washing away the noise from the pub.

Paul takes my hand, and begins kissing my fingers. Little shivers run up my arm. He pauses. "Judith, I hate for this night to end. It's been wonderful having you to myself. And I wanted you to meet some of my friends. How'd you like visiting with the group? I hope it wasn't too much for you." He smiles. "I think the guys are all jealous of me."

I chuckle, and lean into his shoulder. "Oh sure. Seriously, I loved it. Dinner out was amazing and it was so lovely to have you to myself.

And I really like your friends, Paul. Beth was so nice. She told me she wants to be friends and she gave me her phone number. I'm looking forward to spending more time with her. It'll be so nice to have a woman friend. Other than your mother, I mean."

"I'm glad you like'em. We've all been friends for a long time and they're a great bunch of people."

We're quiet for a couple of moments, just enjoying being together. He reaches up and caresses my face, then gently kisses me. Gradually, the kisses become more urgent and I can feel both our temperatures rising. I am being submerged in a whirlwind of passion and longing that almost carries me away. Almost. I feel his hand slip under my sweater in back and slide up towards my bra hooks. Startled, I come up for air, and firmly push him away.

"Wait, wait! What do you think you're doing? I'm not ready for this," I gasp, my heart pounding. "Please, Paul, I think we'd better call it a night."

He groans. "I'm sorry Judith. I just got carried away. I so much want to make love to you. I'm crazy about you, you must know that."

I sigh. "I love you too, but I was taught that I have to wait until we're married for that. Isn't that what your religion teaches you?"

"Yeah. It does. But that's a hard rule to follow. Not many do anymore."

"I don't want my first experience to be having sex in a car. I want it done right, on my honeymoon, in a proper bed. If that's not what you want, I'm sorry."

"I shouldn't have gotten so carried away. I'm sorry, Judith. I'd better take you home." He slams his hand on the steering wheel.

"Don't be upset. You know this is my first date. Everything is "firsts" for me now. I'm trying to keep my head and figure out what's going on in society. It'll take time but I'm really trying to get my life together. I have to consider Kali in everything I do too. You must realize that."

He puts his arm around me. "I'm not upset with you. I'm upset with myself. I'm just frustrated because I'm ready for our future and you're not. I know I'm pushing it. I'll try to be patient. I do love you,

Judith, and I love Kali too. She's a great kid and I want to help you raise her. I'll do whatever you want, and take as much time as you want. I'll wait for you as long as it takes. But I want us to be a family."

He kisses me lightly on the forehead. "Let's go home. It's been a great night. I hope I didn't spoil it for you."

I give him a smile and kiss him fully on the mouth. "It's been wonderful. I love being with you, Paul."

"We have plenty of time for getting to know each other better and get used to life on the "outside." Let's do something fun together again soon. Just the two of us."

"I'd love that."

He backs out of the parking spot. "You know, Judith, there's one thing we haven't discussed yet. You need to learn to drive."

I'm taken aback by the quick change of subject. "Um, I haven't really thought about it much. I suppose you're right. I'll need to be able to drive to a job, when I get one, and take Kali places. But that'll mean I'll have to get a car. Oh man, there's no end to stuff I've got to do, to learn. Will you teach me? I won't be able to get a car until I get my inheritance, but I could start learning now."

"Sure. You can learn to drive my pickup. It's a stick shift, but if you learn to drive that you can drive anything. We'll start lessons tomorrow after work."

I'm delighted at the prospect. Here in this little town there's no public transportation and everyone drives. It will give me freedom that I don't have now. "I can't wait. Tomorrow, after dinner. Okay?"

"It's a date." So, the evening ends on a high note.

10

Meanwhile ...

It's November, and the rains have settled in for the duration, it seems. But I'm busy, always busy, catching up on my life. I'm already thinking about Christmas. I have to come up with gifts for everybody. I still have some savings, but I'll have to be careful not to overspend. I haven't a clue how to go about it. What could I possibly get for Paul and his family? Kali will be easy. I can always get her something new to wear. Or, maybe a bicycle. I'll bet she'd love that. I've seen kids riding them around town. Or maybe a skateboard? I've seen lots of kids using those too.

Maybe I'll give Beth a call and she can help me figure out what to get for Sharon and Doug.

Since I passed my tests with good results, I plan to start taking classes in January to earn my GED. That will mean long drives to

Coos Bay to the community college to take classes. Meanwhile, I manage to get my learner's permit, and I'm studying for my license, while Paul and Sharon work on teaching me to drive. I'm having a hard time getting used to traffic, and working the clutch with my left foot while I work the brake and gas pedals with my right, all the while staying on the road where I belong and handling the gearshift. I've begun to think I'm totally uncoordinated.

I'm learning that there's a limit to Paul's patience, as I'm jerking along and he's shouting terrified instructions at me. "Stop, stop! What do you think you're doing?"

"Left foot, left foot! Okay, easy, easy! You have to step on the clutch to shift!"

Our first two or three sessions have led to tears more than once, with Paul apologizing profusely. "Geez, I'm sorry, Judith. I didn't mean to yell. I just get carried away." Then gently starting over. We do our practicing on quiet country roads at first, until Paul decides that it's safe enough for me to chance busier streets. I'm sweating right through my sweatshirt as we slowly make our first death-defying trip through town. Right on Highway 101. My hands are trembling. People are honking behind me and I want to yell at them. But we make it to the market parking lot. As log trucks scream by on the highway, I park the pickup and jump out. Paul gets out and leans on his door, watching in amazement as I run around and around his truck. People are staring but I don't care. Finally, having worked off the quivering nerves that drive me, I stop, panting.

Paul puts his arm around my shoulders, concern on his face. "Judith, what in blazes are you doing?"

"Working off steam. Do people have to be so rude with the honking? Do you think I'll ever get the hang of this?"

"Anyone who can fight off a bear can handle driving." He puts his arms around me and I lean my head on his chest. "It just takes time.

Trust me, you'll get it. We just have to keep practicing. Maybe that's enough for today. D'you want me to drive home?"

I clamp my arms around him and wearily say, "Yes, please. I don't think my nerves can stand any more right now." After a long moment, while my nerves steady and the solid comfort of him begins to turn into heat, we reluctantly separate and hop in the truck, headed for home.

Sharon is very patient with me when we go out in the daytime. Her Volkswagen is a stick shift too, and, gradually, it becomes second nature to me. Between the two of them, I actually find myself driving with more confidence every day. But I don't think I'll ever be comfortable with parallel parking. I study the driver's manual whenever I can, and practically have it memorized.

Meanwhile, I'm waiting to hear from the sheriff's office about exhuming Gramma's body. I know we won't be able to get in until the snow is gone from the passes. So, it will probably be April or May before we can get it done.

Then, out of the blue, Paul decides to move back into his rental house. His parents had kept up the payments when he disappeared, in hopes that he would be needing it again.

He tells me this while we're watching TV alone one evening. He clicks off the TV and shifts in his seat, and takes my hand. "Judith, I have something important to tell you." He hesitates. "Um, I think it would be best for us if I move back into my old place. There's no use leaving it empty. I'm back on my feet and doing fine. And I'm finding it hard to be so close to you all the time without wanting to make love to you. A little distance will give us both a breather. When you're ready to accept a proposal from me, we can move in together. Or maybe we'll buy a house of our own. We'll still be seeing each other most days. I'll just be sleeping at my own place."

My heart sinks. I can feel my face heating up. He really wants me. And I have to admit that I have a restless desire for him too. I think about it for a while. Finally, "I love having you here, but maybe it's for the best. It'll be easier if we're not sleeping in the same house. Once I get my GED and my driver's license, and get through this trial, maybe I can get my head cleared and look to the future. Have you told your folks? How do they feel about it?"

He pulls me close and kisses my cheek. "They think it's a good idea. Anyway, this gives us breathing room and we have plenty of time to figure out where we're going. I love you, Judith. I want us to be on the same page when we get married."

Tears dampen my cheeks. I am so grateful for this man. We sit closely for a while and let the idea sink in.

And so, Paul moves out the next day, taking the few belongings he's packed in to his bedroom. The house feels empty once he's gone, even though I see him most days at dinner. I miss our morning chats over our breakfast coffee. I miss knowing he's in the same space at night. When I hear the owls call at night, through our open window, it reminds me of how lonely I was out in our cabin.

To keep myself busy, I decide to go take the driver's test. Sharon takes me and Kali down to the DMV office in Brookings. Although very nervous, I manage to pass the driving exam, in spite of a frazzled job parallel parking, which I had to attempt twice before I did it right. My examiner is patient with me, and before I know it, I have a license. Sharon and I are both grinning from ear to ear and hugging. I feel victorious and validated at the same time. I have to restrain myself from doing victory laps in the parking lot. This gives me identification when I need it. As soon as I have some money, I plan to get a car of my own. I'm really going to need it. Sharon lets me drive back to Gold Beach.

We all celebrate that night over a fantastic pot roast Sharon prepared, with wine for the grownups, except for Kali and me. We have ginger ale. Afterwards Paul and I go out to the local pub to meet his friends and celebrate some more. I feel warm and included in his circle of friends. It's amazing to have people to share my experiences. Someone once said, "Friends divide our sorrows and multiply our joys." I understand that now.

Beth and I meet for coffee the next day at the café on the waterfront. This is exciting for me, as I really need her friendship. I need to know what I've missed while I was hidden from the world in the Kalmiopsis. We find that we have more in common than I imagined. We both love the outdoors, especially the wilderness. She has backpacked many of its trails. She likes to read, and promises to give me a list of her favorite new books.

"I like some romance novels, like Danielle Steel books and also fantasy fiction by Tolkien and Andre Norton but also scary stuff like Stephen King writes. I'll give you a list the next time we get together. Then we can visit the library."

"I'd like that. I haven't been to the library yet." We discuss some of the books I've read while hidden in the Wilderness (and my passion for Charlotte Bronte). My parents had really stocked up on a lot of classics. But I have other things on my mind. Changing the subject, I ask her if she plans to marry Robert.

"Maybe. We've been dating for six months and we seem to be a good match. We have similar tastes and interests, and he's a great kisser. I think I'm in love with him. We're comfortable with each other. Yeah, I think we'll end up getting married. What about you and Paul?"

"I don't know. He wants to get married and I think I love him. But he's the only guy I've ever dated, and how do I know if what I feel is love? I'm very grateful to him for all the help he's given me and Kali, and we also share a lot of the same interests. He's so handsome and my heart speeds up when he walks into the room. I'm really drawn to him. I feel like this is love. But how do you know when the guy is the one you want to spend the rest of your life with?"

Beth eyes me closely. "You really haven't had any experience with men, have you? God, I can't imagine the life you've had. But I can see why you'd hesitate. How do you manage to stay so in control of your life?" Suddenly she rears back in her seat and her jaw drops. "Omigawd! You've never 'done it' have you? Had sex?"

I glance around quickly to make sure nobody heard that and I'm blushing furiously. I hiss, "Of course not. I'm not married.

I'm a Christian. And I want to be a virgin when I do get married. I want my relationship to be exclusive with my husband. Don't you?"

She laughs. "It's a little late for that. However, whatever floats your boat is fine with me. But, maybe you need to get more experience dating before you settle on one guy. I really don't know what to tell you. As for love, it just feels right. You can't see living the rest of your life without him. Do you feel that way about Paul?"

I sit back in my chair. "I think I do. But I'm so confused and I've got so much to learn. Maybe, once I graduate, and get my bearings, decide what I want to do with my life, I can figure it out. I have to keep a lid on myself for Kali's sake. I can't afford to make mistakes. I've taken care of us for so long, I can't let up now." We're both silent for a moment. My mind wanders into my latest puzzle.

"Not to change the subject, but I'm excited about Christmas. Maybe you can help me figure out what to get for Paul and his parents for Christmas? I just haven't a clue. Back in the wilderness, I would make something for Kali. But I haven't had to buy presents before for adults. What do you think?"

"Sheesh! I don't know. Let me see if I can worm some hints out of Paul the next time I see him. As for his parents, that's a tough one. I know his Dad loves to fish and hunt. His Mom is into quilting, I think. Why don't you ask Paul? He might have some ideas."

"You're right. He should be able to help me. As for Kali, I have an idea what I want to get her. Do you have your Christmas shopping done?"

We chat for over an hour and I realize how hungry I've been for a woman friend my own age to talk to. She asks me about how I preserved food in the wilderness for the winter months, and how I educated my silent sister. I ask her about her interests. She's into running, and said she'll help me train for a 5K run if I want to participate. I think that'll be fun. We agree to get together again, just before Paul comes by to give me a ride home.

I ask Paul to help me find a bike for Kali for Christmas. We have two weeks to go before the big day and I'm anxious to get my shopping done.

"Sure, we can do that. Let's swing by the hardware store on the way home. They have a small selection of bikes."

At the hardware store we find a beautiful, metallic blue girl's bike that's a good size for Kali, and is adjustable as she grows. It has something they call a "banana seat," which I think looks uncomfortable, but decide to buy it anyway. I take out my wallet and pay for it. There goes $95. I've got $800 of my stash left. I feel a moment of panic. I need to find a job.

We put the bike in the back of the pickup. Paul will hide it in his apartment until Christmas. I turn to him. "Can you think of anything I can get for your parents? I'm drawing a blank when it comes to them. What do you think your Dad might like?"

He puts his arm around me. "I know what I'd like." He leers at me, wiggling his eyebrows up and down.

Blushing, I push him away. "Paul, get serious. It's important to me to get the right thing. I love your parents and want to show them I appreciate all they've done for Kali and me."

He sighs. "Well, it was worth a try. Okay, let's go by the sports shop and take a look. I think he might really like a flannel shirt. He loves those for his fishing and hunting trips, and I think his is gettin' worn out."

With Paul's help, I find a forest green, heavy flannel shirt. So, that takes care of Doug. I decide to keep my eye out at home to get some hint of a gift for Sharon. And maybe she can give me some idea of what to give Paul. As we drive home I feel a shiver of anticipation through my body.

This year we'll have people to celebrate with us. What a joy! I make plans to do some Christmas baking. The last couple of years I didn't have much in the way of baking supplies. But Sharon's kitchen is well equipped.

Sharon has been spending her spare time at her sewing machine, working on some special project. So, while she's busy with that, I take care of the house and delve into baking. She shows me her favorite Christmas recipes, and how to use the mixer. Soon Kali and I are baking up a storm. We make dozens of cookies, including gingerbread men, and I turn Kali loose with the decorative icing. She spends hours decorating the various cut out cookies, and is thoroughly enjoying the whole process (except for the cleanup). I ask her, "Remember how we used to have to grind the flour and stoke up the range and mix everything by hand at our cabin? It's so much easier to cook here."

She nods happily, icing smeared on her face, and bounces in her seat. "Easy." We both grin at each other.

I make Gramma's favorite applesauce cake, so we'll have something familiar. We're filling up their freezer with baked goods.

Doug comes in from work in his stocking feet, having shucked his muddy boots on the porch, wearing a sweatshirt and heavy work pants, and sniffs appreciatively. "Wow, you girls must be starting a bakery! It smells wonderful in here."

I hand him a plate of cookies, smiling. "I hope you like'em. You can be our taste tester."

"I'll take that job any day." He stuffs a gingerbread man in his mouth. "That's terrific. You're hired."

I laugh. I'm pleased that he likes them. And that he seems light hearted. He's usually so serious and doesn't joke a lot. "Only until after Christmas. Then, I'm going job hunting. There must be something I can do in this town."

He turns serious. "I might be able to help you there. You'll have to figure out your school schedule, though. I'll ask around and see what might be available."

"That'd be great! I'd really appreciate that, Doug."

"No biggie. I'll be glad to do it."

"You and Sharon have been so kind to us. I want you to know that I really appreciate it. Once I get a job I can pay you some rent."

"Don't be silly. We love having you here. And you need to save your money for other things. For example, we need to get you a car."

"Yeah, I can't wait. I have so much to think about. My schooling is first on the list, though."

"All things in good time. You're doing great so far. Your life has changed tremendously in the last few months." He looks down at his muddy jeans. "I guess I'd better get outa these. It was a mess surveying that woodlot today. I'll just take a couple of cookies for the road."

He smiles and grabs a couple of cookies and heads for his bedroom.

I feel so good about our conversation. I've been fearful all along that we're imposing on the O'Brien's. I knew Sharon was enjoying our company, but was afraid that Doug thought we were a nuisance. He seems to like having us here now.

I peek in on Sharon. She's completely engrossed, hunched over her sewing machine, the needle rushing through the fabric at lightning speed. There are bright scraps of fabric spread out everywhere. She's concentrating so hard I don't want to disturb her. I decide to surprise her by making dinner. I know she was planning on "Spanish Rice" tonight, and I have the recipe laid out. As I tiptoe back to the kitchen and start to work, I feel a thrill of excitement. Christmas is coming and the air is electric with secretive, mumbled conferences and good cheer.

I must find something wonderful for Sharon and Paul.

After dinner, (which delights Sharon, who stays engrossed in her project until I call her in to eat), I approach her in her sewing room. "Sharon, can you tell me what would be a good Christmas gift for Paul? I want to get him something but have no idea what."

She sits back in her chair. "Well, he loves to fish when he can. Ask Doug what he thinks Paul could use in the way of fishing gear. Other than that, maybe he could use a new sweater, or maybe a new fishing vest?"

"Okay. I'll quiz Doug. Thanks, Sharon."

"Sure. And thank you for cooking dinner. You're really a big help around here."

"My pleasure. I know you're busy with your projects."

When I corner Doug, later, I ask him my question. He thinks a bit, rubbing his head as if to pull something out. "He actually could use a new fishing reel. His old one's about caput. Why don't I take you to the shop tomorrow after work and we can pick out a good one?"

I clap my hands. "Super! Thanks so much, Doug." I give him a quick, impulsive hug and he pats me awkwardly on the shoulder.

The next day we head down to the store after Doug gets home from work. Carefully, we look over the reels, and Doug helps me pick out the one he thinks is best. It looks much more complicated than the simple one I used in the Kalmiopsis. But I'm sure Doug knows what Paul would like. Then, looking around, I select a fishing vest, with Doug's approval, and have my shopping almost done.

"I have one more problem, Doug. What can I get for Sharon? I'd like to find something really nice for her but have no idea what. Do you think she could use a new sweater or maybe some jewelry?"

Doug frowns and thinks hard. "Gee, I don't know. I don't even know what I'm going to get her. She's a hard nut to crack. If you figure out something, let me know. Maybe you can come up with an idea for me."

That evening, while Sharon and Doug are watching TV, I snoop around her sewing room a bit. There must be a clue here. I see fabrics lining the shelves, and a project sitting on her sewing machine. Apparently, she's making a quilt. She seems to have all the tools she needs. Anyway, I wouldn't know if she didn't. Maybe I'll head up to Bandon or Coos Bay and see if I can find a fabric shop. Or find her a pretty sweater set. I'll take Kali with me. She'll want to give her something too. I take a quick, guilty look in her closet to see what sizes she wears, and what colors she likes. That should help.

The next day I ask Sharon if I can borrow her car to go shopping in Coos Bay. She looks surprised, but gives me permission and hands over the keys with a smile. "Try to be back by five, okay?"

"I'm sure we'll be back by then. We don't have that much shopping to do." I suspect that she's eager to have us out of the house so she can work on her projects.

Kali and I head north. Kali had been so excited when I conferred with her the night before. At the word "shopping," she'd lit up like a Christmas tree. "Presents," she'd said with glee. Again, a new word. Wonderful!

11

—— CHAPTER ——

Christmas With Family

I nervously follow the same route Sharon used when she took us to Coos Bay. It's the first time I've driven this far on my own. The traffic is scary, with log trucks roaring by and people creeping up behind me and zooming around me the first chance they get. I'm careful to keep to the speed limit but most of the other drivers pass me like I'm standing still. My hands are sweating on the steering wheel. Nevertheless, we make it into town, and I feel a vast sense of relief when we find a place to park.

At Penney's we look around carefully at all the women's clothes and finally settle upon a lovely sweater set. Kali smiles when we pick it out, and touches the soft knit, nodding her head vigorously. It's a soft, pastel green with a floral pattern on the cardigan, and will go beautifully with Sharon's strawberry blonde hair. I feel triumphant. And relieved. Kali also picks out a pretty scarf to go with it. I let her find it all by herself. She grins happily and waves it around with glee.

After that, we pick up wrapping paper and ribbon at the nearby drug store. I want our gifts to look pretty under the tree. I decide to treat Kali to lunch out at the little café where we went with Sharon before. We sit down in the vinyl booth and peruse the menu. Kali points at it and says, "Hamburger. French Fries." My heart jumps. She's adding to her well of words every day. I order that for us both, along with a couple of milkshakes. I'm feeling suddenly more in charge of my life. This is going to work. Kali *will* speak, and I will take care of us both. I'm learning more each day and feeling more confident as well. Just knowing that I can handle a car by myself is a major step. We will survive. Kali and I are going to be fine.

After I pay for our meal, I realize I'm down to my last three hundred and fifty dollars. Our money will be gone soon. Anxiety grabs my stomach, and I feel an urgent need to find a job.

On the way back, I take the time to drive through old town Bandon, just to see what's there. I fill the gas tank at the station on the corner. The street leads down to the river, and I follow it until I see the road to the beach. I park by the river's mouth, near the jetty, and we watch the waves crash in over the huge boulders. I love watching it. Kali sits for a while and then grabs my arm and points down to the beach. I shrug and say, "Why not. But just for a little bit. It's raining and it's cold, and we really need to get on home."

So, we spend a good half hour walking on the beach, enjoying the gulls floating and squealing overhead, and watching the sea throw itself against the huge pillars of stone standing off the shore. Finally, shivering in the cold wind, with rain pelting us, I'm ready to retreat. "Come on, Kali, we have to go. I'm freezing." She rolls her eyes and makes a face but follows me back to the car.

When we arrive back at the house in the late afternoon we hastily sneak our packages into our room. Sharon looks up as I pop into her sewing room to give her the keys.

"Thank God," she snaps, frowning. "Where have you been? I was expecting you back an hour ago. I was getting really worried."

My heart sinks with remorse. "I'm so sorry. I didn't mean to worry you. It was just so lovely. We really enjoyed shopping and we took a little time to check out Bandon on the way home. I love the beach there. I just couldn't resist taking Kali down to it." I hand her the keys. "Thanks so much for trusting us with your car. I really do appreciate it."

She looks somewhat mollified. "Well, okay. I know you're a good driver, even though you're new at it. I'm glad you got there and back safely." She leans back and stretches her arms up over her head. "And I've had the whole day to just work on my projects and had a great time." She relaxes her arms. "It's just—I'd really like to have an idea of when you'll be home after this."

"I promise I'll keep it in mind in the future. I'll go ahead and put dinner on if you'd like. I wanta make it up to you for worrying you. What would you like me to fix?"

"Well," she grumped. "That would be helpful. Um, how about a salad and there's green beans in the freezer and make mashed potatoes to go with the roast I have in the oven. We can thicken the juices to make gravy to go with the potatoes. Can you handle all that?"

"Oh sure. I'll start right on it."

So, with Kali peeling the potatoes while I whip up a salad and prepare the beans, we manage to get dinner on the table by 6:30 after the men get home.

After dinner and cleaning up, we watch a couple of hours of TV before Paul heads out for his apartment and I suggest to Kali that it's bedtime. It's been a long day, we're both tired and slide quickly into sleep.

The following morning, Kali has a conference with Sharon. Then she begs ten dollars off of me and the two of them leave to "get groceries." I'm suspicious but don't question them. I busy myself straightening up the house and then have a wood chopping session. I enjoy the activity out in the open air and it feels good to work those muscles. After that I do our laundry and am folding it when they come back in the door. Kali heads straight for our room with a mysterious bag of goods and Sharon, after a quick, "We're back," drops her groceries on the kitchen counter and proceeds to put them away.

Eyebrows raised, I sidle into the kitchen from the dining room where I've been folding clothes. "Hmmm. What have you two been up to? I smell a rat."

Sharon gives me an innocent look in return. "Why, whatever do you mean. We were just grocery shopping. Kali loves to do that."

I laugh. "Uh-huh. And why did she need money?"

"I think she needed some school supplies. Sharon stuffs a box of cereal in the cupboard. "We've gone through a lot of paper and she wanted some new colored markers. You know she's been having a great time creating art with me. I think she's really talented."

I know better than to point out that she's changed the subject, so I go along with it. "I'm so glad you've been helping her. I've never had much talent that way but I'm happy she's developing hers. You've been so good at teaching her."

"It's been a thrill to see her blossom and develop. You know, I've grown to really love her. And it's nice to know that I still have my teaching chops. It's been good for *me* too. You girls have really enriched our lives. I'm happy you're here."

I tear up, overwhelmed. "It's been a joy to get to know you too. And Doug. I'm really looking forward to having a family Christmas this year. Our Christmases in the wilderness were pretty lonely."

Sharon's mouth wobbles. She touches my arm. "Well, we're going to have the best Christmas ever. You'll see. I can't wait."

The next day we all go out into the woods behind the house and pick out a Christmas tree. After tramping around for half an hour or so, we find a young fir that we all agree is perfect, and cut it down. That evening we have a great time putting on the lights and ornaments. The lovely fragrance of the tree takes me back to our wilderness Christmases, when we hung the tree with our homemade ornaments. Those were happy times with our family. Sharon and Doug's ornaments are much fancier than ours were. They're really pretty and sparkly. I force my mind back to the present as Kali and

I stand back to see the results of our collective handiwork. Kali's eyes are big. She looks up at me. "Lights."

I laugh and hug her. "Yes. Lights. Aren't they pretty?" She nods happily. "Yes."

Sharon claps her hands and says, "Let's have some hot chocolate and cookies to celebrate the occasion." We all head for the kitchen.

The days fly by and before we know it, it's Christmas Eve. We're all dressed up, me in my new dress and Kali in her pretty red one. Sharon is wearing a slim navy skirt with a lighter blue, soft looking sweater. We all don our coats, as it's cold outside. The men are wearing slacks and sweaters too and look very handsome. Then we all head out to midnight mass. It's pouring, of course, so we're glad to have the hoods on our coats.

Midnight mass is wonderful. When we enter the church the brilliant poinsettias around the altar and the fragrant pine and cedar bunting down both sides of the church lift my spirits and I almost gasp at how pretty it is. There are beautiful banners on the wall on each side of crucifix. The banners are quilted, with golden angels flying over a blue background. I lean over and ask Sharon if she made them. She nods. I whisper, "They're beautiful." She beams at me.

I feel embraced by the warmth of the congregation and the beauty of the service. This time Kali and I walk up at communion, arms crossed over our chests, for a blessing. After the joy filled service, and wishing our new friends "Merry Christmas," we all head back home.

There, we continue the celebration with hot cider and Christmas cookies. Kali is excited but still nearly falls asleep over her plate. I put my arm around her and haul her off to bed.

When I come back out, Sharon and Doug have gone on to bed, leaving Paul and me alone. We just stand and hold each other for a few minutes. Finally, I murmur, "The service was so beautiful tonight, wasn't it?"

His arms tighten around me. "Sure was. Do you think you might be interested in joining our church?"

"I've thought about it. I really like the calmness of the service, and the reverence. The people are so nice. I feel at home there. It's so different from what I remember. There's no bombast or threatening. I like the way I feel when I'm there."

Paul takes my hand, raises it to his lips. It sends a thrill down my arm. "I like the way it feels when you're there with me. Do you think we might get married there some day?"

Tears form in my eyes. Let's face it. I love this man. Why keep putting off the inevitable? With a sigh, I manage to whisper, "I think so. But not until I get my diploma and have some idea of what I want to do with my life. You can understand why this is important to me, can't you?"

"Yeah. Like I told you, I'll wait. I just need to know that, in the end, we'll be together."

I lean my head on his chest and he holds me close. "That's what I want too. It'll all work out, you'll see."

Finally, I say, "We really need to put the presents under the tree. I want'em to be there when Kali wakes up."

"Oh yeah, I almost forgot." Paul goes out to his pickup and brings in Kali's bike. It has a big bow on it and a tag that says To Kali from Santa. A bike helmet hangs from the handle. I grab Paul's arm. "Did you get her that? I never thought about a helmet."

He nods. "We want her to be as safe as possible. And I wanted to give her something extra." I kiss his cheek.

"Thank you for thinking of it."

I've gathered Kali's and my packages from our room and placed them under the tree.

Together with what's already there they make quite a pile.

We admire the sight of the loaded tree for a moment. Paul points out several crude ornaments that he'd made when he was a child. There's a pinecone reindeer and a blown-out egg shell that's painted to look like a Santa. I chuckle, remembering the ornaments our family made when I was small. I know they're still in the cabin. Then, reluctantly, we head to our own rooms. He's spending the night here, as in the morning we'll all be celebrating together. He holds me close at my door and I feel so warm and loved that I hate to break away. Finally, I push him gently away. "We have to get some sleep," I whisper.

"I know. But I wish we were doing it together."

I sigh. "The time will come. Now get some sleep."

He touches my cheek and heads back to his own room.

The next morning Kali's up at seven. She yanks on my arm until I drag myself out of bed.

She's so excited she's twittering like a bird. I laugh and grab her in a bear hug. "Merry Christmas, Kali. Wait until I get some clothes on so we can go out there." I wriggle into my jeans and red sweater and slip on my tennies. Kali has rushed into her clothes too, and I run a brush through my hair and hers. Then she races out the door and into the living room. As I walk into the room, she's standing stock—still and staring at the bike.

"Well, Kali, what do you think? Do you like your bike?" She looks at me, her mouth drops open.

"Bike? My bike?" I'm getting used to her speaking, but it's still a thrill.

"Yes. It's yours. Go look at it."

Paul and his parents drift into the room in their robes and slippers. We all watch as Kali walks over to her bike and caresses the handle bars and seat. Her face lights up in a huge smile, and she says, "My Bike."

We are all smiling now. Paul says, "Try sitting on it. See how you like it. Try on the helmet."

She lifts a leg over the bar and tries sitting on the seat. "Hmmm. I can see it needs a little adjustment," Paul says. "I'll help you with that after breakfast and we'll take it out for a spin. How would that be?"

"Yes! Yes! Ride." She hops off and gives him a hug.

Then she hugs me. "Thank you, Judy." It hits me hard, and I catch my breath. It's the first time she's said my name, or "thank you," since she went mute. I'm overwhelmed. I fight back the tears. I look at Paul and our eyes meet. He knows what this means to me. I see his own eyes glisten.

I hug her back. "Merry Christmas, Kali. And thank Paul too. He got you the helmet." I blink rapidly as a memory of our last Christmas as a family stabs my brain. I see Mamma, Dad, David and Gramma all together with Kali and me, happily opening our homemade gifts for each other. It was our last celebration as a family.

Kali turns and tells Paul, "Thank you."

He grins. "My pleasure, Kali."

Sharon sniffs and walks over to the tree. "Well, let's see what the rest of us got." She starts handing out presents. Soon we're all exclaiming in delight. Kali is given a checkers set from Doug and Sharon, and a rod and reel so she can go fishing with them. Doug seems to really like the shirt I bought him. He and Sharon exchange gifts, more fishing gear for him, a pretty necklace and bracelet set for her. Sharon loves the sweater set, exclaiming over the color and texture. She makes a big fuss over the scarf from Kali. And Paul is delighted with his new reel and vest.

Kali hands me a lumpy package, tied with a big bow. I carefully unwrap a pretty hair ornament that I recognized from the drugstore display. It has silk flowers attached and will match my dress. I make sure to praise it and put it in my hair.

"I love it, Kali. Thank you so much. It'll go great with my dress." I give her a warm hug. Then Sharon hands me and Kali each a large package.

Inside are matching quilts, beautifully done in forest greens with colorful yellow and red blossom designs. I gasp, "Oh Sharon. They're so beautiful. You must have spent hours on them. I love them." Kali nods vigorously and caresses her cheek with the fabric. We both give Sharon hugs. "Thank you so much. We'll cherish them forever."

Sharon is beaming. "I'm so glad you like them. I wanted you to have something special this year."

"Well, you really outdid yourself." I snuggle the quilt to my chest.

The room is filling up with wrappings. Paul has given me a beautiful, butter yellow cashmere sweater set. It's my first introduction to cashmere. "Oh Paul, I love the color. They're so soft. I'll wear them today."

I take the sweaters to my room and put them on. When I return, I can see his approval in his eyes. He smiles and waggles his eyebrows. "That's a winner. It looks fantastic on you."

I feel my face heat up. "I love it. And it's so warm. Now you'll have to take me somewhere to show it off."

"That's a promise. I brought you something else too." He dives behind the tree and comes out with a new rod and reel for me. "We're going to have a fishing date soon, so you need to be prepared." I'm delighted. I love to fish and have missed doing it. "You'd better not wear that sweater, though." I laugh and thank him happily.

"I can't wait."

He grins, looks at his mother. "Not to change the subject, but when are we going to eat around here? I'm starving. I'll put on the bacon if you'll start the coffee."

She laughs. "Okay, it's a deal. I'll go get dressed and maybe the rest of you can clean up all these wrappings while we get to work." Paul heads for the kitchen while Kali and Doug and I make a quick clean up. Sharon soon reappears and before long we catch the scent of bacon and fresh cinnamon rolls wafting from the kitchen, and we go in to help, setting the table. We have a feast of orange juice, rolls, bacon and eggs. It's such a wonderful start to our first Christmas with a family in so many years, it's almost overwhelming. I keep fighting back the tears, but I haven't felt this content and happy in a long, long time.

We eat and laugh and talk for an hour and a half. Well, except for Kali. She finally gets restless and leaves the table. A few minutes later she comes into the dining room, bike helmet in hand. She looks imploringly at Paul. He laughs. "Okay, Kali, let's take that bike out and go for a ride."

Sharon jumps up. "Let's all go and see Kali take her first ride." So, we all throw on our jackets and pile out the door. Paul puts the bike in the back of his truck, and Kali and I hop into the cab with him. Sharon and Doug follow in her VW, and we drive to the paved grade school parking lot. It's wet, but the rain has let up and the sky is clearing. There, Paul gives Kali her first wobbly lesson in riding her bike. "Hang on, Kali, I'll balance you while you get the feel of it. That's it, that's it. You've got it." He's so kind and patient with her, it melts my heart.

It takes her several attempts, along with a couple of falls, but, scrambling back up, she ignores her bruises and is back at it. Her face is set in total concentration, her mouth a firm line as she frowns at the space in front of her. She catches on quickly and is soon cruising around the lot, a big grin on her face, with us cheering her on. After half an hour Sharon and Doug go back to the house while Paul and I stay with her. Kali swoops around in circles for another half hour, and the happiness on her face fills me with joy. Paul and I keep yelling encouragement to her as she moves in an ever-widening arc. Eventually, we decide that's been enough for one day. She stops reluctantly but she's still smiling as we head home. Home. It really does feel like home now. I'm praying that this one will stay safe.

12

CHAPTER

New Year's Eve

Sharon decides to have a party on New Year's Eve. The idea scares me a bit. There will be a lot of people and I'm not sure what will happen. I can't remember ever being at a party. But it can't be much different than having drinks with our friends at the pub, can it? Sharon has invited several of her and Doug's friends, as well as Paul's. Together we work at making party food, something else I've never done before. We make something called "hors d'oeuvres," small pastries with various fillings, and "dips," for chips. We've stocked up on chips and beer and soft drinks. There are large bottles of champagne, which I've never had before either. It looks like it'll be a big night. Kali's as excited as I am and flits about, helping wherever she can. I put her to work dusting the living room. That keeps her out from under foot for a while.

As evening nears, and dinner is cleared away, Kali and I go to our room to get dressed. I put on my dressier slacks and my Christmas sweater set that Paul gave me.

Kali opts to wear her red dress with her Mary-Janes and preens in front of the mirror. She looks adorable. I brush her hair and pull it back with a red ribbon I had snagged from Sharon's sewing room. Just the finishing touch!

Turning my attention to my own hair, I decide to imitate Kali's "do," using the hair ornament that Kali gave me, add a touch of lipstick, and we're all set. Kali's eyes shine. Her first party! Sharon has invited Al and Gerry Lucas and Lucy. Lucy, Kali's new little friend, will have a sleepover with Kali, another new experience for her. We plan to give Lucy my bed and I'll spend the night in Paul's room, while he sleeps at his own place.

Paul, who's already here, whistles when we come out of our room, "Hubba-hubba, you ladies look gorgeous. Looks like we're havin' a party." He wiggles his eyebrows up and down and grins at us. I blush and Kali twirls around, giggling. We help Sharon set out the food and she puts on some lively blue grass music before people begin arriving. The music really ramps up the atmosphere and I find myself dancing around the kitchen.

I'm on edge, as always when meeting new people and not knowing what to expect. I know that everyone I've met so far has been kind to us so I'll probably enjoy the evening. I just want to be sure I don't make a fool of myself—must watch and observe and keep quiet.

People begin arriving about eight o'clock, and we're busy taking coats and handing out drinks. Lucy arrives with her parents and the girls take Lucy's bag to our room then head for the family room, and are soon engrossed in a game of checkers. I'm relieved when Beth arrives with Robert, soon followed by Jack and Grace. I feel more at ease with friends my own age here. I'm content to listen in on the cross-conversations and join in the laughter.

Soon, the doorbell rings and Paul lets in a good looking man about his own age. He's a little shorter than Paul, about five feet eleven, with blond hair and blue eyes. They greet each other loudly, with a strange handshake that includes fist bumping and back slapping, and Paul takes his coat. Then he brings him over to me. "Pete, I want you to meet the woman I hope to marry. Judith Johnson, I want you to meet my old college roommate, Pete Green. I managed to lure him down from North Bend. Beware, he thinks he's a lady's man. He'll try to sweep you off your feet."

Pete's piercing blue eyes stare into mine. He takes my hand. "Wow, Paul. Where've you been hiding her? Judith, whatever he says, he doesn't deserve you. We really should get to know each other."

Paul laughs, puts his arm around me. "Hey, man. Back off. Find your own girl. I think there're a couple of singles milling around here."

I don't know how to react to all this and just smile, pulling my hand away. I can feel my face heat up and inwardly cringe at my inability to control my blushing.

Paul grabs Pete's arm and guides him away. "Come on and meet the rest of my pack. You know my Mom and Dad." They smile and greet Pete with hugs. Then he introduces him to the rest of the group.

People are milling around and chatting, and I'm sticking by Paul and listening. After a bit, Pete sidles up to me. "So, Judith, Paul hasn't told me much about you. I saw you on the news, though. It looks like you've had quite a different life."

"I guess you could say that. Um...Would you like something to drink?" He smiles toothily. "Sure. What've you got?"

"I'll show you."

He follows me into the kitchen and selects a beer from the ice chest on the counter.

"Thanks, Judith."

"There're refreshments on the counter and on the kitchen table, if you're hungry. Please help yourself."

"Actually, I could use a snack. Let's see what you've got."

I give him a tour of the food, and hand him a plate. "Enjoy. The napkins and forks are over there. We're all just snacking out wherever we land. Feel free to join us in the family room or living room. There's the dining room too, of course."

"Thanks, Judith. This looks great."

I hesitate and then rejoin the group in the family room. They're standing around with drinks in hand, and the noise level is rising. The older adults have gravitated to the living room, or the dining room, while the younger crowd are in the family room. I note that Kali and Lucy are ignoring the adults and still enjoying their checkers. I join Beth and their group. Beth pulls me aside and whispers, "Beware of Pete. He thinks he's God's gift to women. He'll probably make a move on you."

Surprised, I ask, "But he's good friends with Paul. Would he really do that?"

"Not sure, but you might not want to let him get you alone. I'll introduce him to May Atwood. She's single and attractive and may keep him at bay."

Pete ambles in with a plateful of food and his beer and finds a comfortable spot to sit. Some of the group decide to start up a poker game. Paul turns to me. "Hey, Judith, would you like to learn to play? It's a lot of fun and I suspect you'd be good at it."

"I'll watch you play a while and see if I think I can handle it." I sit by him as the group becomes involved in the game at a card table in the living room. I can't say that I'm interested. Paul tries to explain to me what's happening, but it seems quite complicated to me, and it entails too much sitting. I whisper to Paul that I'm going to mingle with the other guests. He nods and gives my hand a squeeze. He whispers in my ear, "Do you want me to come with you?"

I whisper back, "That's okay, you enjoy your game. I'll find Beth and the girls." He nods his head with a smile, gives my hand another squeeze, and says, "Okay. I'll join you in a while."

I wander into the family room. They're all eating and visiting and just enjoying each other's company. I feel kind of lost, not sure how to mingle. I curl up in an easy chair.

I notice Pete set down his empty plate, and he comes over and sits near me on the nearby sofa. He leans towards me. "You must not be a party animal. Do you find this difficult after being by yourself in the forest for so long?"

"I'm afraid that I'm still trying to get used to socializing."

He shifts forward in his seat, forearms on his knees, and glances towards the table where Paul's sitting. "When Paul disappeared last fall I was really worried. I figured he'd run into trouble either with pot growers or maybe had an accident. I helped out with the search until I had to get back to work. Even then I went back on weekends with his Dad and looked for him. We couldn't find a trace of him. I guess we were lookin' in the wrong area." He smiles, and his handsome face relaxes. "You must've done a good job hiding out."

"Well, I was afraid of the guys camping out at the grow, and Paul was injured, so we just kept to ourselves at our cabin while he healed up. I don't know what would've happened if Kali hadn't run off and been kidnapped."

He grins. "I can think of worse fates than being holed up in the wilderness with a beautiful woman. He really lucked out when you found him."

Again, my face heats up and I'm tongue-tied. I don't even know this guy, and he makes me uncomfortable. Is he flirting with me? In spite of myself, I can't help feeling a little flattered. Finally, after a dead pause, I tell him, "I don't know about that. It was a lucky accident for us both."

"Are you two goin' to get married?"

I don't want to answer that. It's none of his business. My answer is short. "I don't know. Maybe."

"What was it like, living out there all alone?"

"I wasn't alone. I had Kali, and my grandmother before she died. And Don dropped in once in a while and brought us supplies. It was lonely but we were busy and time went by fast. We had our animals and were comfortable in our cabin. We had nowhere else to go."

He shakes his head. "I really admire you for managing to survive out there. I haven't had a chance to talk to Paul about it much. But I think he actually enjoyed the experience."

I smile at that. Pete's easy to talk to. "I think we all did. It was great to have company. And as for surviving, we had no choice. We did what we had to do."

"So how are you adjusting to life back in civilization? Has it been difficult?'

I pause, think about it. "Well, I'm finding all the noise and hustle of town life to be an adjustment. It was so peaceful out in the woods. But I'm happy to be around people again. Paul's friends have all been so nice and welcoming. Doug and Sharon have been wonderful. I don't know what we'd have done without them. Sharon's been working on bringing me up to date. Everything's changed a lot since we went into the wilderness. I've had to learn how to operate new machines, like the washer and dryer, and phones, and drive a car, and a whole new way of life."

"I'll bet. I never thought about that. You have a lot of catching up to do. Yeah, Doug and Sharon are great. I've known'em since Paul and I were freshmen."

"So, what kind of work do you do, Pete?"

He tells me that he works for a Coos Bay engineering firm, and describes what he does there. I listen with my ears but my brain wanders off to where Paul is playing poker with his pals. He looks like he's having a good time. Personally, I can't sit still that long concentrating on cards. I realize that Pete has stopped talking. "That sounds like an interesting job. Do you like living in North Bend?"

"It isn't much of a town, but the rent's reasonable. And I like the proximity to fishing and hunting and the beach. Do you still fish and hunt?"

"I haven't since I've lived here. But Paul gave me a new fishing rod for Christmas so we'll probably get out there as soon as the weather permits."

"Maybe we can all do a fishing trip together."

"That could be fun." I glance around. "Would you excuse me? I should see if Sharon needs help in the kitchen." I stand up.

"Sure. I'll check on how the poker game's going."

I head into the kitchen. I'm feeling tired already from trying to make conversation. After years of silence I have a hard time thinking of what to say. There's so much talk about people and events that I know nothing about. I try to listen carefully to learn whatever or whoever the conversation is about. But it's a strain, trying to keep up.

I check on the refreshments and refill some of the platters. I peek into the living room. The older adults are sitting around a couple of card tables, chatting and laughing. I grab an hors d'oeuvre and wander back into the family room. Some of the group including Pete and May, are dancing to the music. Pete seems to be enjoying himself and chatting easily with the other guests. Kali and Lucy have put aside the checkers and are dancing too. I'm enjoying watching them and soon join them, doing my best imitation of what I've seen on TV. It seems to me that anything goes as long as we're moving. Beth has joined us and we're all having a great time. She shouts, "Hey, Judith, try the 'monkey'," and goes into a set of jerky movements. I'm laughing and trying to follow her without much success.

Before long, a loud rock 'n roll song comes on and everybody is whooping it up. I back out and plop down on a chair. I'm feeling really thirsty and pop up to head toward the kitchen for a cold glass of water. Pete follows me in and takes a glass too.

"You're a natural dancer, Judith. You picked that up fast."

I laugh. "Well, it's nice of you to say so. I'm afraid I'm a rank beginner."

He points to the ceiling above the sink. "Do you know what that's for?"

I look up. It's a bunch of mistletoe. "Oh no."

"Oh yes." He bends over and kisses me on the mouth.

Stunned, I register his firm lips on mine just long enough to realize that this kiss doesn't feel at all like Paul's. I feel … nothing. Then I'm angry. I push him away. "What're you doing?"

He raises his eyebrows in surprise. "Well, you're supposed to kiss when there's mistletoe over your head."

"Well, I don't agree with that. Don't try it again."

"Sorry. I wasn't trying to start anything. I wouldn't move in on Paul's girl. It was just an impulse."

"Well, control your impulses. Let's just join the others." I bolt out of the kitchen.

Before I know it, people start gathering around the TV set. They're watching a mob of people in New York being entertained while waiting for a ball to drop at midnight. This strikes me as an odd tradition but they seem to be intrigued. Someone starts singing "Auld Lang Syne" and the people are swaying and waving their arms. I'm hit with a vision of our family in the cabin, playing games and singing as the New Year begins. A pang of missing them almost overwhelms me. I swallow hard and blink back the tears, bring my mind back to the present. It's almost midnight. Once the ball drops, Kali and Lucy will have to go to bed. We're all waiting. Pete's standing next to May.

Sharon begins handing out glasses of champagne, and everyone's watching the ball. I give her a hand until everyone has a glass of champagne or soft drink. The poker players end their game and filter into the room. Paul slips into the crowd and puts his arm around me. They all start counting as the ball starts sliding down. Suddenly, everybody starts cheering and kissing, and Paul pulls me into his arms. "Happy New Year, Judith." He plants a long, enthusiastic kiss on my lips. I kiss him back. Everyone holds up their drinks and toasts the new year. There's much cheering and backslapping and hugging going on.

Finally, I break away from Paul and turn to Kali and Lucy. "Happy New Year, girls. Now it's time for bed. Let's get you settled down for the night. I look at Paul. I'll be right back."

The three of us head for our room. The girls are dragging their feet. "Go to bed now? It's new year," whines Kali.

I'm startled. It's the first time I've heard her say a full sentence. A great way to start the new year. I'm elated.

"Yes, now. Or you won't be able to get up in the morning." I hustle them along and see that they get ready for bed and are tucked in for the night.

"Okay, girls, you'd better get some sleep. Tomorrow's the first day of the new year. We'll have a lovely breakfast of pancakes and eggs when we're all up. Nighty-night." I turn off the lights and close the door. But I hear giggling as I head down the hall and figure there won't be much sleeping for a while. It's a joy to hear Kali having fun with Lucy. She's embracing our new life with more and more enthusiasm. And she's speaking more every day. She and Lucy seem to get by with a combination of sign language and simple sentences. I love Lucy for sticking with Kali.

The party is winding down, and the poker game is done. People are milling around. Everybody heads for the kitchen for a midnight snack. Paul joins me and puts his arm around me. "Hey, Judith, want to step out on the patio for some air?"

I nod and we head out through the sliding door. It's cold outside and rain is pounding on the roof, but it feels good after being in the crowded house. We stand with our arms around each other. "Did you enjoy your game?"

"It was fun. But I'd rather be with you. I need to give you a proper New Year's kiss." Our lips meet and I realize that these are kisses that I will enjoy forever. We stand there, holding each other close.

He asks, "Are you enjoying the party?"

"I guess. I find it hard to concentrate with all these people around. Would you believe this is the first party I've been to that I can remember? It's almost overwhelming."

It'll get easier, Judith, I promise. You'll get used to being around people. I want you to enjoy my friends. What do you think of Pete?"

I hesitate. "He seems nice. He likes to fish and hunt. You two should have a lot in common."

"Yeah. We've been hunting partners for several seasons now."

"He kissed me under the mistletoe."

"He did? What did you do?"

"I told him not to do it again, and bugged out of there. Are you jealous?"

"Depends. Did you enjoy it?"

"Well no. But what if I did? How would you feel?"

He pulls me close. "I'd probably punch his lights out. I'm glad you didn't like it, though. I want you to save your kisses for me. But I trust you, Judith. I'd trust you with my life. After all, you saved it once. I know you. You're loyal to the end. I know you'd never cheat on me. That's one of the reasons I fell in love with you."

I tighten my arms around him. I simply say, "Yes."

"Yes what?"

"Yes, I'll marry you." I'm overwhelmed by longing and joy and, even a little fear of the sheer finality of it. "I know now that's what I want. I don't want to be alone anymore."

He steps back. "You mean it? Are you sure?"

"Yes. But I still want to get my diploma first, and maybe even get some further education. Would you mind if your wife goes to college? And of course, Kali's part of the package."

He grabs me in a bear hug. "You can do anything you want, be anything you want. I promise not to hold you back. We'll work it out, you'll see. And Kali's the kid sister I never had. I love her and wouldn't expect anything else." His voice cracks. "We're a great team. We can do anything." We just hold each other for a while. "Shall we tell my folks? We've already popped the champagne."

I'm not ready to tell the whole world yet, I think. And I want Kali to be the first to know, anyway. "I'd rather wait until we've set a date and just let the family know then."

"Whatever you want. I'm just over the moon because you said 'yes.' Let's make it official." He drops down on one knee. "Judith Johnson, will you marry me?'

I giggle. "Of course, Paul O'Brien. I'm all yours."

He stands up and grabs me in his arms and lifts me off my feet. "You've just made me the happiest man alive. I can't wait to tell my folks." He puts me back down. "But it'll be our secret until you think the time's right."

He kisses me thoroughly and I feel myself responding down to my toes, my doubts floating away.

Some of the guests have started leaving by the time we get back in the house. I'm sure Sharon realizes that something is up, but she's busy handing out coats and doesn't say anything as she bids her guests "Happy New Year, and good-night."

Paul, Doug, Pete and I start cleaning up and putting things away. We're nearly finished when Sharon says, "Okay, people. You've done enough. We'll finish it in the morning. Let's all get some sleep and start the new year fresh."

I protest. "But, we're almost done."

"That's okay. We have to wait for the dishwasher to get finished before we can put those few dishes in it. Just stack'em in the sink. I'm exhausted and Doug and I are going to bed."

"Okay. It was a fun party, Sharon. We had a good time."

She looks at me, eyebrows raised. "I'm glad. It looked like you and Paul were really enjoying it."

Dammit. My face is turning red. What does she mean? I glance at Paul and he's just standing there, looking innocent. "Um, well, we did. Didn't we, Paul?"

He grins. "Yeah. I won three bucks at poker." He looks at Pete, who's been lingering. "We'd better get on down to my place, Pete. I've got a bone to pick with you. And you look like you need some sleep." He faces me. "Pete's staying at my place tonight. We'll see you in the morning." He gives me a big smooch, right in front of everybody, and, throwing on his coat, sings, "G'night, Mom and Dad. Thanks for the party. Happy New Year." And drags Pete out the door.

Sharon stands looking at the door quizzically. "Well, what do you suppose those two are up to?"

I laugh. "I hope they're going home to bed. And that's where I'm headed myself. Thanks so much for the party. It was great."

"Thank *you*, dear. You and Kali were a big help. I couldn't have done it without you."

"Well, I learned a lot ... how to make hors d'oeuvres, and party food. It was really fun. My first adult party." I pause. *And I learned that all kisses aren't the same*, I tell myself. "Well, goodnight, and thanks again."

I give Sharon a hug and head for bed. But it takes me a long time to get to sleep. I keep going over my conversation with Paul and the sensations of our kisses. I'm suddenly filled with the desire to get on with my life and fall asleep making plans for finishing my education so we can be together.

13

— CHAPTER —

A New Year

I wake up to the first day of 1985 with hope and joy lifting my spirits. I spring out of bed and jump in the shower before the girls can wake up and beat me to it. Once dressed, I head to the kitchen to help get breakfast started. I put on the coffee for the adults. As I glance out the sliding glass patio door, I notice something strange hanging from the tree that shades the area, something gray and red and limp, like a rag of some sort. I don't like the looks of that.

I walk out to get a closer look and recoil in horror at what I find. One of Kali's cats has been strangled and gutted and left hanging there. I suppress a scream and my mind goes into overdrive, as does my heart. What's the meaning of this? Who could do such a horrible thing? I've killed animals for defense or food purposes, but am stunned by the savagery of this. Why kill an innocent animal? So brutally? One of Kali's pets? It's a warning to us. How did they do this in the dark? Are they watching our house? They must have been lurking outside while the party was going on. Whoever sent those notes to me must have done this. "Keep yur mouth shut!" flashes through my mind. My stomach is churning, but I have to make sure that Kali never sees this. With trembling hands, I quickly take the poor mangled, bloody ball of gray fur down from the tree. Stumbling to the tool shed, I find a shovel and head into the woods behind the house. I have it buried long before Kali and Lucy come shuffling into the kitchen.

I take a deep breath and brace myself. "Good morning, girls," I chirp, as cheerily as I can muster. "Did you sleep well?" Sleepy nods. "Okay, how about a nice pancake breakfast with scrambled eggs?" Big grins and definite "Yeahs," resound in unison.

I'm preparing pancakes, eggs and bacon for the family when Sharon and Doug join us. I wait until breakfast is over and the mess cleared up before I surreptitiously whisper to Doug to step outside with me. I lead him away from earshot of the house and tell him about my discovery that morning. He clenches his fists. "Oh my god! Unbelievable! That's horrible, Judith." He reaches out and squeezes my shoulder. Pauses. "What on earth will you tell Kali?"

I shiver, and choke out, "I don't want her to know. We'll just say that a coyote or something got her, or maybe she just ran off. She'll understand that, even though she'll be really upset. It's nature's way. She's seen enough evil at the hands of humans. I'm really frightened that this might be a warning that they could harm Kali, though. I just don't know what to do."

He frowns, crosses his arms. "I think we should let the sheriff know, and we may have to have them patrol the area more often. I can't believe they could carry this off without any of us noticing. That's really worrisome. I don't think they'd dare attack you or Kali, personally, but we'll be on our guard, nevertheless. I'm so sorry about this, Judith."

"I'm just afraid that having us here puts you and Sharon in danger. Maybe we should leave."

He sticks out his chin, puts his arm around me and gives me a light hug. "No way," he snaps. "You girls are part of our family, now. We'll handle this together."

I repress a sniffle. It's such a relief to know that they have our backs. "You don't know how much that means to me. I'm so scared for Kali. I can take care of myself but I'm afraid they'll come after her."

"We won't let anything happen to either one of you. We've been warned and we'll be on the lookout. Now, what do you think we should do about the cat?"

"I'm just going to wait until she notices that it's gone and then tell her that it may have wandered off or been taken by a predator. Maybe we can go back to the shelter and get her another one."

"Okay. I'll follow your lead. And I'll let Sharon know what's happened. We'll call the sheriff as soon as Kali's not around to hear."

It takes Kali just a couple of hours to realize that something is wrong with her pets. Only one showed up for her breakfast, and it's acting nervous, meowing, complaining, circling Kali's legs a lot. Kali's puzzled and begins searching through the area around the house. I pretend to help her look, hunting through the woods behind the house, checking under the front porch. Finally, she picks up her remaining cat, which will let only Kali touch her, and sits down on a deck chair, cuddling her. I sit down beside her. "I'm so sorry, Kali. I think maybe she went off to find a mate. Or maybe she's just exploring. You know they're still pretty wild."

Tears slide down her cheeks, and a sob escapes her lips. She clutches her remaining pet and cries inconsolably. It breaks my heart and it's all I can do not to cry myself. Finally, when she's calmer, I say, "Honey, if she doesn't come back, would you like to go to the shelter and pick out another kitty?"

She shakes her head, then, slowly, nods. "Okay, we'll wait a few days, and if she doesn't come back, we'll get you another cat. Meanwhile, we'll keep an eye out for her, okay? She may have just wandered off."

She nods sadly, cuddling her cat, Stripey. Kali isn't very imaginative when it comes to naming her pets.

"So, we need to give Lucy a ride home. Shall we do that now?"

Another slow nod. She hugs her pet and lets her go. There's a flash of gray fur as the cat races into the undergrowth. Lucy has been hovering, looking worried. "I'm so sorry, Kali. I know you loved your kitty."

Kali sniffs and wipes her eyes on her sleeve. "Thanks, Lucy."

I wait three long days, while she mopes around the house. Meanwhile, I've notified the Sheriff's department, since we're out of the city limits, and they reassure me that they'll increase patrols in the area. I have my own plans to keep watch and keep my gun handy.

When I tell Paul what happened, he's outraged. He slams his hand on the counter and rages, "Goddamit! That's a shitty thing to do. If I find out who did that I'll make him sorry he was born. How's Kali taking it? Can I do anything?"

I'm shocked. I've never seen him this angry. "Shhhh! Calm down. Kali'll hear you. The Sheriff has promised to give Gimpy and Bart's relatives a warning. I'm sure it's got to be someone related to them."

"Maybe I should move back up here. I can't just stand by and do nothing. I can protect you better if I'm here."

"I have my shotgun handy in my closet. And I'm keeping a sharp eye out. I think it might be best if we just carry on as usual. I don't want'em to think that they've got us scared. Besides, we've got your folks here too. And remember, you're a witness too. They might come after you. I think if we're all together we make a more inviting target. We'll have to all be on guard."

I finally persuade him to calm himself and carry on as if nothing has happened. A week later, we take Kali back to the animal shelter to pick out another cat. There's actually one of Kali's original group that we had left there, still there—a black and white neutered male. He comes right up to Kali and lets her pick him up. I feel relief and joy for her as she cuddles him. So, she takes him home, naming him Tom, for tomcat. He has calmed down during his stay in the shelter, and filled out beautifully, and lets her hold him all the way home. She takes him out to meet his companion, and I watch her petting them and making cat talk with them. She perfectly mimics their cries and they seem to understand her. She really loves them and I'm glad she's able to accept the replacement cat. It may take a while for his gray striped female companion to accept him, though. Stripey turns up her nose and retreats into the underbrush. I'm sure Kali can bring her around.

This month proves to be momentous in several ways. The court date is set for the trials of Bart and Gimpy for mid-February, to be tried separately. That means I'll be tied up at that time to deal with the situation. But for now, I begin classes to work for my GED. I'm taking accounting and biology to get some science and math credits. It means driving all the way up to Coos Bay to the community college twice a week, but Sharon lets me use her car and, so far, it's working out.

Doug comes home one evening with news of a job opening at the Skipper's Landing Cafe near the docks for part-time help. I drive down there the next morning to apply. I like the looks of the place. It's homey, with wooden tables and chairs in the middle and booths along the sides, and big windows looking out over the bay. Nautical pictures and artifacts adorn the walls. There's a counter with six stools on one end of the room near the kitchen doors. Hank, the cafe owner, mans the cash register and desk at the entrance. A big, burly, balding guy with a middle-aged gut hanging over his belt, he hands me a form to fill out, and looks me over. "Aren't you the girl who was living in the Kalmiopsis?"

"Um, afraid so. Is that a problem?"

"Hell no. You'll probably bring in curiosity seekers. Should be good for business. Have you had any experience waitressing?"

"I'm sorry but I haven't. But I'm a quick learner. And I'm a hard worker."

"Go ahead and fill out the application. Can you work a morning shift from six to two? You'll be taking orders and serving the food, and lots of coffee, and cleaning up when business is slow. Do you think you can handle that?"

"That would be perfect. I'm taking afternoon classes to earn my GED so that'd work out with my schedule."

I sit down at a booth in the corner and fill out my first job application. It takes me a while to work my way through it. I put down Doug as my contact. None of my experiences so far have been related to waitressing, unless you count waiting on Kali and Paul. I watch the activity around me and check out what the waitresses are doing. It doesn't look that hard. I should be able to handle that. I hand the application in with trepidation.

"I'll look this over and let you know in a day or two."

"Thank you. I really need a job. I appreciate your considering me." I hesitate. "There's just one thing. I need to tell you that I may have to take some days off to be a witness at two murder trials that are coming up. The men who killed my family will be on trial and I'll have to be there."

He hesitated. "Well, let's see how it works out. If I hire you, and you're a good worker, we can probably work around your schedule. Maybe trade shifts with some of the evening workers. I appreciate your honesty."

His call comes that evening and I'm hired, to begin the next day. I'm so excited, elated and scared all at the same time. I don't even ask him what the pay is. I just want a job. I feel like my life is taking shape. As soon as I make some money I plan to get a car. Once the trials are over, I can concentrate on the next phase of my life.

So, I settle into a routine. Up at 4:30 every morning, down at the cafe by a quarter till six. I like to be there early.

We don't have uniforms, just tee shirts and jeans, so it's comfortable. It takes me a few days to catch on to the lingo, ("Order up," "Pigs'n blankets," "Poached on a Plank," and more, terms unfamiliar to me,) memorize the menu, and learn where everything is. And I find myself enjoying the easy comradery of the kitchen crew and fellow waitress, Cedar.

Cedar is a tall, skinny, twenty something blue-eyed blonde. Her hair is in a long braid down her back. She has a sharp, pointy nose and a wide, impish grin. Her high pitched, little girl voice makes me smile. She notices my surprise at her name.

"Yeah, I know. My name is weird. My folks were hippies who wanted to be 'at one' (she rolls her eyes) with nature, so they named me Cedar, after a tree, and my brother, 'Forest,' and my little sister, 'Aspen.' I've never quite forgiven them for that. My friends call me "Ce." She notices my nervousness.

"Don't you worry, Sweetie, if you have any questions, just ask. We're all family here. A word of warning …," she points to a table where four elderly men are sitting. "Those old coots come in here three times a week and sit there schmoozing over their breakfasts for at least two hours. Several times, when they left, I seen one of'em holdin' back and pocketing the tips the others left. So, what I do is, I swoop in the minute I notice they're about to leave and busy myself at the table, and pocket the tips before Ernie can snatch'em."

"Wow! Thanks for the tip, Ce. I really appreciate whatever advice you can give me." We become great working partners after that. Eventually, my nerves calm down as I gain confidence.

A couple of shifts later, the four old guys come in. They sit in my area. So, following Cedar's advice, I keep an eye on them. Sure enough, once I give them their bill (paid at the cash register up front), they begin preparing to leave. As the first two get up, I swoop in and start clearing away their dishes, pocketing the tips left on the table. I say, "Oh, thank you guys," as I pick it up. One of the two remaining frowns but doesn't say anything. *Thank you, Cedar.*

Hank is a kind boss. He doesn't yell when I spill a whole tray of water glasses all over the floor. Just grabs a mop and helps me clean it up.

At first some of the customers are curious about me, asking questions, wanting to know about the Kalmiopsis and our lives there, but that peters out soon enough. I find I enjoy being around them because most of the customers are nice. Once in a while I'll catch a bit of conversation that shocks or embarrasses me because of the filthy language. I try to ignore it but can't keep my face from burning.

The first round of people to come in are usually fishermen, in their warm flannels and boots, and the occasional tie wearing salesman or tourists.

Later the retired guys wander in and over breakfast spend a couple of hours telling yarns. They like to flirt; "Hi there, Sweetie, howya doin'?" "'Bout time they got some good lookin' women in here," and I do my best to just josh them along. I'll say something like,"I'll bet you say that to all the girls. What'll you have today?" I've watched how Cedar handles her customers and learn to give as good as I get. We usually have a really busy lunch hour, from 11:30 on. I find that I'm making a surprising amount of cash every day in tips and, once home, stash it away in a jar in our closet. A few more dollars and I'll open up a bank account.

One day three guys come in for breakfast. They're dressed like loggers—flannel shirts, cut-off, sturdy, dark jeans, heavy work boots. When I go to take their order one of them looks at me speculatively. "Ain't you one of them 'wild girls?'"

I stare at him. "I assure you I'm quite civilized."

He guffaws. "You sure about that?" He reaches out and puts his hand on my butt. Enraged, l instinctively grab his hand in one quick movement and bend it backwards until he screams, "Hey, yer breakin' my hand. Ow, Ow, Ow! Dammit, let go."

I hiss, "Do that again and I'll break your arm."

Hank hears the ruckus and hustles over to the table. "What's happenin'?"

"She damned near broke my hand."

"Jack, you've been warned before to keep your hands off of my waitresses. Now get out and don't come back."

"What the hell! I didn't hurt 'er. I want my breakfast."

"Sorry, your money's not good here anymore. Just leave."

"Dammit, Hank. You don't have to get huffy. I'll behave."

"Sorry, Jack. You can apologize to Judith and leave. That's all there is to it."

The man, his face purple with anger, not looking at me, snarls, "Sorry, lady." He reluctantly gets up, glares at me, and slowly walks out with Hank walking behind him to the door. His companions look at each other.

"Well, I want my breakfast," says one.

"Yeah, me too." They look at me, "Sorry, lady. Jack's a jackass."

"Well, then, he's got the right name, doesn't he?" They laugh. I smile and take their orders.

It's late February when I have to ask Hank for the trial days off and he's nice about it. "You've been doing a good job here. If you need time off to get through this thing, you've got it. We'll get by somehow."

The first trial is two days away and it's weighing on my mind. It's pouring rain as I'm driving home late after my class, about nine o'clock. Suddenly there's a large vehicle in my rear-view mirror. I speed up a bit and so do they. My heart races as I try to figure out what's going on. All I can see are bright headlights as their vehicle suddenly rams into the rear of Sharon's car. I scream as the car lurches forward and step on the gas. They speed up too and, suddenly, race around me and sideswipe the car. I'm knocked into the ditch, coming to an abrupt halt, ramming me forward, as they roar on down the road. All I can see as they go by is the black outline of a large pickup. My seatbelt has kept me from going through the windshield, but my head and shoulders are yanked back. My heart's pounding and I'm shaking as I try to back out of the ditch. It doesn't work. I'm stuck. I lean my head against the steering wheel. Whoever is threatening us is serious. What am I going to tell Sharon? I feel sick about her car. She's been so generous, lending it to me. Will she be mad at me?

I turn off the engine, gather my bag and books, and, still shaking, climb out of the driver's seat with difficulty, as the car's at a slant. Using the flashlight from the glovebox, I can see a deep gash down its side, and the headlight's smashed. Is it ruined? Whimpering, I pat its crumpled fender. I fight to tamp down my growing hysteria. Groaning, tears streaming down my face, I head out on foot. As I trudge home in the pouring rain, shivering, I keep a wary eye out in case whoever it was comes back to finish me off. I jump off the road in terror and hide in the bushes whenever a car comes by. Fortunately, it only happens twice. It takes me about forty desperate minutes to reach the house. Sharon and Doug are watching TV and stare at me as I walk in the door, having removed my muddy shoes on the porch. I'm drenched, and thoroughly splashed with mud from stumbling through puddles in the dark.

"Judith, my God, what happened to you?"

I take off my jacket and, leaning against the wall, burst into tears. "I'm so sorry, Sharon. I'm afraid your car is ruined. Somebody ran me off the road. I'm so sorry."

They both jump up and pull me into the living room to the sofa. "What do you mean, they ran you off the road? Are you all right?"

"Oh my God. Let me get some towels." Sharon dashes off.

So, while I mop myself off, I tell them what happened, and as soon as they're sure I'm not hurt, except for a sore neck and shoulder, Doug goes to call the sheriff while Sharon wraps me in an afghan and goes to get me a hot cup of tea and a cold compress for my neck. "Oh, Judith. Are you sure you're okay? Is there anything else I can get you?"

"This is great, Sharon. I feel so bad about your car."

"Forget the car. Cars can be replaced. People can't. I'm sure the insurance'll cover it."

The Sheriff's department sends a deputy out to take my statement. Then, Doug puts on his rain gear and goes with him to check out the car. He gets back about midnight and looks pale as he walks into the room. "Judith, we're really lucky you didn't get hurt worse. They made a mess out of the car. But I think it can be fixed. Good thing we have insurance. But until these trials are over, I don't want you goin' anywhere by yourself. The sheriff's department was supposed to step up patrols in the area. Tomorrow they're goin' to investigate the relatives of both the defendants and see if they can hunt down that pickup. He pauses. Meanwhile, I suggest that we all get some sleep and survey the damage in the morning. I'll take you to work, Judith."

Sharon chimes in, as she dithers nervously. "Yes, let's get to bed. We all need some sleep. We can sort it out tomorrow. Judith, are you sure you're, all right? Would you like some aspirin to help with the neck pain?"

"That might be a good idea. Thanks, Sharon."

So, I take two aspirin, have a quick, hot shower, and, after checking on Kali who's sound asleep in her bed, crawl into mine and drown myself in sleep.

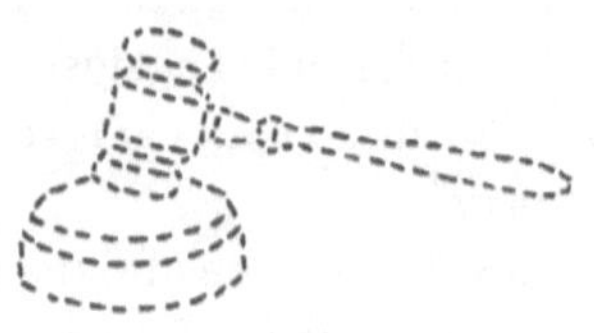

14

— CHAPTER —

The Trial

The Sheriff's department so far is unable to find the pickup that ran me off the road before the trial. I know they've obtained warrants and searched the properties of Bart and Gimpy's relatives, and known associates. So far, no luck. But the trials go on.

In early February, Paul, Kali and I find ourselves in the Gold Beach county courtroom. Beforehand, the prosecutor thoroughly questioned all of us about what happened and I'm apprehensive. He will explain Kali's condition to the judge and see that I can accompany her to the witness stand to interpret for her if need be. He needs her to point out her abductor. Just the interview he had with her in his office was hard on her. She endured the whole thing with an iron grip on her chair arms, head down except when she nodded or shook it. She's been quiet and moody ever since, mostly hanging out in our room or outside playing with her cats.

We're seated in the bench behind the prosecutor's table. I'm doing my best to remain calm and not think about the tough looking crew who file into the wood paneled courtroom after us. There's an old, tiny, weather-worn lady, wearing jeans and a heavy jacket, along with four burly men, ranging in age from about thirty to forty-something. They're dressed in an assortment of gear, from camouflage pants to jeans, boots and flannel jackets or hunting vests. I have no doubt that it was one of them who ran me off the road. I shiver as my mind flashes back to that black pickup.

There are a couple of younger women with them, one of them in black slacks and a heavy sweater, the other in faded jeans and a gray hoody sweatshirt.

The Judge, a handsome, forty-ish man with just a fringe of gray at his temples, enters, and we all rise. Soon the jury selection is underway.

It takes nearly a week for them to select a jury. The questioning of the candidates is long and relentless. Just when you think they've settled on one, one of the lawyers will hand the judge a note and the prospective juror will be dismissed. It goes on for days, but finally they have a jury. Next week, the trial begins.

I have to admit I feel a twinge of sympathy for Gimpy when he comes into the room. After all, he had shown some modicum of kindness to Kali after his associates had tied her to a tree, when Bryce kidnapped her. He had argued against killing her, and I picture him giving her a drink. Later, he put his jacket around her shoulders. But I harden my heart when I remember that he has that limp as a result of my father shooting him when his gang raided our camp. Gimpy is charged as an accessory to murder and kidnapping. Of course, he has pled "not guilty."

Time drags while the prosecutor lines up the evidence against Gimpy, whose real name turns out to be Arthur Blake. I had overheard his associates calling him "Gimpy," and that's how I have always referred to him. Both men have been charged with second degree murder, kidnapping, and drug trafficking. Eventually, they call me to the stand. Once again, I have to tell our story— how my father, struggling with PTSD, took us into the Wilderness when I was a child and he was growing pot because we needed money.

My mind flashes back to that horrible night, and I fight to maintain control as I tell them how Bryce and his gang came in one night to raid our grow. They ended up shooting our mother and father and brother, as Kali and I trembled in terror in the brush. How Kali and I escaped and hid out in the Wilderness with our grandmother. Holding back tears, I explain that Kali stopped talking after the killings. "We lived with our grandmother until she died."

I can't hold back the tears. Someone hands me a box of tissues, and the judge kindly tells me, in a low voice, to take my time. Getting hold of myself, I blow my nose and wipe my face and continue. "After that we were afraid to leave. We had no family outside the wilderness, and nowhere to go. We were afraid of the men who raided our camp. They knew that we had escaped, but they couldn't find us. Then, years later, the killers came back into the forest looking for us. Bryce found Kali and kidnapped her." I describe the shoot-out when our friend, Vietnam Don, leapt out of the brush and shot Bryce, who simultaneously returned fire and shot him right in front of me. I point out the defendant as one of the raiders and explain his involvement in the kidnapping. I keep everything as matter-of-fact as I can, even though re- living the events cuts my heart into shreds.

The cross examination is over rather quickly. Gimpy's lawyer doesn't seem very smart to me, asking what I consider to be dumb questions. "How do you know it was your father's bullet that crippled Mr. Blake?" "How do you feel about Mr. Blake?" "Why did you not go to the authorities after your parents were shot?" *Really?* I've already explained all that. Once should be enough. I doggedly go through the story once more.

When I'm done, the prosecution explains to the court that Kali doesn't speak much. Because of her young age and the trauma she has endured, he wishes to allow me to accompany her as she has great difficulty speaking. The defense agrees with that.

By now it's late. The judge decides that the trial will adjourn until tomorrow morning. The jury is admonished not to speak about the proceedings to anyone and to be back in court the next day at 9 o'clock.

The next day, Kali is called on to testify. I go up to the witness chair with Kali, and hold her hand while the judge kindly asks her, "Now Kali, do you understand how important it is that you tell us the truth about your kidnapping? That you will need to point out the person who was one of your kidnappers?" Kali looks at him squarely and nods, her face solemn. "Good. Then we shall proceed."

She nods her assent when she's sworn in. Her face is strained and serious, as she stares straight ahead. She looks small and scared, and squeezes my hand hard. I squeeze hers back.

The prosecutor walks up to the witness stand and smiles at her. He gently but clearly asks her if one of her kidnappers is in the courtroom, and she nods, looking at the floor. He asks her to point him out, and, squeezing my hand, she glances up and points at Gimpy. He continues to ask her "yes" or "no" questions about the kidnapping, and she manages to say "yes" or "no" as they proceed. He makes sure the jury understands her answers. When he's finished, he smiles at her again, says, "Well done, Kali, thank you," and returns to his seat. She looks at me and clutches my hand.

The defense lawyer attempts to ask her more complicated questions and she refuses to say more than, "Yes" or "No." When Kali starts crying, he finally gives up, shrugs, says, "No further questions," and sits back down. The judge excuses her and we return to our seats.

Paul is next, and corroborates my testimony, filling in the details of how we tracked down the thugs. "Kali ran away, and we followed her to where we could see that she had been taken by someone. Someone brutal." He glances nervously at Kali. "First, we came across her dog, which had been horribly beaten." He gives me a pleading look. I nod my head slightly. He describes putting down our devoted dog, Pepper, when we found him mortally wounded by Bryce. I had left that painful part out. I put my arm around Kali. "Then we found the spot where she'd been picked up." He shoots another pained look my way, looks down at his feet. "There was a lot of blood," he rasps, "and one of Kali's moccasins. We were really afraid for her." Paul shifts in his seat and glances at me again.

Kali tugs on my sleeve, looks at me beseechingly, holding her stomach as if she's going to be sick. I hurry her out of the courtroom and to the restroom. She vomits into the nearest toilet. I'm feeling sick myself, with worry over her. When she's done, she's pale and cries for several minutes. I cradle her in my arms as she shudders and sniffles, and wipe away her tears.

"Just hold on, Kali. It will be over soon and you can relax." Her grip tightens on me. "Don't worry, Honey, nobody can hurt you anymore. Take a couple of deep breaths."

She leans her head on my shoulder and her breathing slowly calms down. We hold on to each other for another five minutes or so.

"Are you ready to go back in?"

She hesitates, then nods. I pull off a couple of paper towels and dampen them, and wipe her tear-stained face. She leans over the sink and scoops water into her mouth and rinses it. I straighten her pony tail and give her a smile. She smiles back, faintly, nods and we head back into the courtroom.

The defense lawyer questions Paul for nearly an hour, going over the same territory we had already covered, and finally sits back down. The Judge decides to continue the proceedings tomorrow, bangs his gavel, and excuses Paul.

The next day, the defense calls up "character witnesses" for questioning. They're not a convincing bunch, mostly relatives and old hunting buddies. Gimpy's sister is called to the stand to give her version of what happened. She's a mousy, skinny girl with thin, stringy hair hanging down to her shoulders. Her face is gaunt and weathered. I'm sure she's had a hard life. She's wearing jeans and a gray sweater, which makes her look even more colorless. She looks cowed by the attention, head lowered. I feel a surge of pity for her. When questioned, she nervously wipes her hands on her jeans, insists that Gimpy shot himself in a hunting accident. "That's how he got his limp." She glances nervously at Gimpy.

When the DA questions her, he asks if she actually saw Gimpy's shooting accident. She clears her throat, quietly says, "No. Um. But his buddies told me what happened."

So, the DA says, "In other words, you took his *co-conspirators'* word for what happened." He looks at the jury to see that they register that.

She looks at her hands in her lap and nods her head. The judge reminds her to speak clearly so the jury can hear.

She glances up. "Yeah, that's what they said happened."

I check out the jury. Most of them are impassive but I see a couple of them shaking their heads. The tension has worn me down, and suddenly I'm exhausted. I can't wait for this to be over.

The trial drags on for two more weeks, during which the sheriff and deputies and forensics experts testify. It turns out that bullets extracted from the bodies of my family and Don, and retrieved from the earth around the bodies, matched the guns that Bryce and Bart had used. Nothing conclusive on Gimpy's firearm, though. Finally, after the closing statements on both sides, the jury is dismissed to decide on the verdict. John Collins, the D.A., assures us that it looks good for a conviction, and suggests we go to lunch.

We go to a cafe nearby for a sandwich and coffee. Sharon has sat in on today's session and sits across the table from us with Kali. Kali wants her usual hamburger and fries, which makes me smile. She's been more upbeat today, and spent most of her time absorbed in a Nancy Drew mystery, ignoring the proceedings. She seems to enjoy her lunch, tackling it with gusto.

When they're finished, Sharon volunteers to take Kali for a walk and they head out into the unusually sunny weather.

Paul and I linger. We don't talk much. I'm reliving my testimony in my head and hoping that the jury doesn't take too long. The clatter of dishes and chatter of conversations around us barely register on my mind. I toy with my food. The suspense is like a rock in my stomach. Paul reaches out and takes my hand. "Worried?"

"I am. What if they don't convict him? Gimpy's family and friends are such liars. And Bart? Will they keep making our lives miserable? Will we still be in danger? Somebody evil doesn't want us to talk. I can't wait for this to all be over so we can have our lives back. Everything's on hold until it's done. I'm constantly on edge."

He leans forward, takes my other hand and squeezes them both. Looking deeply into my eyes, he says, "I'm sure they'll end up in jail. Don't see how the jury can *not* convict. I'll do everything I can to make sure you and Kali are safe. We'll fortify the house if necessary. I'll get a machine gun. Or some vicious watchdogs. Nobody's goin' to hurt my women. Try to relax."

"I'm trying." I sit back, take a sip of my coffee. "You know, if you put enough cream and sugar in this it tastes pretty good."

Paul chuckles. "I figured you'd develop a taste for it. Did Don bring you coffee when he visited you at your cabin?"

"He brought us some, but he was the only one who drank it. I just never developed a taste for it till now."

Paul takes my hand, smiling, raises it to his lips. I feel a warm tingle shimmy up my arm. He keeps hold of my hand. "It's so much fun introducing you and Kali to new things. I love to watch your reactions. You've really had a lot to take in since you came out of the woods. I think you're amazing, the way you've handled it."

My anxiety melts a bit. "I couldn't have done any of it without you and your family. I can't tell you how much I appreciate and love you all. I feel more comfortable in this new environment every day." I pause, and shift gears. "D'you think we should be getting back to the courthouse? Who knows how long the jury will be?"

"I'm sure there's no reason to rush. These things usually take a lot of time. Especially in a serious case like this."

We hang out at the cafe for another hour, sharing a piece of apple pie, chatting sporadically, and finally head back to the courthouse, where Sharon and Kali find us a few minutes later.

"It felt good to get out and stretch." Sharon finds a chair and Kali sits down by me, pulling her book out again. Sharon has brought some knitting and proceeds to work on the sweater she's making for Kali. I love her for doing that.

It's a long wait in a small room, furnished with a table and sofa and chairs. There are a few old magazines but nothing of real interest to read. I'm wishing I'd brought my homework with me to fill the time. I close my eyes and lean my head on Paul's shoulder, as we sit side by side on the sofa. I start to pray, hoping to speed things up. It takes three more hours before we're called back into the court room, and the jury comes back with a "guilty" of kidnapping, unlawful use of a firearm, theft and drug peddling verdict. The relief that flows through my body leaves me limp, and tears slide down my cheeks. I can't wait to get out of that courtroom and don't even pay attention to the defendant's reactions, or his supporters. Paul and I thank Mr. Collins profusely and, arm in arm, we all head for Sharon's (newly repaired) car, filled with quiet gratitude that it's over.

15

CHAPTER

Life is For the Living

That evening, Kali is very quiet. I try to comfort her, telling her how proud I am of her, and what a good job she did when the D.A. questioned her. And now she doesn't have to worry about Gimpy ever again. I'm worried that her speaking progress has been set back. I put my arm around her and begin singing "Puff, the Magic Dragon." She leans her head on my shoulder cuddles up next to me. Tears run down her cheeks. My song trails off.

"Kali, do you remember what Gramma said?" She shakes her head. "Gramma said, 'Life is for the living.' We have to go on. We will mourn for our family forever. But we have to find a new life and love and help each other through it."

I pause. No response. "More than anything, I want us to get past this whole, awful thing, and enjoy our lives. That's what Mama and Daddy would have wanted. We'll always miss them. But we just have to be brave a little while longer, and get through the next trial, and we can be free of the whole thing.

"I want you to be able to talk to your classmates when you start sixth grade next year. You really need to do that to live your best life. You've been gradually finding your voice again. Do you think you can 'carry on,' like Grandma said?"

She nods her head, slowly. "Are you tired? Would you like to head for bed?"

Again, she nods. "Yes. Tired."

"Come on, Hon, I'll keep you company until you go to sleep."

Once she's in bed, I pull her covers up, like I did when she was little, and lie down beside her. She snuggles close, murmurs, "Gramma," and is soon fast asleep. I watch her for a while, filled with tenderness and heartache for her. Finally, I join the family in the living room.

Sharon waves her hands in the air. "I'll be glad when this is all over. Do you think Kali will need to be in court for the sentencing? I could stay here with her while the rest of you go."

"Let's wait and see what she wants to do when the time comes. The sentencing won't take place until next month. And Bart's trial starts next week. Another month or so and we should be done with this."

The next day, Saturday, after my morning shift, I'm restless. I ask Paul, who's driven me home, if he'd like to go for a run. "That's a great idea. Just let me stop by my place to get into my sweats and running shoes and we'll take off."

"Good. Give me ten minutes so I can change too."

I ask Kali if she'd like to come but she shakes her head. She points to a book she's reading, still Nancy Drew. Reading. I chuckle. I'm delighted she's enjoying her book. She was enthralled when Sharon took us to the library, small though it is. We both came home with a stack of books and have been blissfully plowing through them in our spare time.

I hurry into my running shoes and sweats and accompany Paul to his place so he can change. It's the first time I've been to his apartment, which is really the bottom half of an old house that's been converted. Sandy greets me noisily when we come in the door. I pet her and make a fuss over her while Paul heads to his bedroom. I nose around his living room while he changes. So, this is how he really lives? It's actually pretty tidy but spare, just the basic necessities. He has a bookcase full of books, both fiction and non-fiction. There are a couple of framed nature photos on the otherwise bare white walls and a TV set in the corner. A jacket has been flung over the easy chair which matches the sofa along the wall. It looks comfortable. A coffee table is strewn with magazines and a book. I check out the title. It's a book about native American tribes of the Northwest. I wonder if he's looking into the Modoc history. I'm pleased.

The kitchen has a few dirty dishes in the sink, and there's milk, eggs, bread, some fruit and peanut butter and beer in the refrigerator. I guess he doesn't need much because he has most of his main meals with us. The kitchen looks clean.

When he comes out of his room, I feel like I know him better. It's nice to know he's not slovenly. "You could use some decorating," I suggest.

He grins. "I thought I'd leave that up to you."

I can feel the blush coming up my face. "I guess I'll have to study up on the current decorating trends."

He puts his arms around me and pulls me in. "I can't wait until we're married and doing these everyday things together." He kisses me on the lips and I'm thinking that we might not make it out for our run. I push away.

"You're just trying to get out of running. Come on. How far can you go?"

He groans. "Well, I still have some weakness in my leg but we'll see. I've only been working out the last couple of weeks."

We walk out the door with Sandy on our heels. As we step out on the wide front porch, Paul stops me with a hand on my shoulder. "Hold on a minute, 'Wild Woman,' we have to stretch first."

This is news to me. I usually just start moving. "Okay. Show me, oh wise one." So, he leads me through some stretching moves and then we head out through the neighborhood. It feels freeing to run off the anxieties that have been piling up, in spite of the light drizzle. I put my worries about the road incident and the letters on the back burner and we just run for a couple of miles, until Paul starts to lag. We slow to a walk and walk hand-in-hand for a while before turning back. Sandy stays with us, with frequent side trips to sniff out the area.

"Feeling better?" he asks.

"Definitely. We need to do that every day."

"We'll have to see if we can work out a schedule. It'd be good for us both."

"Beth's been wanting to go with me too. Maybe we could get a group going together. That'd be fun."

"We lucked out on the weather today. We'll have to see how we can work out around that. It's not much fun to run in the pouring rain. They open up the high school gym in the evenings, when there's not a game going on, for people to use. Maybe we can run laps there when it's too nasty out."

"That might work."

Paul drops me off at the house, with an enthusiastic good-bye kiss, and I get showered and settle down to do my homework.

The next day is February 14. This means nothing to me. I am unaware it's Valentine's Day. But Paul has made plans. I'm working on my homework, planning a budget, at the dining room table when he walks in after work, his hands behind his back. When I look up, he whips out a fistful of red roses and a card from behind his back. "Ta-da! Happy Valentine's Day."

Startled, I rear back. "What's this? What's Valentine's Day?"

He smiles, the corners of his beautiful hazel eyes crinkling. "It's the day you let your loved one know how much you love her. Haven't you ever heard of it?"

I stare at him. "No. I guess it's something we never celebrated in my family." I search my memory for a moment. "Well, now that you mention it, I remember making valentines in grade school and distributing them. I'd forgotten all about that."

"Well, I'm remembering for you. We're goin' to celebrate it in style. Get on your gussiest duds, madam. We're goin' out to dinner at the best place in town."

"We are? But I didn't get you anything. And I still have homework to do."

"Don't worry. It's my chance to woo my woman. I won't keep you out too late. You still have to eat. I want some time alone with you."

I laugh. "Okay. But you'll have to wait while I change."

"No problem. I'm not goin' anywhere."

I open the card. It's very red, with mushy proclamations of love. My heart skips a beat. "Wow! This is lovely. Thank you." I stand up, sniffing the roses. They don't have any scent. "Okay, just let me get these roses in some water. They're beautiful, Paul. That's so sweet of you." I give him a quick kiss and head to the kitchen to find a vase.

"Where's Kali? I've got something for her too. And Mom."

"That's so sweet. Thanks for thinking of her. I should have made her a valentine too. I'll send her out. She's reading in our room."

Kali's sitting on her bed, engrossed in her book. This time she's reading Beverly Cleary's *Ramona*. "Kali, Paul has something for you. Go see what it is."

Her face lights up and she hops off the bed and flies out the door. Soon she's back with a big valentine and a large, heart-shaped box of chocolates, and a big smile on her face.

I manage to change at lightning speed, while Kali fires questions at me. "Where you going?"

"I'm going out to dinner with Paul, Kali. I won't be out late."

Her face lights up. "Me too?"

I give her a hug. "Not this time, Sweetie. Paul and I need to spend some alone time together. I'll see you when I get back. You'll be fine here with Sharon and Doug."

She frowns and retreats into her book, sulking. I hesitate. "Happy Valentine's Day, little sister. Next year I'll know to get you a valentine. But aren't those lovely chocolates that Paul got you? You can have them all to yourself. Just don't eat'em all at once. And maybe tomorrow we can think of something fun to do together, okay?"

She nods her head but doesn't look at me. Again, I pause, but decide to leave it at that. She has to get used to the idea that we will be doing more and more apart from each other as time goes by, not like in the Kalmiopsis, when we only had each other.

Paul and I go to the "Sea-View" restaurant where we went on our first date. Once again, seated where we can watch the waves wash in, I feel excited and yet comfortable. I order something new to me, seared sea scallops, while Paul orders his old standby, steak. I tease him. "Don't you want to try something different? Who knows, you may find that you love something you haven't had before."

"Well, I've tried other things in the past and figured that their steak is their best meal. Why 'fix what ain't broke,' as they say? I love steak."

"Okay for you. But I need to try new things. I've got a lot of exploring to do. I've never had scallops, so I'll have the adventure of trying'em."

He grins. "And I'll have the pleasure of watching your reactions. You'll probably love'em."

I sit back and eye him. His short, curly brown hair is tousled by the wind. I have to fight the impulse to run my hand through it. I think he is the handsomest man I've ever seen. "I'm glad you take pleasure in watching me slog my way through modern civilization. Sometimes I feel like a fool and really 'out of it.'"

He leans forward and takes my hand. "One thing you're not is a fool. You'll find your way, Judith. I can't believe how well you've adapted."

I squeeze his hand. "It's been a crazy year. I don't know what I'd have done without your help. And your parents'."

"I think my Mom wants to adopt you and Kali. You know she lost two babies before I was born. She was forty when I came along. She quit working until I was in school. You could say she's a 'hover mother.' It's a relief to me to have you taking some of the attention off of me. It's good for us both."

"Well, I know it's been good for *me*. And Kali."

Our dinners arrive and they smell wonderful.

He has a glass of wine while I stick to iced water. The meal turns out to be my idea of fabulous, and we both enjoy it to the full.

But, eventually, my mind drags itself back to the trial. "You know, Paul, I'm worried about our safety. Whoever has been harassing me could come after you next. And I'm really afraid for Kali. What if they try to snatch her again? It would be devastating for her. And me."

He leans back, worry lines creasing his forehead. "I've thought about that. I don't know if we can trust the police to keep a close enough watch. I think I'll keep my .45 handy from now on. I've got a concealed carry permit for it. But maybe we should get one for you, too. I'd feel safer if you were armed, especially when you're out by yourself."

"I don't know about that. Maybe I could just get some pepper spray. I've seen it advertised in the paper. I put my shotgun in my closet so I have it handy in case of a break in at the house. But I don't want to shoot anyone. I'm hoping it won't come to that."

"Pepper spray isn't very practical in this windy location. You could get it blown back in your face. But I'd feel better if you had some form of defense. Maybe we could look around at the gun shop to see what they might suggest."

I sigh. "I can't wait for this next trial to be over. Maybe then we'll be free."

He leans over and takes my hand. "We'll get through this. We've got our whole lives ahead of us and I can't wait to move on to the next step. It won't be long now."

We change the subject and talk about my schooling and Kali's progress and Paul's latest project at work. Finally, it's time to leave and we walk out hand in hand.

It's dark out now, but I notice that Paul's pickup looks awfully low to the ground. A curse escapes Paul's lips. "Shit. They've been busy while we were eating."

I realize that all four of his tires have been slashed. My heart sinks. "Oh no, Paul. They're after *you* now. What'll we do?"

He looks quickly around the lot. Of course, there's no one there. "First, I'm goin' to call the cops, then I'm goin' to get you a ride home. This'll take some time to straighten out and I want you home safe."

"I can stay ..."

"No, Judith. I can handle it. I'm sorry our first Valentine's date turned out like this. But I'll feel much safer knowing that you're home with Mom and Dad. I'm goin' to call Jack. He'll take you home. Come on, let's go inside so I can use their phone."

I think better of objecting and we go back inside. Paul called the police and then Jack, who came promptly and gave me a lift home. I thank him profusely. "Hey, no big deal. What're friends for? I'll go back and see if there's anything I can do to help Paul."

At the house, I wave goodbye and hasten inside. What will they do next?

I quietly pull Sharon and Doug aside into the kitchen and tell them what happened while Kali's occupied watching TV in the living room.

They're both aghast, and Doug is livid. "This is the last thing Paul needs. I'm goin' to run down there and see what's goin' on. This has got to stop." He grabs his jacket and heads out.

"I'm sorry, Sharon. I didn't mean to spoil your evening. But I thought you should know. I'm really concerned that we're putting you and Doug in danger. Maybe we'd better move out."

"No. I won't hear of it. They won't dare attack you while you're here with us." Her face has a fierce, intent look. "And we can keep an eye on Kali while you're working and at school. I'm so mad at these awful people, I could scream." She leans her elbows on the kitchen counter, her head in her hands. Then she straightens up, her face grim. "We'll get through this together, Judith. That's all there is to it. I won't let them win."

I give her a hug. "I'm eternally grateful to you both. I had no idea this would become such a threat to all of us."

She hugs me back. "We'll handle it, you'll see. Meanwhile we'll keep our doors locked and our eyes open. We'll find out what's being done when Doug gets back."

"Okay, but I want you to know that I have my shotgun in my closet, in case there's any more trouble. I've really had it with these people. Is there anything you need me to do before I hit the books again?"

"No. The dishes are all done. I'll just go work on my sewing until Doug gets back."

I return to my homework, but my mind isn't on it. I just keep trying to figure out what our tormentors will cook up next. I just can't imagine. I'm determined to see my parents' killers in jail. Or at least these remaining two.

It's two hours later when Doug comes back in. His face is grim. He hangs up his coat and comes into the kitchen where I'm getting a drink of water.

He leans his six-foot frame against the counter, wearily removes his glasses and rubs his eyes. "Well, they really did a number on those tires. Paul'll have to buy four new ones. I talked to the police and they seem as frustrated as we feel. Who knows what they'll try next?"

"I intend to be prepared for whatever that may be."

"We all will, Judith." His lips tighten. "Paul told me about the shotgun in your closet. Probably a good idea." He looks at his watch. "Well, I'm goin' to bed. You probably could use a good night's sleep yourself."

"Yes, good night. I'm ready to settle in." I head for bed. It's been a long day, and I'm suddenly exhausted.

16

CHAPTER

Living on Edge

That Saturday, after my morning shift, Paul and I seek out the gun shop. I'm resisting the idea of buying another gun. On the other hand, I want to be able to defend myself and Kali. We look for viable alternatives for self-protection. The pepper spray idea seems minimal, but I purchase a canister anyway. I just have to remember to be upwind if I use it.

I look over the small arms, thinking that Paul may be right about the added protection. I finally settle on a used, small Smith and Wesson .38 special. It looks like a toy, but carries a five-shot load, and it's cheap. I'll be able to carry it tucked away in my jacket pocket. But first I have to get my concealed carry permit. This means I must take a training class at the shop, pass the exam and fill out my certificate after which I need to apply at the sheriff's office. Now all I have to do is find the time to do all that. Thankfully, the class is short and I can finish it in one night.

Paul looks serious but pleased that I've conceded to necessity. "I'll feel better about your safety now that you have that. Thanks for going ahead with it. We'll do a few practice rounds when we get a chance."

"I'm not happy about carrying this thing, but better safe than sorry. Thanks for helping me choose."

"With Bart's trial starting on Monday, we'll have to be extra careful this weekend. I think I'll stay at the folks' house until this is over. We'll have to keep our eyes open. Sandy'll help too. She always makes a racket whenever anyone comes around."

We're edgy throughout the weekend, checking out every noise, keeping tabs on each other. With the exception of church, we plan to stick to the house. Finally, though, feeling restless and housebound, I suggest that we go out to visit our animals on Cheryl's farm. Kali lights up at that idea, jumping off the couch and shouting, "Yes!" We three load into Paul's pickup, along with Sandy, for the ride out.

At the farm, Kali runs to her goats and Fret, who leaps up on her with joy, licking her face and almost wriggling out of his skin. She looks happy and free for the first time since the trials began. "Star," the little kid, has grown a lot and is as big as the yearlings were when we brought them here. Amigo comes running up to Kali, braying the whole way. She hugs him, as he rests his chin on her shoulder. Then she swings up on his back, like she used to do and, with a gentle kick, encourages him to trot around the pasture. We spend a long time there, petting and romping with the goats, Amigo, and Fret. Paul joins in on the fun, getting reacquainted with Fret, who sniffs and licks his hands and wags his whole body with his tail. I vow to myself to bring a grooming brush next time so I can give Amigo a good brushing. He's been such a dear and loyal member of our "family" for so many years. I settle for petting and sweet-talking him.

Sandy and Fret joyfully get reacquainted, chasing each other around. Kali finds a stick and throws it for the dogs to retrieve. They both race off and, Fret getting there first, brings it back and lays it at Kali's feet with a happy grin on his face. Paul and I watch as they repeat the process. Cheryl comes out to join us and we chat a bit.

"I love to watch her with the animals, so relaxed and happy. Look at her running with her goats."

"Yes, she adores her pets, and misses them terribly. I hope to have a home someday where we can keep'em. Kali relates to animals like most of us relate to people."

"They must understand her non-verbal language."

"I think so. I really appreciate you keeping them here, Cheryl."

"They're no trouble. I figure Mama goat's milk pretty much pays for their care."

"Nevertheless, I want to pay you for their upkeep. I'm working now and can afford it." I hand her a wad of bills that I had in my pocket, amounting to $300. "I suspect you've spent more than that keeping them here. And I plan to pay for their care from now on. It's not fair to expect you to keep doing this for free."

Her eyes grow big. "Are you sure? They really haven't been any trouble. But I must admit that the vet did charge me to check'em. Thanks, Judith. This'll be really helpful."

"It's nothing. You've done so much and it's the least I can do. I really hope to take'em off of your hands as soon as I can get settled somewhere with a little property."

We chat for another fifteen minutes or so and finally head out. As we head for home from our visit I feel revived. Kali seems more relaxed, stretches out, head laid back, a smile on her face. We'll get through this.

Bart's trial is a duplicate of Gimpy's, with Paul and me testifying, and Kali, with my assistance. We go through the process and wait for a verdict. Once again, the angry relatives are lined up in the seats, glowering at us. And, again, we're concerned about our safety.

The night of the first day of the trial, someone shoots our mailbox full of holes. They want us to know they're still around, I guess. I'm just glad they didn't shoot up one of our vehicles.

We all work that next morning to clear out the garage so we can get both vehicles inside. Doug's and Paul's trucks are parked in the big shed behind the house where Doug has his workshop.

Our nerves are on edge as we plod through the trial. The slow process seems to take forever. When we see car lights go by below the house at night we check out the window to see what's going on. Sharon and Doug are feeling the tension. Sharon spends a lot of time in her sewing room, keeping her hands busy. She's irritable and fidgety in her daily chores. She seems to be banging the pots and pans and dropping things a lot. I'm concerned about her. Doug sticks around the house at night instead of working in his shop as he often does.

I tend to jump at any noise after dark. We check and double check to make sure everything is locked up at night. When a branch snaps in the woods behind the house one night, it jerks me awake. I decide to keep our window closed and locked after that.

The sheriff has deputies patrolling by our property off and on at irregular intervals. It seems to work, because that was the last of the vandalism. Until mid-way through the trial.

We're into the second week when, around midnight, I suddenly hear Sandy going crazy, barking frantically, followed by shots fired and glass shattering. I jump out of bed, grab my shotgun and run out into the living room, my heart racing. I see headlights in the driveway, piercing the broken living room window, reflecting off the walls, and hear three more shots explode and bullets thud into the front of the house.

Paul runs out and grabs me, pulling me away from the doorway into the kitchen. "Judith, keep out of the line of fire," he yells.

I'm suddenly filled with overwhelming rage. I've had enough!

"They're not gettin' away with this," I snap. And before he can stop me, I'm out the sliding door to the patio. Not even registering the cold patio floor against my bare feet, I run to the corner of the house. The truck they're driving is turning around to leave and is clearly visible in the floodlights from the porch. I fire a blast with both barrels at them. It's hard to see where I'm aiming in the dark but I don't care. I just want to scare the hell out of them. I hear the shot hit the back of the truck and the sound of taillights exploding. At least I hit something. Paul yanks me back behind the house as the truck rockets down the driveway and onto the road below.

"Judith, watch out, for God's sake. Are you crazy?" he snaps. "They might fire back."

"They're gone. I just wanted to give them a taste of their own medicine. I'm furious," I yell back.

"Let's get back inside and check on the damage and call the cops. I've had it with this bunch too. But now, at least, we can identify the truck if they can find it."

We go back in, and by this time everybody is up and gathered in the living room. Doug and Sharon look bewildered, their faces reflecting shock as they survey the damage. The big picture window is shattered, and one of the table lamps is smashed and on the floor. There's glass everywhere. Turning on the lights, we can see three bullet holes in the wall opposite the window. Sharon is shaking and yells, "What's going on? Judith are you all right? What happened?"

Doug puts his arm around her and holds her tightly. "My God, Paul. They're getting more extreme. We've got to put a stop to this."

"I'm calling the Sheriff right now." Paul grabs the phone from the kitchen counter and dials the number.

Kali is pale and shivering in her pajamas, tears streaming down her face. She scrambles to me and latches on for dear life. I hold her close and reassure her that everything's all right, even though I'm shaking myself.

"They're gone, Kali. They were just tryin' to scare us but it won't work. They won't come around again. The Sheriff'll see to that."

She hides her face in my shoulder and continues to shake, making snuffling sounds. I just hold her, trying to soothe her as she slowly calms down. But she doesn't let go of me, her face buried in my shoulder, sniffling off and on. I fear that our attackers have traumatized her all over again.

"We'd better leave the mess until the sheriff's people see it," says Doug. "Sharon, why don't you put on a pot of coffee? The deputies might want some. I know I do. I'm goin' to look outside and see what else they shot up. Good thing we've got the cars tucked away."

Sharon is still trembling as she heads for the kitchen, but the act of filling the coffee pot and putting in the coffee seems to calm her as she busies herself around the kitchen. Kali sticks to me like a burr, and I do my best to reassure her.

After calling the sheriff's office we spend an hour waiting for them to arrive and, then, explaining what happened. They've sent out two deputies. One of them looks quite young, tall, dark haired and earnest. He carefully checks out the damage, asks questions and writes down his report. The other one, older, with a graying beard, shakes his head in disgust and follows Doug outside to check for damage. It appears that all the damage was limited to the living room window and wall. They dig the bullets out of the wall and put them in a baggie, take some pictures, then assure us that they will be patrolling the rest of the night but they don't expect further violence. They figure it was just another warning. In the morning they'll do a search for the pickup again, send the bullets to forensics, along with casts of the tire tracks. We're urged to not drive over the tracks until the team can come out in the morning to take casts of them. They finally head out and leave us to pick up the pieces.

I help Sharon clean up the glass, and the men put a sheet of plywood over the broken window.

I try to apologize to the family. "Sharon and Doug, I know this is all our fault. If it weren't for us, you wouldn't have to put up with this nonsense. I really think Kali and I should find an apartment and get out..."

Sharon interrupts. "I won't hear of it. I'm so angry and upset at those people I'd like to shoot them myself. But it's not your fault, Judith. It's theirs. You're the innocent party here. We'll manage somehow. I think if they wanted to hurt us physically, they could have picked us off in the daylight. They're trying to scare us and I won't let them. Don't you agree, Doug?"

He puts his arm around her. "She's right, Judith. You're safer with us around. We'll just have to take precautions until the trial's over. So, no more talk of leaving."

"I just feel so bad that you're putting yourselves in danger for us. But you don't know how much I appreciate your support. It's wonderful to know we're not alone in this."

Paul hugs me. "Don't forget that I'm a target too. It's not all on you. Don't worry, Judith, we'll handle this."

I hang on to him a while, and Kali stays close to me.

To distract her, I lure her into the kitchen with the promise of hot chocolate. While she drinks it, I blather on with whatever comes into my head, trying to calm her. "Good thing I had my shotgun handy. I let them have a blast. They won't try that again. I'll bet I scared the bejeebers out of 'em. The trial'll be over soon and then they'll have to give it up. Um, how's the hot chocolate?"

She nods, makes an 'okay' gesture with her hand, but doesn't say anything. Her face is despondent, and I see tears still sliding down her cheeks. I'm really worried that she's suffered a setback. Will we have to start all over from square one? I start singing the first song that pops into my head, an old gospel tune that our mother sang to us, 'Shall We Gather at the River?' I see the hint of a smile. I go on to Mr. Rogers theme song, "It's a Beautiful Day in the Neighborhood"... and she relaxes and her lips curve up more. I keep up the chatter while she finishes her cocoa, bid everyone good night, and take her back to our room.

When we go back to bed, I snuggle in with Kali, like I did when she was little. She gradually settles back down to sleep. I hear the others drifting off to their bedrooms. As for myself, I spend the rest of the night wide awake. I'm up before the alarm goes off and get ready for the day. I quietly leave Kali to sleep in and head off to work.

In the days after that, I go through the permitting process on my handgun in my spare time. It takes over a week to go through the whole thing, fitting everything in between the trial, school and work, but I finally have my concealed carry permit. Paul takes me out to an old quarry, miles from town, and we practice shooting at tin cans that he's brought. It's so different from a rifle, it takes me an hour of target practice to feel comfortable with it. Paul's a good shot and coaches me. "Hold it steady, pull the trigger slowly. You've got this." Eventually, I decide that I can use it safely and efficiently.

Kali knows not to touch it, but I promise to show her how to use it when she's older. We're not afraid of guns, as they were essential to our survival in the wilderness. And my Dad had drilled safety precautions in me thoroughly before he died. Nevertheless, I hide it on the top shelf of my closet. I plan to carry it whenever I'm out alone at night. Our tormentors seem to only operate in the dark.

In the end, after weeks of the lawyers niggling back and forth, interviews of law officers and forensic experts, then closing arguments and the judge's instructions, more waiting for the verdict, Bart is finally found guilty of kidnapping, conspiracy to murder, and attempted murder. There is pretty strong proof that he shot at my family, since one of the bullets pulled from my parent's grave matched his own gun. And he did fire at me the night I rescued Kali, plus he plotted to kill us with Bryce, so that nailed him for the conspiracy and attempted murder charge. Again, we have to wait for the sentencing until next month.

So, drained but relieved, we all go out for a celebratory soda and let our hair down. Kali is quiet as we celebrate, but she loves the chocolate milkshake and slurps it blissfully.

For myself, I'm still wary of what our tormentors might do. Will they give up, now that the trials are over? I hope so, for all our sakes. But I plan to still keep my weapon on hand when I'm out alone. Having gone through all the hoops, I'm free to carry it with me when I need to. I can't forget how I was warned by Cedar, at work, when we had a break and time to chat. She asked how the trial was going. I told her I thought it was going well.

"Well, I hope that Bart gets many years to cool it in jail. That bunch has always meant trouble around here. They're nasty and vindictive, and inbred. You don't want to be their enemy. Nobody in town likes'em."

That evening, Sharon asks me whether Kali has had all her vaccinations. And, for that matter, whether I have. No one ever mentioned this to me before. It hadn't even occurred to me. "No, I know Kali hasn't had any. And I haven't since I was a baby. Is it important?"

"While you were in the wilderness you weren't exposed to common diseases. But now that you're mingling with people, you both need to be brought up to date. I'll make an appointment for you with our family doctor, Dr. Olson. It'd be good to have him check Kali over anyway. Perhaps he can suggest a therapist who can help her with her speech problem."

"That's a good idea. You're so thoughtful, Sharon. She's regressed since the shooting incident. I'm afraid it brought back all the bad memories."

"We need to get you both signed up for a health insurance plan. Maybe we can do that this week too. Kali needs more help than we can give her here. We'll get the name of a therapist who can help her. One more thing, we'll have to look into getting Kali a birth certificate."

"I don't have a clue how to do that."

"Did your parents write the date of her birth in their Bible?"

"Yes. We're all registered in there."

"I'm sure we can use that to get her a birth certificate. I'll look into it for you. She'll need it to get into school in the fall."

"I never thought of that either." Big sigh. "There are so many complications to living on the 'outside.' I'm glad I have you to help me figure it out."

"We'll get there. It all takes time." Her blue eyes smile as she puts her arm around me and gives me a squeeze. I feel so lucky to have her in my life. I hug her back.

The following day we go through the process of getting us signed up for a health insurance plan. I hate to spend the money, but Sharon assures me that it's necessary in case we need medical treatment in the future, so I concede to her knowledge of how the system works. There goes a big chunk of my precious savings. Everything costs money on the "outside."

The next week, we go in for our first physicals. Dr. Olson, who is comfortably middle aged, a little paunchy with just a whisk of hair on his scalp, and a kind smile on his face, pronounces us extremely fit, and brings us up to date on our vaccinations. Kali makes a sour face when she's vaccinated but doesn't make a sound. He's very gentle and kind with her. "Now, don't you worry little girl, it'll pinch a little bit, but it's better than getting the measles, or whooping cough, or Diphtheria." I decide I really like and trust him. He hands Kali a popsicle, and she smiles at him shyly before she goes out into the waiting room with Sharon.

When we're alone, I confer with him about Kali's speech problem. He tells me that a good speech specialist would be a big help, but the nearest one would be in Coos Bay. He gives me the name of the one he prefers, Dr. Louise Allen. "She's the best we have on the coast here. You'll like her."

So, we make an appointment for Kali for a Friday afternoon, in two weeks, after I'm off work. I can't miss any more workdays, as I lost so many during the trials. We'll see if this brings back her speech to a normal level. I can't wait to have an actual spoken conversation with her.

The last day of March, Paul is giving me a ride home from work when I suddenly realize that my birthday had passed the previous month. Paul hears me gasp, and asks, "What's wrong?"

"Do you know that in all the worry over the trial, I forgot about my birthday? I turned twenty-two on the thirteenth of last month. It completely slipped my mind."

He raises his eyebrows, eyes wide in a shocked expression. "Holy cow! I'm so sorry, Judith. I didn't realize. That's crazy. We'll have to have a celebration to make up for it."

"Oh, that's okay. I don't want a fuss. I just realized how old I am. Once I get this schooling done, I'll have time to think about birthdays."

"Well, we'll see about that. I can't let the love of my life be ignored on her birthday. I say let's have a party."

I laugh. "It's a little late for that. I'm surprised Kali forgot. She must've been as distracted by all that's been happening as I was. Let it go."

He frowns. "No way. We're going to celebrate."

"Please don't make a fuss. I'm fine, really."

"Okay, if you're sure."

"I'm sure." Inside, I wasn't really. I was sad that the day had slipped by and none of us realized it. But I was determined to be a grown-up about it and just not think about it anymore.

"At least, let me take you out for a nice dinner. We have lots to celebrate and this's a good excuse to do it. Okay?"

I smile. "I'd love that."

"It's settled then." He grabs my hand and kisses it. "Love you, Judith."

With a lump in my throat, I reply, "I love you too."

That Saturday I put on my one nice, blue dress and best dress shoes and pin my hair back with the pretty clip that Kali gave me for Christmas. I'm feeling festive as we head out for a celebratory, quiet dinner. Paul takes a side detour by his house, saying that he's forgotten something. He gives me a quick kiss and opens his door. "You stay here, I'll be right back." He pops into the house, and soon reappears, carrying something in a plastic container, and hands it to me. Inside is a pretty little flower arrangement. Another new experience.

He grins at me. "D'you like it?"

"It's really pretty, Paul. Thank you. Um, what do I do with it?"

"You pin it on and wear it on your dress, like, on your shoulder. It's called a 'corsage'. It's like a sign of celebration."

I open the box and try to pin it on, but I'm clumsy. "Help me with it?"

He takes it and awkwardly pins it to my dress. It feels funny, a slight weight on my shoulder. I give him a kiss in return. He grins, kisses me back and starts the motor. "We'd better get along. Don't want to be late for our reservations."

As we walk over to our table, I'm shocked to see balloons waving over it, with "Happy Birthday" inscribed on them. And sitting at the table are Kali and Sharon and Doug. They clap as we enter, singing "Happy Birthday to You" at the top of their lungs. I'm stunned. Then I can feel my face turning beet red as I quickly glance around to see the other customers watching and grinning at us. I slide into my seat.

I can't help smiling. I look at Paul. "I thought I said no fuss."

He's smiling from ear to ear. "Hey, this is an occasion to celebrate, and we're goin' to do it."

Sharon chimes in. "We felt sorry when we found out that we missed your birthday, Judith. We want to celebrate with you."

My eyes are swimming. "This's so nice. You've all been so wonderful to Kali and me. It's been a long time since we've had family to celebrate with. Thank you all so much."

Kali jumps up and comes around and gives me a hug. I hug her back. "I heard you singing with the others, Kali. It was beautiful. Are you ready for some dinner?"

She smiles and nods vigorously. "Yes." I'm thinking, *maybe next year she'll be able to tell me "Happy Birthday."*

We all enjoy a wonderful dinner, (with Kali stubbornly ordering a hamburger and French fries, her all-time favorites). When the dishes are cleared away the waiter comes back to the table carrying a cake with "Happy Birthday, Judith," inscribed on the top and twenty-two candles lit up. Again, I tear up, and have a hard time blowing out the candles while they sing "Happy Birthday" all over again. I'm so full of mixed emotions, my head is swimming— happiness that we have these loving people around us, sorrow that my own parents can't be here, excitement for our future.

While the waiter hands out slices of cake, Sharon pulls out a brightly wrapped package from under the table, and so does Kali. "It's not a birthday without presents, Judith. We hope you like'em."

"I know I will." I unwrap Kali's first. Inside is a play clay heart, painted bright red with tiny blue flowers on top, strung on a black cord. She's made a flowery card that says "To Judy from Kali, happy birthday." I place the pendant around my neck. "Oh Kali, I love this. Look, it goes with my dress. It's beautiful."

She grins happily and nods her head. Sharon takes a picture of the two of us.

The other package turns out to hold a new sweat suit set, which I've been needing for running. Sharon has her camera out and is taking more pictures. I'm never comfortable with a camera aimed at me. But I concentrate on the sweat suit. It's a soft, pale shade of green and warm. "Thank you so much, Sharon and Doug. I really can use this. Such a pretty color. Love it."

Sharon looks pleased too. "So glad you like it. There's not much available here in town but I know you need workout clothes."

"I sure do. This has been wonderful. Thanks so much, everybody."

We have cake and coffee and the evening slides by. Then we all head for home. Except Paul doesn't drive straight home. He drives down to the beach parking spot instead.

"I've got something for you too, Judith. I hope you like it." He pulls out a tiny box. "If you don't like it, we can take it back and you can pick out something you like better."

I open the box and there sits a beautiful diamond engagement ring. It's a simple style, with a slim gold band and one large diamond. "Oh Paul, it's beautiful."

"Are you ready to wear it?"

I hesitate. "Yes, it's time. But we can't set a date until I'm finished with school, okay?"

"Agreed. I just want the world to know that we're goin' to get married. I want to tell my folks."

"Yes. Let's do it."

He slides the ring onto my trembling finger, and it fits perfectly. I am flooded with a feeling of, what? Completeness? It's official now. I stifle the doubts that pop up, wondering if this is the right thing for me. I don't ever want to be alone again, I know that. I'm twenty-two and it's time to plan a future. And I do want to be with Paul. When he kisses me, I feel little tingles all the way to my toes. My doubts fade away.

Sharon and Doug are quite happy when we show them the ring. I don't think they're surprised, but make a show of congratulating us. Sharon squeals "Really? I can't believe it."

Doug shakes Paul's hand and says gruffly, "Way to go there, son. Been wondering when this would happen. Your Mom has been speculating for months."

"Doug, I have not." Then, giggling, "Well, maybe a little."

There are hugs and back slapping going around. When Kali realizes what's happening she jumps up and down and hugs Paul and me both. I'm delighted when she shouts "Happy, Happy." I have to laugh as she twirls around the room.

Sharon gets all excited at the prospect of a wedding in our future. "I've waited so long for this. I can't wait to get started on wedding plans."

"Don't get too excited yet, please. I have so many things to take care of before we can set a date. I have to get my GED and settle my Grandmother's estate and get Kali in for treatment."

Sharon sighs. "I know. But we can still think ahead and start making lists. You don't know how much goes into planning a wedding."

"I know that I want to keep it low key and easy. Just you and a few friends. I like to keep things simple."

"Of course, Judith. But even 'simple' takes planning."

I laugh. "We'll figure it out. I'm still getting used to the idea."

And so, we've celebrated my birthday big time, and I can see a hopeful future blooming ahead for the three of us.

It takes me a long time to get to sleep that night. Visions of our future dance through my head. Then I start thinking about how excited my parents and David and Gramma would have been to know that I'm engaged. An almost physical pain brings a lump to my throat. I begin picturing our past in the Kalmiopsis. David and I had such fun, running through the woods, fishing and hunting with Daddy. And scavenging in the wild with Mama and Gramma for nature's food. Mama rocking Kali in the rocking chair and softly singing lullabies until she fell asleep. Tears wet my pillow and I let them flow. I'll never stop missing my family. I wonder what David might have become had he lived. And I'd love to have my parents here to meet Paul.

What would they think of him? I'm sure they'd like him and approve. My parents had such a good marriage, in spite of Dad's PTSD. Mama stood by him through all the pain and suffering he endured. And she followed him into the wilderness. It wasn't easy for her. And Gramma. She came with us in spite of her misgivings. She wanted to protect Mama and help her. And us children. Gradually, exhaustion takes over and merciful sleep blots out the memories at last.

17
CHAPTER

Bad News

As the trials are over, and the sentencing, (Bart got thirty years with the possibility of parole after fifteen years, and Gimpy got fourteen, with possible parole after eight years), things quiet down. So far, no more threats.

That is, until I get another misspelled note in the mail. "Were not dun with yu yet," was all it said. It feels like a blow to my stomach. Will they never leave us alone? I don't show the note to anyone. After work the next day, I take it into the sheriff's office.

The sheriff reads the note and shakes his head in disgust. "This is the last straw. I'm goin' to give a warning to both of these families, personally. If any more harm comes to you or your family, we'll search their places top to bottom, and we'll come after them. This's gotta stop."

I leave the office, un-reassured. But I have other things to worry about.

We go to see Dr. Allen in mid-March. She's sixty-ish, tall and slim, in a sober gray pant suit with a frilly pink blouse. Her smile is warm and her eyes empathetic. I ask to see her alone first, and, with Kali staying in the waiting room with Sharon, I explain what caused Kali's mutism. "She was starting to talk again until the trials, and now she seems to have had a set-back. She'll only say one or two words at a time. I hope you can help her."

"I can understand how seeing her parents killed would affect her so deeply. The shock was enormous. I haven't treated anyone with this problem before. I'm not sure our usual techniques will work for her. We have the advantage of her speaking normally until she was five, when your parents were killed. So, she should still have those nerve connections and speaking ability. Why don't we try my strategies, and if they don't work, I'm afraid you'll have to take her to a psychiatrist. She may need a different approach."

I tell her about how Kali was open to singing her words before, and how she can do bird calls and imitate animal sounds.

She raises her eyebrows. "That's a therapy I haven't tried. Interesting. We may try including some musical training. And her animal vocalizations may have helped her keep the brain connections active so she can regain her voice. Good to know."

We bring Kali in to meet Dr. Allen. She hangs back behind me at first, finally shaking the hand that Dr. Allen proffers. She keeps her eyes on the floor. Dr. Allen invites her to sit in the armchair next to her desk, seating herself beside her. After a few minutes she manages to gently coax Kali to look up into her eyes, and smiles warmly at her. Kali flits a half smile back. "Kali, your sister tells me that you need to be able to speak better. I'd like to try to help you regain your voice. Wouldn't you like to be able to speak with your friends and family?"

Kali nods. "Would you like to work with me to bring your voice back?"

Again, Kali slowly nods her head. "Well, let's see what we can do today, okay? We can spend some time together while your sister and Mrs. O'Brien relax in the waiting room. Would that be all right?"

Kali looks at me, and I nod my head in return. "Why don't you give it a try, Kali? You know that I've always missed your voice very much. It would be wonderful if we could really talk together."

She gives Sharon and me a "thumbs up" sign, straightens up, chin high, and turns a determined face to Dr. Allen. Sharon and I quietly head for the waiting room.

About an hour later, Dr. Allen opens her door and invites us back in. She turns to Sharon. "Mrs. O'Brien, would you mind keeping Kali company in the waiting room while I confer with Ms. Johnson?"

Sharon takes Kali out and I take a seat while she sits behind her desk. She leans forward, clasps her hands on her desk, and eyes me sympathetically. This doesn't bode well.

"Ms. Johnson, I'm not sure I can get through to her. She has been silent for so long that I may not be able to bring her back. I'd like to set up a schedule to work with her. If I decide I can't help her, I think hypno-therapy may be the next step. It could take her back before the incident, so that the psychiatrist could help her cope. The closest doctor who's equipped to do this kind of therapy is in Eugene. We may need to set up an appointment with him. If he can help her overcome the trauma, then I could help her with her speech patterns. Let's see how it goes. I'll do my best to bring her around. It *is* encouraging that she speaks a little already."

I'm stunned. "I'll get her here, somehow. Thank you for your honest assessment. I'll do whatever it takes."

"Let's set up three appointments for the next two weeks, then re-evaluate." She stands up and we walk out to the waiting room, where she asks her secretary to schedule our next visits. Then she turns, takes Kali's hand.

"Kali, I'll be seeing you soon, and we'll work together to bring you up to speed. Is that all right with you?"

Kali nods, and solemnly shakes the doctor's hand. Dr. Allen turns, shakes my hand and Sharon's, says her good-byes. We settle on appointments for the next two weeks and are on our way.

Sharon looks at me with questioning raised eyebrows. "I'll fill you in later, Sharon, if you don't mind. Meanwhile, as long as we're here, maybe we could have dinner at our favorite cafe? We both know how Kali loves their food."

"Sure. Why don't we do that? The guys can fend for themselves." She gives Kali a hug and we head out for hamburgers all around.

After we place our orders, Kali looks at me expectantly. Sharon is eyeing me too. I look down at my hands, clamped on the table top. "I know you both want to hear what the doctor said. She said we might need to see a different doctor. She said if she can't help you, Kali, you might need to go to another specialist in Eugene. So, we may have to figure out how to get you up there for treatment." I look at Kali, who is eyeing me without expression. "But I'm sure she'll be able to help you talk, Kali. You liked her, didn't you?"

Kali nods, focuses on her food.

Sharon is quiet for a few minutes, but I see conflicting emotions flitting across her face, first concern, then acceptance. She shifts in her seat and says firmly, "Well, we'll just have to do what's necessary. We'll figure it out and get Kali speaking before school starts. Dr. Allen seems to be very personable and capable. I'm sure she can help." She gives Kali a reassuring smile, and I do my best to put on a cheery expression. It feels insincere.

As soon as we're back home I check my meagre savings. I have $1200 in my checking account, and $105 in my tip jar. I doubt that this is enough to pay for a trip to Eugene, plus a motel, plus a consultation with the psychiatrist. I'll check in the morning to see if our health insurance will cover the doctor. I suspect not. I've got to claim my inheritance, that's all there is to it. Unfortunately, we still won't be able to get into the valley until the snow thaws.

18

Free at Last

After that, I go through my normal routine, work in the morning, study in the afternoon, and classes twice a week. I am wary now about going to my classes. It's usually dark when I drive home. I keep my pistol in my purse. On the way home, I pull it out and keep it on the seat beside me. I reach over and feel it's comforting, cold presence whenever a car happens to come up behind me. If anyone tries to run me off the road again, I'll be ready.

But the more I think about it, the more enraged I become that I have to live in fear like this. The sheriff doesn't seem to be getting any closer to who's behind these frightening incidents. I decide I'll try to lure my tormentors out in the open. I will set up a running routine in my non-school afternoons to see if they'll come after me. And I'll be prepared for them if they do. I don't tell anyone what I'm planning.

The next day, after my shift at the cafe, I quickly scramble into my sweats and head out for a run. I've worked up to four miles so far, and try to increase it every time I go out.

Several days go by as I stick to my schedule: work mornings, run, study, or go to classes. In between I do my best to help out around the house, vacuuming, mopping the kitchen and bathrooms, washing dishes, whatever needs to be done. It makes my days very busy. As I gradually increase my running range, I follow the road along the river, where traffic is pretty light. I realize that I'm not only getting stronger, but increasing my endurance and speed. Always, I'm on high alert for anyone following me, listening for engine sounds, checking over my shoulder frequently. My heart speeds up whenever anyone drives by, and I am always looking for that black pickup.

Paul runs with me on the weekends, and he's building up his strength too. But he's upset with me for running by myself.

"There's just no other time for me to work out, between my job and classes. Besides, I always carry my gun with me."

"I still don't feel comfortable with you doing that. But I suppose it won't do any good to argue with you about it. You're a stubborn woman, woman."

"You know it." I laugh and give him a kiss.

During the week he runs after work. We've both equipped ourselves with rain gear to wear over our sweats. It makes our runs feel like taking a steam bath. We don't talk much once we're on the road. We egg each other on, though. "Come on, Paul, let's make it up to that next bend before we head back."

"Hey, Judith, time to slow down for a while. Are you tryin' to kill me?"

I laugh and trot ahead, hollering over my shoulder, "I hear you were quite the athlete in high school and college. We need to get you up to speed."

"Well, I can't do it all at once. Slow down, wait for me." And he pulls up beside me as we jog the last leg of our run.

"Paul, you're doing so well. I'm really proud of the progress you've made. You don't even have a limp anymore."

"I'm pretty happy myself. And I love running with you."

We arrive back home, legs aching, gasping for breath, and head for the sink for cold drinks. Then we exchange a sweaty hug, and head for the showers. It feels so good afterwards, when we relax on the couch. Paul has regained the strength in his leg beautifully.

Three weeks go by. Sharon and Doug have voiced their reservations about my running alone, but I haven't told them about that last note, and I assure them that I'll be fine. I've worked my way up to nearly five miles. I'm feeling really good about my progress. I'm beginning to think that our tormentors have given up and am relaxing more on my runs.

One afternoon, I'm running along easily, feeling relaxed and strong and free. The air is cold but I'm starting to perspire under my windbreaker. My mind is elsewhere as I'm thinking that, since it's the middle of April, the snows will be gone soon and we'll be able to mount our expedition into the Kalmiopsis, when I become aware that I'm being followed. I turn to look and see a battered, putrid green, old Ford pickup creeping up behind me. At first, I'm unconcerned, as it's not the black truck I'm looking for. I'm thinking they're slowing down to go around me. I try to wave them on by, but they hang back. I round a corner and realize that this stretch of road is deserted with no houses in sight. The truck speeds up and I pick up my pace. I don't think they're trying to go around. Feeling a rush of adrenaline, I slide my hand into my pocket, grasp the cold steel of my gun, pulling it out as I run, and releasing the safety. They're coming after me. The driver guns the motor and heads straight at me. I look for an escape. There's a ditch to my right and an embankment going up from that. I turn and fire wildly towards the windshield, then leap over the ditch and up the embankment, twist around, and as I slide back down on my butt, I fire off another round at the front of the truck. It veers sharply, over correcting away from the ditch, and sails off the road, down the brushy river bank, bounces through the brush and launches into the river. I can just see the back end of the truck sticking up out of the water, but the cab is completely submerged. I see then that the tail lights are broken. *It's the same truck from the night of the shooting.* I stare in amazement, trembling violently, and am tempted to just let them drown. But I know I can't do that. I have to do what I can, or I won't be able to live with myself.

A white sedan pulls up to the side of the road and the driver hops out.

"Help me," I yell. "They'll drown." I dash across the road, after the truck. The other driver jumps out and follows me. I pull off my windbreaker and sweatshirt, hiding my revolver inside the jacket, kick off my shoes, and jump into the water. It's freezing, and the current is strong. I realize that I can't be in here long, or I'll drown too. I dive down, grab onto the door handle. I see the driver, a blurred lump, slumped against the windshield, a dark, red rivulet streaming from his forehead. I yank on the door. It pulls open and the driver slumps out. He's huge. I grab him by his coat and pull. Just then, the cab shifts downward another foot. That's when I see that there's a passenger. Heaving with all my strength, I drag the man towards the shore. He's incredibly heavy, but the strong current helps push us towards the bank. The good Samaritan who stopped, has waded hip deep into the water, and I shout at him to take my burden so I can go after the passenger. He grabs the guy and starts dragging him to the shore, as I dive back in. The woman's white, terrified face is peering out from the vanishing bubble of air, as she flails about. She's managed to unlatch her seatbelt and is floating free as I grab her arm. Fortunately, she happens to be small and light. She's zipped into a red windbreaker, and I grab the sleeve and pull her out, just as the truck shifts downwards. She's thrashing around, and I'm not sure I can manage her. I hook my left arm around her neck, push to the surface, and head for shore with her. Struggling against her thrashing, I do my best to keep her chin above water.

It seems to take forever, even though we're only a few yards from shore, as she's fighting me, taking in water, but we finally hit bottom and I drag her clumsily out onto the ground. I pull the now silent and floppy woman up the bank and lay her on her stomach. Gasping for breath myself, I start pumping on her back until she sputters, coughs, vomits, and gulps for air.

My fellow rescuer has managed to revive the driver himself. When I turn the woman over, I recognize the matriarch of the Leland bunch. She's attended every day of Bart's trial. I will never forget that wizened, sour, little frog face. She's shivering and limp.

The driver is sitting up, holding his bleeding forehead. I recognize him too, as one of the thuggish members of the clan. I turn to the man who stopped to help. He's medium height, gray haired, wearing heavy black work pants and suspenders over a red plaid flannel shirt. His eyes are huge, and full of questions as he looks at me.

"Thanks so much for your help. I probably couldn't have gotten her out in time if you hadn't been here. Um, I don't have a car with me. Will you help me haul these two into the sheriff's office? They tried to run me down."

He frowns and shifts on his feet. "You're kiddin' me. They tried to run over you?" I nod. "Well, I don't know. I'm not sure it's safe to have'em in my car."

"Don't worry. I've got my pistol, and I'll keep an eye on'em."

He looks at me like I'm from another planet. I realize that I'm a mess, my wet hair hanging down, my soggy, muddy shirt sticking to me. I use my "take charge" voice. "I really need your help. Besides, we should get them in out of the cold. I'd be so grateful."

He looks at the ground, thinks about it, rubs his jaw. Finally, "Okay, I guess. 'In for a penny, in for a pound.'" He yanks the sputtering driver to his feet. "Let's go, buddy."

"Oh, and do you have a blanket or coat we could wrap the lady in? I'm afraid she'll get hypothermia."

"Yeah. I've got a blanket in my trunk. Hold on, while I get this guy in the car."

As they turn away, I yank off my wet tee-shirt, shivering uncontrollably, and pull on my sweatshirt, and jacket, slipping the gun into the pocket. Then I pull off my sweat pants, wring them out as much as possible, and reluctantly pull them back on, shivering all the while. I pull on my running shoes, not easy to do since my feet are wet, and wad up my tee-shirt with my soggy socks. Holding them in one hand, I lift the old lady to her feet. She looks pretty bedraggled, her hair soaked and sticking out, her skinny frame covered in wet jeans and her red jacket. We squish and shiver our way towards the car, as I support her feeble steps. When the stranger runs back with a blanket, I take off her wet jacket and shirt and wrap her up. She's still shivering as I help her into the back seat with her kinsman.

I plop into the front passenger seat, turn to the rear, and pull out my gun. In my most authoritative voice, I tell them, "If either of you makes a move, I'll have to shoot you. Please don't make me do that." The driver gives me a startled look, eyes wide and mouth open.

"You know how to operate that?"

"Yeah, I have a license and am qualified."

"Jesus H. Christ! What have I gotten into?"

He turns up the heater as we take off for town.

Our passengers look quite subdued. The big guy is holding his bloody head, leaning back against the seat. I wonder if he banged his head against the windshield, or if I had grazed him. The old lady is slumped into her corner.

The ride into town is uneventful. The driver introduces himself to me. "Marv Helleck. I live down the road a coupla miles. I was shocked to see the truck go into the drink. Are you some kind of cop? Why were they trying to run you down?"

"I'm Judith Johnson. It's a long story. Short version: I was a witness at the trial of one of their family members, and they've been harassing me since before the trial began. You don't know how much I appreciate your help."

"Hey, yeah! I've read about you. This Leland bunch has a nasty reputation. You've been in the news a lot. Glad I could help. Does this mean I'll be famous too?" He barks a short laugh.

I can't help a bitter chuckle. "I imagine. Once the story gets out the press'll want to know what happened. You might not like being famous. I think we should take them to the emergency room. This guy's head has bled a lot. I'll call the sheriff from there."

So that's what we do. Marv stays around to give the officers a statement, and takes his leave with my profuse thanks. The man from the truck, who, it turns out, is Wayne Leland, receives a few stitches in his head before he is hauled off to jail by the deputy. The old lady is kept for observation.

The sheriff offers me a ride home, and, as I am about to leave, the nurse comes out of the cubicle of the emergency room and taps me on the shoulder. "Mrs. Leland would like to speak with you."

I hesitate, look at our six-foot-plus, middle aged sheriff. He rolls his eyes and nods, waving me off. I go in to see what the woman wants. She looks at me out of sunken eyes. "You didn't have to risk yer life to save us," she rasps. "We were tryin' ta harm ya."

A surge of anger wells up in me and I snap, "Well, unlike you and your brood, I'm not a killer. I can't stand by and watch people die, even if they've done me wrong."

She turns her eyes away from me. "You don't have to worry about us no more. You done us a good turn. We won't bother you again."

I stare at her. "I hope not. I only did what I had to do to get justice for my family. They didn't deserve to be gunned down. Kali and I were just kids when it happened. And we didn't deserve to be orphaned, or persecuted by you and your clan. At any rate, the sheriff has all the evidence he needs if it happens again."

She pulls the blankets up around her neck. "It's over. We won't seek no revenge from now on."

I feel a huge surge of irritation and relief well up in my brain. I snap, "I hope you mean that. I don't know what the sheriff will do, but I'll tell him what you said."

She closes her eyes. Says no more. I turn, walk out into the breezy but sunny day with Sheriff Blake. I feel light, as if a great burden has been lifted from my shoulders. We can all stop worrying. Get on with our lives. "Yippee!" I raise my arms to the sun and twirl around.

Sheriff Blake looks at me quizzically. I explain what Mrs. Leland had said. He nods his head but looks serious. "Yeah, I was eavesdropping. I heard what she said. We'll see how that goes. But we'll have to bring new charges of attempted murder and harassment against 'em."

I hadn't thought about that. Will it start up all over again? I hope she meant what she said. Anyway, I'm cold and damp and need to get home.

"You might check out that truck. I think it's the same one that went through our yard in the middle of the night. It's been painted but it's a rotten paint job. And the taillight is still broken from when I shot at them."

"We'll get someone out there to fish it out."

As I walk into the house Kali and Sharon look up from the dining room table, where they're working, with alarm. They both jump up. Sharon asks, "What happened to you?"

I burst out laughing, as the absurdity of it all hits me, until tears are streaming down my face. I finally regain control, "I had an altercation with the Leland Clan and went for a swim."

They stare at me, mouths open. "It's all right," I assure them. "We won't be bothered by them anymore. They're in the custody of the Sheriff's office. I'll tell you all about it when I've had a chance to shower and change." I head to the bathroom.

The hot shower feels heavenly, and I just stand in it and let the water run off of me for a good ten minutes. Finally, I scrub off my entire body and wash my hair. When I step out of the tub I feel wonderful. Relaxed. Free. Also, exhausted. I flop on my bed and wrap myself in the bedspread. I'm free from the ever-present worry of what our tormentors will do next. Free of the trials. I'm almost giddy. I lie there for about ten minutes as I gather the energy to get up.

I dry my hair, get dressed and throw my wet, muddy clothes into the washing machine.

Ah, the luxury of modern life! I throw some used towels in with the wet things and start the machine.

Sharon and Kali have waited long enough. They both take an insistent stance around me, hands on hips. Sharon snaps, "All right, young woman, I want the whole story. What happened to you? Why did the sheriff bring you home, and why were you such a mess?"

I fill them in on my big adventure, and they stare in amazement. Sharon, fists on hips, gasps, "How could you do that? You took an awful chance! You could have drowned. I'm *horrified*. Those people tried to kill you and you still went in after them."

"I didn't drown and I'm fine. Besides, I truly believe we're free of them at last." I proceed to tell them about my conversation with old Mrs. Leland.

Kali throws her arms around me and I hear her sniffle. I hug her tight and tell her that everything is good. "We don't have to worry about those people anymore, Kali."

"So, it's over," Sharon breathes. "I'm so glad. I can't believe you went in after them like that, Judith. That was *insane.* But, my God, you're an actual hero. You'll have the newspapers after you again."

"I'm hoping it won't turn into a media circus. I've had enough of that."

Kali finally lets go of me and gives me a big smile. "You did good, Judy." A complete sentence. We're back on track. Thank God!

Sharon shakes her head. "Wait until we tell the men. They'll have fits."

I grab Kali's hands and whirl her around. "I'm in the mood to celebrate. We have our lives back. And I don't have to worry about my friends and family getting hurt anymore." I turn to Sharon. "Is it okay if I put together a cake?"

"Oh yeah! We're goin' to celebrate. Come on, girls, let's see what kind of a special dinner we can put together. I'm glad you don't have school today, Judith." Sharon practically skips into the kitchen. Kali grabs my hand and trots after her.

At first, when the men hear the story, Doug claps his hands on his head as if to say, *This woman is impossible.* "Good God, Judith. What were you thinking?"

But Paul is livid. Slams his hands on the kitchen counter and shouts, "What the hell were you thinkin' Judith? You could have been killed. Did you ever think of that? We're family here and we back each other up. You deliberately put yourself in danger. I'm totally pissed at you." He glares at me.

I feel somewhat contrite. "I'm sorry Paul. I didn't want to worry you all but I just had to find a way to put a stop to this. And I didn't want to put anyone else in danger. Can't you see that?"

He's still glaring at me. "You have to learn that you don't have to take on the whole world by yourself. We're supposed to be a team here. Whatever affects you affects me and all the rest of us. Don't you ever do anything like this again. Please! We could have lost you. Did you think about how I'd feel, or Kali? Or Mom and Dad?"

"I knew that Kali would be cared for. And you have to realize that I'll do what I think is right no matter what you think. I will defend my family."

He takes my hand in his. Sighs. "In the future will you at least talk it over with me? Let me know what you're thinking and want to do? We have to be open with each other, Judith. You're not alone now, living just for yourself and Kali. There are others' feelings and lives involved. Can you accept that?"

Chastened, I lean my head on his chest. "I... You're right. I do have to remember how my actions affect the people I love. I'm sorry, Paul. I promise to not keep anything from you in the future."

Gradually, I feel his body relax. He puts his arms around me. His voice cracks. "I could have lost you," he says into my hair. Don't you know how devastating that would be to me?'

Now I really am feeling bad. I return his embrace, and we hold on to each other. "I'm sorry, Paul, really. I'm just so used to handling my problems alone." I step back. I can see the pain in his eyes. "I solemnly swear not to take dangerous chances alone anymore. Unless I'm cornered. Then all bets are off."

He resists smiling for a moment, then his lips curve upward. "Okay. I don't expect you to stop being independent. Just to remember that we're here for each other and not go off half-cocked looking for trouble. Okay?"

I smile back. "Okay. Now, can we eat? We've prepared a feast to celebrate. And I'm hungry."

He peers around the kitchen, sniffs. "Smells great. Let's eat."

And we do. We adults, including myself, all have a glass of wine to top off the evening. I'm kind of getting used to the taste and the effect. Kali celebrates with ginger ale. She laughs as I'm kidded about my swimming exploits, and even shouts "Cheers," as we toast each other. I notice that the more she relaxes the more she talks. It reassures me about her future.

19

CHAPTER

The Communing Tree's Legacy

I don't press charges against the Lelands for trying to run me off the road, and they've stayed away from us. But I just want to put all the unpleasantness behind us. There are no more threatening notes. But the sheriff charges Wayne Leland with reckless endangerment, menacing and, after checking out the truck, illegal use of a firearm and assault with a deadly weapon from the firing into our house incident. I suppose I'm going to have to be involved in the court proceedings, but hope to stay out of it for now until my presence is demanded. I've made my statement for the Sheriff.

But now I realize that Kali's birthday is almost upon us, April fourteenth. She'll be twelve years old, and I need to do something special for the occasion. I consult with Sharon.

"Oh my, we have to have a party. We can invite Lucy, and have a nice celebration here at home. We need to bake a cake. I'll get candles for it. What would you like to do?"

"I think we should have a family celebration here, and I'm sure Lucy would like to be included. I don't know much about parties, but we always just had cake and presents at home. I'll make her Gramma's favorite applesauce cake, if that's all right. And I need to get her a present. I thought I'd get her some clothes for when she starts school. Some books? And maybe a skateboard. I've seen a lot of kids using those in town."

"Good idea. I'm sure she'd love that. I'll see what I can come up with. We'll have cake and ice cream. And whatever she wants for dinner. You can quiz her on that. Wow. Next year she'll be a teenager. She's growing up. Have you explained menstruation to her yet? She may start at any time."

"Yes, we've had a talk about that. But she hasn't started yet. I picked up the supplies she'll need so we're prepared. But now, I need to go shop for presents. Do you mind if I borrow your car? We only have three days to get this together."

"Oh yes, but I'll come with you. I need to find something for her too. We may have to run up to Bandon or down to Brookings."

After scrambling to get everything together, we have our celebration. Kali wants spaghetti and meatballs, so that's what we have. Lucy is there too, and brings Kali a gift of a board game that's popular at the moment. Kali is thrilled with everything and beams happily when we all sing "Happy Birthday" to her. She loves everything she gleefully unwraps, and her eyes tear up as she seems overwhelmed. She thanks everyone with each gift. Paul has given Kali her very first watch. She gasps, and puts it on, admiring it. "Oh, thank you Paul. L–love it."

The skateboard is unwrapped with glee. She and Lucy take it out on the patio and take turns practicing on it. I can see that we'll have to take her down to the playground so she can really get a good run on it. Kali's twelfth birthday is a happy one for all, and concludes with a sleepover with Lucy once again using my bed. I am so happy for Kali. This is a birthday she'll never forget.

Near the end of April, the Sheriff calls to say that the passes are open and we can go on the expedition to bring out my grandmother's body.

Once again, we find ourselves trudging up the trail to my former home in the wilderness. Kali stays behind with Sharon. The trail has been narrowed by the encroaching brush, since it hasn't been traveled over for several months, and there are a couple of trees that we have to cut through to clear our way. I note changes in the landscape as we make our way forward, the occasional boulder ejected from the steep hillsides near the path, the spread of *Kalmiopsis Leachiana* on the slopes and buckbrush filling in spaces. Small patches of snow in the shadier areas higher up the slopes. Huckleberry bushes are moving into shady areas. I wonder if I can come back in the fall to pick the tiny but delicious berries.

We have a team of two mules, one sheriff's deputy, a man from the coroner's office, myself and Paul, who represents the Forest Service. The deputy appears to be enjoying this as a change from his usual duties. He and Paul chat back and forth, occasionally laughing at some joke. John Olson is young, maybe twenty-six or so, and muscular. The coroner's assistant, a thin, bespectacled, middle aged man with a bad comb-over, seems grumpy and unhappy about this hike and rustic accommodations of the night before, when we camped out. He complained about his back in the morning, as his air mattress had deflated, and griped that the camp coffee was bitter. I can't say I like him very much.

We will exhume Gramma's body and take her out to be examined by the coroner. After that, I'll have the death certificate so that I can proceed with my inheritance. I dread disturbing Gramma. She has lain in peace, under the branches of my "communing tree," for so long. I console myself with the idea that she will be happy to be laid to rest with her only child and family.

As we come over the crest of the trail and look down on our old cabin, I feel a surge of homesickness. Life was so much simpler here, even though difficult. I didn't need to worry about money or taxes or dealing with other people. Nature ruled my life here. Now society does.

We head on down to the lonely little cabin. As we approach, it looks pretty much untouched. It's mossier, and looks like we may have lost a few shingles in the winter storms. Well, I don't have to worry about that anymore.

We unload the supplies and bedding into the cabin before taking the mules to the small paddock my father had built for our own animals. Once they're fed and watered, Paul and I lead the men up to my grandmother's gravesite. The little cross is still standing, which gives me a twinge of comfort. The men take a look and plan on doing the exhumation the next morning.

Paul and I linger a moment while the rest of the party heads on back to the cabin. He puts his arm around me and I flash back to the last time we were together here, where Paul professed his love for me. My first kiss was here. He gives me a squeeze and I turn into him and just hold on to him for a few moments. "I'm so glad you're here. I couldn't have done it without you."

He leans down and kisses the top of my head. "I told you, we're a team. What affects you, affects me. We'll get through this, Judith. I've never known a stronger woman. Together, we can do anything."

We kiss, and it feels like we form a forever bond as strong as steel. I've never loved him more. I step back, shaken. "I guess we'd better go on down with the others. We need to settle in."

"Sure. Come on, Sweetheart."

A shiver runs through me. It's the first time he's called me that. It makes me feel so loved and special. We head on down the path, hand in hand.

When we arrive, the men have lighted a fire in the little cooking range. It works quickly to chase away the chill and damp. I show the men the little room that had been Gramma's, and point out the bunks in the main room where they can sleep. I will use my parents' old room.

We heat up a re-constituted freeze-dried beef stew in the oven, and add some hard tack and a bowl of dried fruit to complete the meal. There are chocolate bars for dessert. Simple and filling. It's good to have a hot meal and sit at the rustic table my father built. It may be nearly May, but the camp-out the night before had been wet and cold. The deputy is interested in the cabin and asks all about it while we eat. Paul is negotiating with the Forest Service to save it for use by backpackers and Forest Service personnel. I like the idea. So does John. Rick, the coroner's man, is sleepily noncommittal.

We've all had a long, hard day getting in here, and all of us head for bed pretty early. Paul takes Gramma's room while the others sack out on the cots. I curl up in my sleeping bag on my parents' bed. The heat from the stove has warmed up the room, but it still smells a little musty. I think about the night Kali was born on this bed. It was a long ordeal for us all, but what a wonderful result. I remember the looks on my parents faces as they cuddled our new baby. Pain shoots through my heart and I curl up in a ball. This may be the last time I sleep here. It's like I'm saying good-bye to Mamma and Daddy all over again. Gradually, I drift off to sleep, awash in memories of our life here.

The next day I'm up at dawn. I get dressed and stoke the fire before I dash out to the spider web festooned outhouse. I grab the old broom off of the porch and brush them away. I don't want to be bitten while I do my business.

When I return, the guys are up and dressed. I wash my hands and put on a pot of coffee. Paul has put a kettle of water on the stove to cook the oatmeal, and breaks a pack of biscuits to bake in the oven. We have a hot breakfast of oatmeal with reconstituted milk and biscuits with peanut butter. As soon as the guys are fed they go on out up the hill with shovels and a pickaxe. I stay behind and clean up the breakfast dishes, before I head out to check on the mules. I pour water into the trough, fill a pan with oats and hunt for a brush in the shed. I like mules. They remind me of Stubborn, the mule my family had to haul in supplies. The pot raiders took him and I never saw him again. I considered him to be a friend, and missed him for years. I pet and brush them down and dally around. I really don't want to go up that hill and see them dig up my beloved Gramma's bones.

Finally, unable to stand the suspense, I make my way up the hill. The men are still digging, very carefully. They're very serious about their work. When they inevitably get down to the blanket wrapped figure, they put aside the shovels and excavate around the body with small trowels and their hands, slowly clearing away enough dirt to try to lift her out. But the blanket is rotten and tears when they pull on it. I catch a glimpse of her buckskin dress with its beautiful beading. I back up and go sit under the tree. Sorrow is roiling up from my gut and I close my eyes.

Paul sits down beside me and puts his arm around my shoulders. "I'm sorry, Judith," he whispers softly. "Are you all right?"

I shake my head. "It's bringing everything back. The day she died..."

He holds me, and I lay my head on his chest while he gently strokes my hair. Gradually, I stop shaking and feel calm returning to my mind. I just have to believe that Gramma would want this for Kali and me, and would be glad to be buried with her only child, our mother. I straighten up. "I'm okay now, Paul. I just want to get this over with."

Since they don't want to tear the rotten blanket further, they bring up a sturdy canvas sheet, and, working carefully, manage to move the remains onto it. It would seem that there are only bones and hair left of her body. They carefully lift the bundle up out of the hole and she's once again lying on the earth. I stand back and avoid looking as they slide her, tarp and all, into a body bag. They set to work, refilling the hole with Paul's help. It doesn't take them long. Paul has taken "before" and "after" pictures to document what we've done.

They place the body on a stretcher, and carry her down the hill. We pack up our gear, placing the bulk of the stuff on the mules. We use our backpacks for a few personal items, including snacks.

The plan is to carry Gramma out on the stretcher, all of us taking turns on the way. She's really quite light, and we don't want to take a chance on damaging her remains.

I go in to check on the stove and it's cold. I have one more look around the cabin, then walk out and latch the door. I wonder if I'll ever see it again. Now that Gramma is removed, there's really no reason to come back. It just makes me mourn all over again. Then I have a thought. I turn to the men. "Paul, I have something to do. It'll only take me a few minutes. Why don't you all go on ahead and I'll catch up with you?

Paul looks at me, eyebrows raised. "You sure you want us to go ahead?"

"Yes. I'll only be a few minutes behind you. Okay?"

He raises his eyebrows in a puzzled look. "Okay. See you soon." He gives me a questioning look one more time and they head out.

I run to the wood shed and grab an old shovel that's still there. Then I run up the hill to my "communing" tree. I search the ground around it until I find what I'm looking for— a small seedling that has sprouted from the mother tree. It's against Forest Service rules, but I dig it up anyway. I will take a piece of my tree, and its surrounding earth, to have with me forever. Back at the shed, I carefully wrap the seedling in an old piece of burlap, gently place it in my backpack, and head on out.

I catch up with the group in only thirty minutes. Again, Paul looks at me with questions in his eyes, but doesn't say anything.

It takes us nearly two days to reach our vehicles. We place Gramma carefully in the back of Paul's pickup and, once the mules are back in their trailer, head on to town.

Once we're on the road, Paul asks, "Judith, are you all right? Why'd you hang back when we left?"

I explain to him about the tree. He frowns. "You know that's against wilderness rules, Judith. You've put me in an awkward position."

"It's just one little seedling. It's like having a piece of Gramma with me. The mother tree drew nourishment from her body, and it feels like the baby tree must have traces of her inside it. I need it, Paul."

"Okay. I get it. It'll be our secret. Please don't tell anyone where you got it."

"Thanks, Paul. I promise I won't tell anyone but Kali when she's older."

He smiles at me, squeezes my hand. "Deal."

When I get back to the house I find a spare plant pot and carefully place my tree in the best soil I can find. I'll keep it in my room until I find the perfect place to plant it permanently.

Within three weeks, I have the death certificate, and Gramma's cremains are released to us. Amazing how so many bones can be reduced to ashes. Once again, we all gather around our family's grave. We don't bother getting permission, and just dig a deep hole with a post hole digger to place the container in with the rest of the family. There's plenty of room. We fill the hole back up and put a bunch of flowers on top. Gramma is with her family now.

We all bow our heads and are quiet for a while. Kali leans into me and I put my arm around her, remembering the first burial, when we were left alone in the forest. I start singing "Amazing Grace" once again, Gramma's favorite hymn. I look out over the scene, down the hill and across Highway 101, to the sea, where the waves are gently caressing the shore. As the final notes float out over the grounds, I feel like I've done all I can.

Kali is pensive, holding my hand. I ask her, "Do you think Gramma will like it here?"

She nods her head solemnly. "Nice. Gramma love it."

Her speech sessions are showing results. I feel an enormous sense of gratitude to the universe, and Dr. Allen. Her patience with Kali has paid off. I give her a big hug and we leave our family in peace.

20

CHAPTER

Emancipation

I contact Virgil to let him know that I have the certificate. I'll get over to the bank in Klamath Falls and transfer my account there to my bank in Gold Beach. I've decided to hang on to my grandparents' property, at least for the time being. He can continue to handle it.

Sharon and I reserve rooms at the same motel as before and, with Kali in tow, go to Klamath Falls. We arrive late in the afternoon, but in time to arrange the transfer of my account over to the Gold Beach Bank.

Then we drop in on Virgil. He jumps up and grins when he sees us, and leads us into his office. I arrange to replace the old roof on my grandparents' house and continue to rent it out for the time being. Future payments are to go into my Gold Beach account. Virgil is content to continue to handle the property and congratulates me on my new status as a land owner.

"You may decide to keep it in the future. At any rate, it's not goin' anywhere. It's like an insurance policy. It's a source of income but it's there when you want to either sell it or move into it."

I thank him for all his help. I'm feeling relieved and happy about my decisions. I ask Virgil if he'd like to join us for a sumptuous dinner to celebrate. His face falls as he sadly declines, since he has plans for the evening already with his wife and kids. He does give us a recommendation for a restaurant nearby, though, and that's where we end up. It's a nice, cozy Italian place with checkered table clothes and candles on the tables. Kali wants spaghetti with meatballs, her second favorite meal. Sharon and I order lasagna, something I haven't tried before. It's a festive evening and we toast our new life with ginger ale (red wine for Sharon). I feel good, treating Sharon for once. I've hated feeling beholden to her and Doug. Now I can pull my own weight.

The first thing I want to do when I get home is find a car for myself. I mention it to Paul and his face lights up. "Yeah, Judith. You need your own wheels. We'll start looking right away. He grabs the local paper and turns to the used car ads. He's like a hound on the hunt. I swear he's more excited than I am. "You need something that gets good gas mileage, and low mileage on the odometer, and is easy to keep up. Something basic. I'm not seeing anything local here but we can run up to Coos Bay on Saturday and look around. Are you game?"

"Absolutely. I can't wait. I hate always having to borrow Sharon's or your car. What kind do you think I should get?"

"I'm kind of a Ford man, myself. I like American made. But you'd get better mileage with a Honda or Toyota, something small. Also, they seem to hold up really well."

We continue our hunt that Saturday, running up to Coos Bay to check out the used cars. We look over the offerings in the lots, and there's a VW Beetle that looks good and a Toyota 4-door sedan catches my eye. We decide to go have some coffee and a snack and talk it over. I grab a Coos Bay paper from the news rack and we check the ads while we sip. There's an ad for a 1980 Volkswagen Beetle, single owner, 40,000 miles on it. "Let's go look at it, Paul. I think it might just be exactly what I need."

He looks at the ad. "Hmm. You might be right. Let's check it out. We call the number and find out that it's still for sale and get the address. Turns out, it's at a home in the hills above downtown. The seller is the grandson of the woman who had owned the car and passed away. We look it over and I am immediately smitten with the little red car. I ask if we can take it for a test drive while we leave Paul's truck for collateral. He agrees, and Paul and I take it for a spin up the hilly streets of the town, then down into traffic. It doesn't take me long to get used to how it works. Paul listens to the engine as it purrs along. We pull over to the curb and inspect it carefully for rust, which can be a problem at the coast. It's clean as a just washed plate. We grin at each other. "This is it," I tell him.

"It's a beauty. Go for it."

We head back to the house. The grandson wants to get rid of it and likes the offer of $1100 cash. He signs over the deed, and hands me the keys. I love the feel of my very own car keys in my hand.

So, twenty minutes later, I'm on the road, following Paul back to Gold Beach.

Of course, there's a catch to my newfound freedom. I have to get insurance, and get my registration validated. Everything has strings attached out here in the civilized world. Ah well, I'm emancipated now.

That settled, I write out a check for $2,000 to Sharon and hand it to her as she is working at her sewing machine. Her eyes grow big, and she immediately hands it back to me, shaking her head. "No, no, Judith. I don't want your money."

"Please, Sharon. I owe you and Doug so much. I'd never have made it through the last year without your help. I know that keeping Kali and me here hasn't been cheap. You've incurred a lot of expenses on our behalf. This isn't even a fraction of what we must owe you. And I want to pull my own weight. I need to know that I'm contributing to the family."

I hand it back to her. She searches my face for a long minute, then reluctantly accepts the check. "All right. If it makes you feel better. But you know you don't have to do this."

"Yes, I do. I have to do my share. I want to be able to support myself and Kali. This is a start."

"I understand. Thank you, Judith." She stands up and gives me a hug. "You know that you and Kali mean so much to me. I love you like my own daughters." She steps back. "Speaking of which, have you and Paul set a date yet? We need to start planning."

I smile at that. "Not yet. But we will soon. I'll graduate at the end of summer. Then we'll decide."

She sighs. "Well, keep me posted."

I laugh. "Don't worry. You'll be the first to know."

I call Beth and arrange to meet her for lunch the next day. I have to show her my car before we go in to eat. She's looks it over. "Wow, Judith. It's a really nice car. I like the color and it looks really clean. I'd say you got a good one here." She opens the driver's side door.

"A stick shift. Good thing you know how to operate that. You'll love it."

"You're right. I love it already. Shall we go in and order before your lunch hour is up?"

"Sure. I'm really happy for you, though, Judith. You can go where you want, when you want now."

We settle down with pizza and salads. Over lunch we cover the usual ground. Beth is excited over my engagement. She looks me over. "Judith, we need to get you to a beauty parlor. You want to look like a modern bride, don't you? It'd be fun. I'd love to do a 'makeover' on you. Make you a new woman to go with your new car."

"Well, I don't know about that. I think Paul likes the old me. What if he hates the new me?"

"Don't worry, he'll love it. I'll make the arrangements with the gal who does my hair, Stacy Barker. She'll have a great time doing you over. You'll feel like you stepped into a different time zone."

This idea makes me a bit uneasy. But, maybe she's right. Maybe it's time for me to think about updating.

So, the following Saturday, filled with misgivings, I'm sitting in Stacy's Beauty Shop, which is in her former garage. Stacy is a perky, thirty-something blond, with teased hair piled high on her head, and little ringlets surrounding her face. She's turned her work space into a cheery ode to beauty care, with a tile floor, pink decorations and curtains, and a waiting area with a pretty, flowered love seat. There are a couple of comfy leather chairs with beehive hair-dryers looming over them, and a counter with a sink on one wall. She seats me in her hair cutting station. There's a mirror in front of me and Stacy wraps a plastic covering around my shoulders.

"Well, Judith," she chirps, "what would you like me to do? Is there a particular style of haircut you'd like to try?"

"I don't know. What do you think, Beth?"

Beth is hovering. "Hmmm! Have you ever had bangs? I'll bet you'd look great with wispy bangs. Want to give it a try? And shorten the hair at least six inches?"

"Let's go for it." I lean back. "I'm in your hands, Stacy."

Stacy's brows rise up, her blue, mascaraed eyes grow big, and, grinning, her ringlets fairly quivering with glee, she takes in a huge breath. "Oh, this'll be such fun. I haven't done a makeover in ages. And you could *really* use some help. Whatever have you been doin' to your skin, Hon? It looks like you've had way too much sun and no face cream or makeup. You really should have a complete facial. This is gonna take some time."

Beth pipes up, "Yeah. And let's give her a manicure too."

Three hours later, I emerge from the beauty shop, a bag of beauty products in hand, a changed woman. And $150 poorer. Beth and Stacy seem thrilled with their handiwork. I'm excited about my new look. My hair has been teased and puffed and sprayed within an inch of its life, in a fluffy "page boy" style. I've never had it this short. It feels cool. They've plucked my eyebrows, and persuaded me to apply mascara and makeup, and a brighter shade of lipstick. My nails are an interesting shade of scarlet. I'm thinking I look "with it" and gorgeous.

When I arrive home, Sharon is startled at the transformation. Her eyes grow wide and her mouth drops as she says "Wow, Judith. You really went all out. You look incredibly ... um ... different."

I'm hoping that's a compliment. But she isn't smiling. "Thanks, Sharon. I hope Paul likes it."

She nods. "Um, we'll see. Sometimes men don't like their women to change their looks. You never know how they'll react."

That gives me pause. I'm nervous about it now. We'll have to wait and see.

Kali cocks her head and looks at me. "Pretty." She stares at my face. Walks around me and checks out the haircut. Pats my head. "Nice."

I give her a hug. "Thanks, Kali. That's what I'm hoping Paul will say."

I get busy on my homework and, later, help Sharon get dinner ready. The men have spent the afternoon on the river, fishing. When we hear them come in I'm suddenly nervous. Will Paul like the new me? I turn my back to the kitchen while I busy myself setting the table.

"Honey, I'm home," Paul calls out loudly. I hesitate, steel myself, and turn to face him. The goofy grin on his face freezes. "What have you done?" He stares at me.

"Do you like it? Beth thought I should look more contemporary."

His jaw drops. "Um, I don't know what to think," he starts slowly. "No, I don't think I like it. I liked you just the way you were. What was Beth thinking? You're not going to keep on with this, are you?"

I feel a flush of fury surge through my body. For this I spent hours in that damned beauty shop? Hands on hips, I yell, "What do you mean? It's my hair and my face. I'll do what I want with it. I'm still me. I just don't want to look like a hick."

He reaches out for me. "I didn't fall in love with a phony face. I fell in love with the real you. Please bring her back."

I push him away. "This is the new me. You'll just have to get used to it." I whirl around so he can't see the tears forming in my eyes, and stomp back to my room, slamming the door behind me. What makes him think he can tell me what to do?

I sit down on my bed and let the tears come. I'm trying so hard to fit in. There's so much I have to learn still. The whole process is overwhelming. I hate being in the "outside." Life was so much simpler in the wilderness. Maybe I should go back there.

There's a tap on the door. "Judith, can I come in?" It's Paul.

"No. Go away."

"Please, Judith. I'm sorry."

"Go away." There's a long pause, then I hear him retreat.

I grab a tissue and mop my face. I notice that it's streaked with black. My mascara is running. I don't care. I don't like the feel of it on my lashes anyway. I sit and brood and feel sorry for myself for a while. Finally, Kali slides into the room and puts her arm around me.

"Sorry, Judy. Love you." My heart melts. Whatever happens, Kali is always on my side. I hug her back.

"Oh, Kali. I'm so glad I have you."

She fingers my cheek and grins. "Funny."

I laugh and cuddle her for a while and then straighten up. "I guess I'd better go wash this goop off of my face."

I look in the bathroom mirror and have to laugh at myself. I do look silly. There are black streaks smeared on my cheeks, and the lipstick looks way too bright. And whoever heard of green eyelids? I really dislike the feel of the makeup on my skin. I hate to admit it, but Paul's right. It's not the real me. I wash it all off. Then I wet down my hair and blow it and brush it into a more natural "page boy," as Stacy called it. I do like the shorter cut, just reaching my shoulders. I'm going to keep it that way, whether he likes it or not.

I return to the kitchen, where the family is still gathered. I'm still a little angry with Paul. He has no right to tell me what to do and he'll have to realize that if we're going to be married. He should have been more supportive.

Paul looks mournful. "I'm sorry, Judith. I didn't mean to hurt your feelings." He looks at my hair. "And I really do like your new hairstyle."

I'm not ready to let him off. "Well, I just want you to know that I'm in charge of my appearance. Not you."

"Sure. I just want *you* to know that I love you just the way you are. I don't care what anyone else thinks. And neither should you."

He tries to put his arms around me but I fend him off.

"I'm not done being mad at you so just keep your distance until I've finished cooling off."

He laughs. "Okay. As long as you forgive me in the long run."

I can't help smiling a little bit. "We'll see. Dinner's ready so we better eat it before it gets cold."

Sharon and Doug look relieved, as does Kali, who has joined us. Sharon picks up a casserole. "Paul's right, Judith. Your new hairdo really is attractive. It suits you perfectly."

Flustered, I tell her, "Thanks, Sharon. I'm glad you like it." We all head for the dining room.

—

21

CHAPTER

Life Goes On

It's June, and we're having a short break before starting summer classes. On my day off I take Kali over to the goat farm to visit our animals. They come running and bleating when Kali calls. It's so nice to see them and spend some time with them. Fret tears over for a petting and I make a big fuss over him, rubbing his tummy and behind his ears. He's a blur of black and brown and white fur as he keeps jumping up and licking my face, while I am laughing and pushing him back down. He's joined by the tail wagging family dog, a blond Labrador who has become his best friend. So, I pet him too.

Kali runs around the field, the goats following her. Cheryl has placed a couple of huge cable spools in the pasture, and there are three platforms of various heights for the goats to climb and jump on. Kali scrambles up on one of them and the goats follow her, then they all jump off. They playfully butt us with their heads, and rub up against us. Star is especially eager to have Kali's attention, pushing the other goats away. Amigo has run up too, braying. We're laughing and petting our goats and Amigo, when Cheryl comes out and joins us.

"It's so nice to see you girls. Actually, Judith, I've been meaning to call you. I want to discuss something with you. Would you like to come in for a cup of tea?" She looks at Kali. "Cookies, too. I'd love to have a chat."

I'm delighted. I need all the friends I can get and we really haven't had much chance to just visit, one on one. Also, I'm curious to know what's on Cheryl's mind. Kali, hanging onto Amigo, is reluctant to leave him. I nod towards the house. "Come on, Kali. Just for a while." I have to grab her hand and pull her along until she gets the idea and reluctantly follows.

The farmhouse is a gracefully aging, white, two story with sky blue shutters and a wide, inviting front porch. The yard is shaded by a couple of huge oak trees, along with some ornamental shrubs. Inside, the furnishings are comfortable and the atmosphere is warm and welcoming. We follow Cheryl into the kitchen. She puts on the teakettle and sets a plate of oatmeal raisin cookies on the kitchen table. "Please, have a seat, ladies. The tea will be ready in a few minutes."

She busies herself putting teabags into a pretty, flowered tea pot, then sits down with us. "I've been wondering how your studies are going, Judith. You must be near to getting your GED."

"Yeah. I should be finished up by the end of summer. I'll be so glad when it's done."

"Have you thought about what you'll do afterwards?"

"I'm really not sure. I'll be getting married in the near future. But I'd like to move on into some kind of career too. I just don't know what yet. I may take some classes at the community college in Coos Bay."

"I know you've had experience working with goats in the past. Do you think you'd be interested in learning how to handle a goat dairy?"

"I have to admit; the thought has crossed my mind. I love our goats and really enjoy working with'em. You have such a wonderful set-up here. It's really tempting to me."

The teakettle whistles and she jumps up to pour the water into the teapot. She sets it on the table, along with three mugs and milk and sugar and spoons. I'm learning to love the aroma of tea.

"Kali, sweetie, have a cookie."

She passes the plate to Kali, who helps herself, smiles, and says, "Thank you." I'm pleased that she's minding her manners.

"You're welcome, Kali. Have all you want." She turns to me. "Well, our hired hand is going back to school in the fall, and I'm goin' to need some help. I was wondering if you'd like to step into the job, once you've got your GED?"

"Wow. What an interesting idea. When would you like me to start?"

"Perhaps when you're done with school and know when your wedding will be. I wouldn't want to interfere with that. Maybe after your honeymoon? Tony'll head out the second week of September."

"Gee, thanks. Wow! Let me think about it and I'll get back to you. It's an intriguing thought." This is a new possibility for me and I'll consider it seriously. I do love the goats and have spent years around them, caring for them, milking them. Cheryl has mentioned that goat milk and cheese are starting to catch on. I wonder if this may be my destiny. I feel a thrill of excitement.

I enjoy visiting with Cheryl, she's so real, so warm. Kali loves the cookies and tea with lots of milk and sugar. Cheryl and I discover a love of books. She reads a lot in her bits of spare time. I'm trying to catch up on more current literature, and she tells me about what she's reading. "Right now, I'm reading *The Color Purple* by Alice Walker. It's great."

"Oh, I read that a couple of weeks ago. I loved it."

"I love it too. I'll give you a list of some of the books I've read lately if you want. Maybe we can exchange lists of books we like."

"That'd be great. Have you read *The Joy Luck Club* by Amy Tan?

As the conversation progresses, I learn that Cheryl was born and raised in Curry County, as was Aaron. They were married right out of high school but they've managed to make a go of it so far. It turns out that Cheryl does most of the goat wrangling while Aaron has a day job in the timber industry. She really needs an assistant.

Our visit gives me a lot to think about. Should I go on for more schooling, or get to work goat farming?

Kali is unconsciously humming to herself on the way home. The animals always cheer her up and give her comfort. Whatever will become of her? She definitely has to improve her speech before school starts in the fall. I plan to increase her sessions with Dr. Allen over the summer. If she can just get through a year of classroom experience, I'm certain that she can make it through high school.

Lucy is my hope, where Kali is concerned. Her friendship has done so much to bring Kali out of her shell. She and Kali have devised their own form of sign language, spelling out letters with their fingers, which gives them added closeness. But Lucy encourages Kali to speak, too. I've heard her say, "No, Kali. Tell me. Don't sign." Her influence has helped immensely that way.

I ask Kali, "Shall we stop by Lucy's house and see if she'd like to go get pizza for lunch with us?" Kali recently discovered pizza, and it has almost overcome hamburgers as her favorite food.

Kali nods her head vigorously. "Yeees! Lucy. I ... like ... pizza." My eyes water. She's working hard on her speaking ability. I love hearing her voice.

I'm so happy to have my own car, and to be able to enjoy my day off with Kali. We stop by to see if Lucy's free. She's excited to join us. Then it's off to the pizza parlor. I told Lucy's mother we'd have her home by three o'clock. After pizza and root beer, we head down to the beach.

It's a sunny day, though breezy, and we're all excited to hit the sand. I pull a couple of shovels out of the little trunk, and a bucket, and we're soon busy building a humongous sand castle. The girls jump in with vigor, furiously digging to build a huge pile of sand.

We all stand back to examine our handiwork when finished. It has four turrets, and a moat with a wall surrounding it.

I thoroughly enjoy the muted roar of the surf, and the fresh scent of the sea, while we scour the beach for stones and shells for decoration. Gulls soar overhead, noisily calling to one another. It soothes my soul. Finally, we insert the shells and stones around our structure. We stand around and admire it. Suddenly, I wish I had a camera to record this moment. Come to think of it, we have very few photos of our lives so far. I wish we had been able to take them while we lived in the Kalmiopsis. I don't have any baby pictures of Kali, or any of the different stages of her life so far. That has to be remedied right away. I know that Sharon has taken pictures, but I want a camera of my own.

After we leave Lucy at her house we head to the hardware store. I figure they might have cameras. They do have a few, but I realize I don't know anything about photography. So I decide to wait until someone can help me pick one out.

That evening, I ask Paul if he knows anything about cameras. He thinks for a minute. "Well, I have an old camera that I use once in a while. But Mom has a nice newer one that might work well for you. Why don't you ask her? "

Later, I ask Sharon about her camera. She shows me her Nikon-FE2. It looks easy enough to operate, is small and easy to carry. She waxes enthusiastic. "I love it. It's light and easy to use. I agree, you should get one. Kali's growing up so fast, and you'll want pictures to remember her special moments. And yours too. Here, let me show you the photos I took of your birthday. I just got them back today."

I look at the photos. They're really good. As I study my picture, I realize everyone is laughing and looking happy, while I have a bemused smile on my face. I must have been thinking about my lost family or something. It's the first time I've seen a photo of myself as an adult, other than the newspaper photos. So this is the me I have become. This is how I look to the rest of the world. I think I look good, like I belong. I like the feeling.

On my next Monday off, I run up to Coos Bay, again, to hunt for the camera. Sharon comes too, as she wants to do some shopping, and Kali tags along. We find a camera shop, and I purchase my Nikon, and film. I'll try it out when we get home. Then we stop by Penney's to look at clothes.

I really want to find another dress so I don't have to wear the same one all the time. I find a simple gray wool skirt that'll look good with the sweater set Paul gave me for Christmas. It's on the sale rack because the new summer line is in. I pick out a couple of blouses and then find a pretty, cotton-polyester dress with a flared skirt that looks really good on my muscular body. It's spring green dotted with tiny white flowers, like daisies. While I'm trying it on, Sharon brings me a couple of more skirts and dresses to try. I pick out another skirt, navy, and a bright yellow, short-sleeved spring dress. Feeling really good about expanding my wardrobe, I grab a new pair of jeans and look at running shoes. I collect a pair of Reeboks. By then I'm ready to call it a day. I find all the sensory stimulation to be exhausting. But we have to get some things for Kali. So, it's on to the junior department. She has a great time looking at *everything.*

I'm beginning to wonder whether we'll ever get out of there. She finally grabs some things to try on, as Sharon and I discuss what she'll need for school. Mostly, the girls wear jeans and sweaters. We decide to wait until it's closer to the school year to stock up on those. We pick out a cute shorts set, and a nice summer dress, and pick up a new pair of jeans. Then I decide to get her a couple of new bras, as she seems to have sprouted since our last shopping foray.

She's really growing up. When I hand one to her, she blushes and shakes her head. I've embarrassed her.

"Kali," I whisper, "you really need this. You're growing up and you can't hide it. Please try it on. If it fits, I'll get you a couple more."

She reluctantly accepts the bra and pushes me out of the changing room. I wait about ten minutes. Then ask, through the curtain, "Kali, did it fit?"

I hear a mumbled "Yes." So, I gather a couple more to add to our pile.

Sharon is still looking, manages to find an outfit for herself and then heads to the home furnishings department. Before we're done she's picked out a free-standing, adjustable lamp to aid her with her sewing.

We finally pay for all our purchases and are happily on our way. Stashing them in the car, we grab a late lunch and head for home.

I realize, once we're on the road, that I'm finally feeling comfortable with this new life. I've learned so much in the short time we've been in town. I know there will be a lot more to discover, but I'm feeling much more at ease with the complexities of civilization. Kali seems to have adjusted faster than I to our new life, now that the trials are behind us. Yes, I think we're heading in the right direction.

22

CHAPTER

Summer Life

Summer flies by as I take classes in geography, U.S. history, and literature. I've met my math requirements and don't want to go on to advanced math. I don't like it and can't see any advantage to taking calculus. I'm also working five days a week at the restaurant. The summer crowds include a lot of tourists who are passing through. They're good tippers, and my savings are adding up to defray my expenses.

I'm really enjoying my work here. I'm meeting new people all the time and getting acquainted with the regulars. The rest of the staff are all friendly and jolly and make the time fly by with their jokes. And my boss is kind and considerate of his crew.

We're also taking Kali up to Coos Bay for continuing speech therapy three times a week. Sharon drives her on the days I can't make it. Kali is making good progress; she's speaking more in whole sentences. She's not a chatter box, but she can make herself understood. "I'm goin' to my room now." "Don't want peas." "Please pass the butter." Everyday messages. I'm encouraged that she'll be able to get by in school.

Sharon sees to it that Kali has completed all her scholastic requirements in order to enter sixth grade. She's given her the standard tests provided by the state, and Kali zipped right through them. I owe her big-time for that. She's been an absolute rock and second mother to us. I really love her like family. Sometimes I wonder if I'm really marrying Paul in order to have a real, live family again. But when I think about him, and spending my life with him, I know he's the right man for me. We just fit like a hand in a glove.

In spite of all the busyness of our lives, Paul and I manage to get away for a Sunday afternoon of fishing on the river. It feels wonderful to be out on the river in their motor boat and relaxing to the rhythm of the water slapping on the sides. We catch and release several fish and the thrill of the catch never gets old. We pull into shore for a picnic dinner in the shade, and just enjoy being together in nature. We talk about planting a little garden in our backyard in the spring. I tell him about the biography of Teddy Roosevelt that I'm reading for my history class, and he wants to read it when I'm done. We're both interested in the local plants growing along the shore, and he's surprised when I tell him about some of their uses.

"Look at all the Salaal around here. It's good for so many things—a tea made from the leaves is good for inflammations and sore throats, even diarrhea, and gas pains. The berries are bland but nutritious and the natives dried them for food. And there are elderberries. So nutritious too. Kali and I enjoyed dandelion greens and cattail sprouts and corms and new growth nettle leaves and mushrooms with our game. And there's Purslane. It's so nutritious and good for a lot of things, like a poultice for scrapes. So many of our wild plants are good for so many purposes. I want to learn all I can about'em."

"I love how much you know about all this. You should teach classes."

"Maybe I will someday. I still have a lot to learn."

We go back to our fishing and head home when it starts getting dark. It's wonderful to spend time together and share our common interests.

By the end of August, I've completed my courses and receive my high school diploma at last. There's a small ceremony in one of the high school class rooms where four other adults and I are handed our GED diplomas. We even get to wear black graduation caps and gowns. I am really thrilled, and with Paul and the rest of the family in attendance it's a wonderful occasion. Sharon's busy snapping photos. I can't help but squeeze Paul's hand as we leave the building, waving my white tassel.

Afterwards we celebrate at home with champagne and a huge chocolate cake with fancy icing that says "Congratulations, Judith." Paul holds up his glass. "Let's drink a toast, to my smart, beautiful, brave fiancée. I'm so proud of you, Judith. You did it. Congratulations!"

Paul and Sharon echo his words, "Congratulations, Judith," as we all clink glasses.

Kali chimes in too. "Good job, Judy." Then sneaks a fingerful of icing from the cake, which makes me laugh. As I sip my champagne, the happiness and relief I feel make me giddy. Now my life can begin in earnest.

As fall nears, the first thing on my agenda is getting Kali started in school, then, second, planning our wedding. We set the date for the second week of September. Paul and I begin taking marriage instructions at his church, so I can understand the Church's views. I like what the priest has to say about the seriousness and sanctity of marriage, and what our obligations will be. One evening, after a session, Paul and I discuss having children.

"Sure, I want kids. Don't you?"

"Yes, eventually. But I've spent so much of my life raising Kali that I think I need a break before I start raising my own kids. Can you understand that?"

"Yeah. But you won't be upset if you accidentally get pregnant, will you? Sometimes that happens with natural family planning."

"As long as I have your full support, I can handle anything. But, as I said, I'd like to wait a couple of years before we have kids."

"I think that's a good idea. I want you to be happy."

"Thanks, Paul. I want that for both of us." We head for home.

Sharon, Kali and I make another shopping trip to Coos Bay. We add to Kali's wardrobe for school, and I start looking for a wedding dress. We check out a couple of smaller boutique dress shops, searching for just the right dress. They're really expensive and too fussy for my taste. Finally, at The Hub store, we find a simple, ankle length dress with long sleeves and a V-neckline that's modest and feels just right. It's satin, with a simple lace overskirt and three-quarter length sleeves. As I look in the mirror, the clerk brings me a veil with a circlet of flowers and places it on my head. I stare at the image in the mirror, feeling a sense of ... what? Joy? Elation? Anticipation, I guess. I'm really going to do it, marry the man I love. A chill goes up my spine.

Sharon looks on, her eyes watering. "Oh Judith, it's perfect. It's you. Can you see it?"

Kali pipes up. "Yes, Judy. Buy it. Beautiful."

"Yep," I say, softly. "This is the one."

That settled, we purchase the dress and look for a nice pair of shoes to go with it. I decide to splurge and buy a pair of white satin slippers with low heels. They're totally impractical but I fall in love with them and they'll go perfectly with my dress. I probably won't wear them ever again but, after all, this is a once-in-a-lifetime event.

Sharon is as excited as I am, I think. She chats about wedding plans all the way back home. "We'll have to get a photographer, and flowers. We'll have to look into arrangements for the reception. I think the altar society will supply the food. And we need to get the invitations out right away."

I listen to her suggestions and let her know that I just want to invite a few friends to the wedding and Paul wants to invite his aunts and uncles, and his six cousins. I have no family to invite other than Kali, as my father's parents disowned him when he married my mother. The wedding keeps getting bigger by the minute. But I can't dampen Sharon's enthusiasm, so I go along with it. We'll have the ceremony at the church and the reception at the church hall afterwards.

Of course, when we bring Paul in on the plans, he goes along with whatever we want. I think he just wants to get it over with and get on with our lives. He's happy to have me meet his extended family. He enjoys his cousins and they love to get together.

Sharon wants him to rent a tux. He puts his foot down. "No way. I'm wearing my good suit. I've only worn it once, to Ed's wedding. And that's what my best man and groomsman'll wear too. They both have dark suits."

When we're alone, parked at the beach one evening, I tell him, "I'm feeling overwhelmed with this wedding stuff, Paul. Your Mom keeps coming up with new ideas and it's making me crazy."

He sighs, and pulls me to him. "I know it's kind of getting bigger than we envisioned, Judith. But I really want my extended family there. I wish you had family you could invite. But it'll still be a small wedding by our standards. And we just have to relax and go along for the ride. Mom is loving every minute of this. You know, she feels like you and Kali are family."

"I know she's excited about the whole proceeding. I really do appreciate all she's doing. I just feel kind of lost in the whirlwind."

He chuckles. "It'll be over soon and we'll be on our way. I can't wait to have you to myself in our own home. And Kali, of course."

He takes my face gently in his hands and gives me a long, passionate kiss. I feel like my bones are melting. Finally, I pull away, before I lose control completely. My voice is shaky when I tell him, "I think we'd better head home and save some for our honeymoon."

He groans, leans back in his seat. "All right. If you insist. But I think you know what I'd rather do."

"It won't be long now, Paul. Just be patient."

So, with so much to think about, I'm pretty distracted on Kali's first day of school.

23

CHAPTER

Kali's First Day

I meet with her teacher, Mrs. Ray, beforehand, and explain Kali's circumstances to her. Her eyes grew big when I told her our story, and she teared up. "I saw much of your story in the paper, and I am so sorry Kali had to go through such a terrible event. I'll do my best to see that she fits in." I feel reassured.

Mrs. Ray's about my height, five foot nine, and sturdily built without being fat. It's hard to tell how old she is, but she has strands of silver in her hair, which she wears pinned back with a barrette. Her eyes are kind, behind dark rimmed glasses, and her voice is soft.

Sharon brings Kali in and we introduce her, so she gets to know her teacher a little bit. Mrs. Ray gives her a warm smile and holds out her hand. Kali smiles shyly and shakes her hand quickly, limply, then shrinks back, twisting her hands together. Her face flushes and she looks at the floor. Mrs. Ray speaks softly, as if Kali is a timid puppy she's trying to coax.

"Kali, I'm so looking forward to having you in my class. I know many of the students and I'm sure you'll like them. And they'll like you."

Kali nods shyly and says simply, "'Kay."

Mrs. Ray, still smiling, places her hand on Kali's shoulder. "We're going to get along famously, Kali. Come on, let me show you around."

We check out her classroom first. It's bright and cheerful, with colorful posters showing places from around the world. She's obviously worked to make it welcoming and interesting.

She points out the desk where Kali will sit, a one-piece affair with a flat surface attached to an arm piece, and a wooden seat. Kali reaches out and caresses the surface.

Then, Mrs. Ray shows Kali the cage where the class bunny lives. She's a small, soft brown and white bundle of fur. Kali is enthralled. "You'll get a turn at caring for our bunny. Would you like to pet her?"

Kali nods her head vigorously, her eyes glued on the creature. Mrs. Ray opens the cage and Kali reaches in and pets the soft fur. She grins up at Mrs. Ray. I can tell that Mrs. Ray has risen highly in Kali's estimation. Then she takes us around the building, showing us the restrooms and the gymnasium, and the cafeteria. The school goes up through eighth grade. After that, the students all go to the high school.

As we walk down the freshly waxed halls, the sights and smells suddenly trigger an attack of nostalgia and pain in me. I remember the last time I was in grade school, with my friends Monica and Maureen. "The Two M's," I called them. My eyes water and I swallow the lump in my throat. I lost so much when we went into the forest. But now, I have to concentrate on giving this experience to Kali. I don't want her to miss out on all the things I did.

Having finished the tour, we bid good-bye to Mrs. Ray. She turns to Kali. "I can't wait to see you in class next week. I'm sure you'll love it."

Kali smiles and nods. I thank Mrs. Ray for taking the time to show us around. Kali is smiling as we leave and I'm hopeful that this is going to work out. Before we head out, we check out the playground. It's a large area with swings and monkey bars and such on one end, and a baseball diamond on the other surrounded by open field. Kali yips and dashes for a swing. We each take one and spend ten minutes or so just enjoying the feel of it. I had forgotten what it feels like. Kali obviously loves it and is reluctant to leave when we have to get on our way.

As we approach the school that first day, Lucy meets up with us, as arranged. Other students wearing backpacks hurry by us. Suddenly Kali hesitates, hanging back, and clutches my hand. "Don't want to go."

"Now, Kali, we've talked about this. You know you have to go to school. You have to learn how to work with others and enjoy making friends. You're braver than anyone I know. You can do this. Lucy's here to help you. You'll be fine." I reach down and give her a big squeeze.

She looks at me, her eyes big with fear. Her lips tremble. Lucy steps up. "Kali, it's going to be fun. You'll love it. I'll be right here with you. Come on." She holds out her hand. Kali reluctantly takes her hand like it's a lifeline, and they walk into school. As they pass through the entrance, Kali looks back, gives me a wide-eyed, frightened look, but flashes me a timid smile. I smile and wave. She stoically turns and follows Lucy in.

I'm so full of trepidation for her. Will she make it through the day? Will the other students be nice to her? I spend the day fretting about it as I go through the motions of waiting on customers and chatting distractedly with my fellow workers. Cedar tries to console me. "She'll be fine, you'll see. That girl has survived much worse than the first day of school."

I sigh. "True. But you should have seen the look she gave me as she went in, like she was facing wild wolves."

"I'll bet she'll be happy as a lark when she gets home. You'll see. The first day is the worst. For you, that is."

I'm praying that she's right as my shift ends.

That afternoon, when Kali hops out of the school bus, Sharon and I are there to meet her. I put my arm across her shoulders as we walk up to the house. "So, how was your first day?"

She cocks her head, considering. Finally, she smiles faintly. "Okay."

"Just 'okay'?"

"Yes."

"How was your lunch?"

"Good."

"Did you meet new friends?"

"Yes. Janice and Arleen."

"Were they nice to you?"

"They let me eat lunch with them and Lucy."

(Wow! A whole sentence.) Sharon and I exchange glances. She asks, "What did you do at recess?"

"Swung."

"Is that what the other girls did?"

"Lucy did."

"Are you tired? Do you feel like you hiked ten miles?"

"Yeah. School's hard. Homework."

We stop grilling her as we go in the front door. Let her unwind and we will gradually get more out of her. Maybe I'll call Lucy to see how she thought it went.

Later, while Kali's doing her homework at the dining room table, and Sharon's working in her sewing room, I take the phone and slip out onto the patio. I dial Lucy's number. Her mother answers the phone. "Gerry. Hi. This is Judith. I was wondering if Lucy said anything to you about how Kali got along at school today."

"Oh, Judith. She was so excited when she got home. She said that Kali made friends with her friends, and they all had lunch together. She feels very responsible for helping Kali get along."

"I'm so grateful to her. This's been such an adjustment for my sister. You're raising a fine daughter there. She's so kind. You must be proud of her."

"Oh, yes. I'm proud of all my children. But thank you. Would you like to talk to Lucy yourself?"

"Oh, yes, that'd be great. I'd like to get her first-hand account. Kali hasn't said much, as usual."

"Hold on."

I hear her calling Lucy. She comes on the line with, "Hi Judith."

"Lucy, you were such a big help to Kali today. It was really hard for her to go into the school and I'm not sure she'd have made it without you. Thank you."

"Oh, that's okay. We did fine. I think she liked it. Mrs. Ray introduced her to the class and told everybody to make her welcome. She was quiet in class but we ate lunch together with my friends and traded desserts and hung out at recess. We had fun and my other friends like her too. We taught her how to play hopscotch. She did really good. She didn't like dodgeball though, and went and played on the swings. But I think she enjoyed that."

"It means a lot to all of us that you're so kind to her. Will you tell me if she has any trouble? I'm not sure she'd tell us. It's so important that she gets along in school."

"Sure. We're buddies. She'll be fine."

As I take the phone inside, I feel that I can stop worrying. I go to report my findings to Sharon. We've made it through the first day.

24

— CHAPTER —

The Torment Begins

The first week goes by and Kali seems to be adjusting well. She is usually cheerful when she gets off the bus, trotting up the driveway and popping through the front door with a loud, "Home."

Then, in the middle of the second week, she rushes into the house and goes immediately to her room without even saying hello. What's happened?

I hurry after her and find her lying curled up in a ball on her bed, her head facing the wall.

"Kali, what's wrong?"

No answer. I sit on the edge of her bed and put my hand on her back. "Kali, are you all right? What happened?"

Her body is shaking. I realize that she's sobbing. "Kali, Sweetie, tell me what's wrong."

No response. I pat her back and let her cry for a while, then gather her in my arms. "Did something bad happen in school today?"

She sniffles, her face twisted with pain. "The boys called me 'Dummy' and 'R–retard.' I h–hate them."

I am filled with such rage that I want to go and rattle those rotten kids' teeth out. I just hold her and try to console her. "Those boys are the dummies. You have to just ignore them and stick with your girlfriends. Stay close to Lucy. Did Mrs. Ray hear them calling you names?"

"No. At recess."

"Where were your new friends?"

Gulping sob. "Playi–ing b–ball."

"Why weren't you playing ball too?"

"Don't know how." My heart sinks. Why hadn't we thought to bring Kali up to speed on group games?

I grab a tissue off of the night stand and wipe her face. "Okay, honey, this isn't the end of the world. First of all, you ignore what boys say. You know you're not dumb. Those are just nasty words they throw out because they don't know or understand you. They're the ones who're dumb. You have Lucy and your new friends to be with. Second of all, we'll teach you how to play ball so that you can join in with the rest of the girls. What kind of ball game were they playing?"

"Ball with bats."

"Okay, we'll figure out how that works and go practice when Paul gets off of work. I sort of remember how to play that, from when I was little. I'm sure it will all come back to me. We'll have you playing like an expert in no time. How does that sound?"

She nods her head, sniffles. "Good. I *hate* those boys."

"Gramma taught us that hate doesn't help anyone and is a useless waste of energy, that it only hurts the one feeling it. What we have to do is show them that they're the ones in the wrong. You're smarter than any of'em. Can they hunt for game and skin and gut it to have something to eat? I doubt it. And I'll bet they can't talk to the birds either. You can do lots of things they can't. You know more about surviving in the wild than they'll ever know. This will pass. You just have to be strong and not let'em get to you." I give her a squeeze. "You know what? I think Sharon baked cupcakes today. Wanna go check'em out? I know for a fact that she'll let you have one."

She nods despondently, but slowly gets up and heads for the kitchen with me. Sharon is busy frosting cupcakes. She takes one look at Kali's face, glances at me. "What's wrong?"

"Kali had a run in with some mean boys today and they called her names. I thought a cupcake might help her feel better."

"Of course. But what happened, Kali? Can you tell me?" She hands Kali a pink frosted, chocolate cupcake.

Kali repeats her tale of woe between bites of her sweet treat. Sharon nods sympathetically. "You know, Kali, you haven't had to deal with people like that before. Sometimes you have to ignore meanness and just go on with your life. You will run into people like that once in a while, so you have to be strong and just be yourself. And you know, when people are cruel like that, it often means that they've been treated badly themselves. They're unhappy and want to take their anger out on someone else."

I explain how I want to teach Kali how to play softball so she can join the other girls. Sharon gets excited. "I have a ball and bats here from when Paul was young. We can practice with that. We'll go down to the beach tonight and have a game of our own. Would you like that, Kali?"

Kali smiles a hopeful smile. "Okay."

So, it comes to pass that we spend that warm September evening playing softball on the beach. Sharon and Paul and Doug help us outline a diamond with bases, and show us the rudiments of the game. I watch Paul as he shows Kali how to hold the bat and swing. My heart turns over as he patiently explains how to do it, his dark hair catching the wind as he talks, and then demonstrates it for her. His concern is so touching. He's such a good influence on Kali. He teases her as she swings and misses the ball the first couple of times. But, it turns out that Kali has an eagle eye and can smack the ball with the best of us. In fact, Paul and I both end up soaked and covered in sand as we chase after it. Sandy, Paul's dog buddy, has a great time running around and getting in the way when we're running after the ball. Once, Sandy trips Paul just as he dives for it and he ends up sprawled in the sand just as a wave comes in and catches him. We're all laughing and having a great time. Sharon runs back to the car for a towel and dry spare jacket for Paul. She's been to the beach many times, so comes prepared.

We take turns hitting, pitching, and catching in the cold sea breeze. Kali is actually having fun and we all end up winded, cold, wet and covered with sand, but happy as darkness sets in. I ask her, "Do you think you'll want to join the girls playing softball tomorrow?

She grins happily. "Yeah. It's fun."

I have to agree. I'd forgotten what fun it was to play team games. But I'm grateful when we're back in the warm house and can change into dry, clean clothes.

Another week goes by. Kali joins the other girls playing softball and seems to be having a good time and enjoying school. Until, one day when I've just walked in the door from work, the phone rings. I hear Sharon answer it.

"Hello. Yes, this is Mrs. O'Brien. You want to speak to Judith? Hold on."

She sees me standing there and holds out the phone. "It's the school. Apparently, Kali's in trouble."

Alarmed, my heart skips a beat as I grip the phone. "Hello, this is Judith."

"Ms. Johnson, this is Mrs. Holden." *The principal. Kali must really be in trouble.* "I'm afraid your sister needs to go home early today. She's been in an altercation, and is being dismissed for the rest of the day."

"Is she hurt?"

"No. Actually, she attacked one of our boys and gave him a nasty black eye and a bloody nose."

I choke back a laugh. Kali's fighting back. I clear my throat. "Can you tell me what happened?"

"If you can come and pick her up, we can discuss it when you get here."

"I'll be right there. Thank you for calling."

I hang up. Sharon looks at me with a worried frown.

"Kali's been in a fracas at school and they want me to come and get her. She's not hurt, but apparently she walloped one of the boys that've been harassing her."

Her eyebrows shoot up. "Do you want me to come?"

"It may be best if I go by myself. I don't want the principal to think that we're ganging up on her. I need to see what this's all about."

When I arrive at the principal's office, I find Kali sitting on a chair with her arms crossed and a mutinous frown on her face. She looks at me, then at the floor, but doesn't say anything.

Mrs. Holden closes the door. That's when I notice a boy with a cold pack on his face, sitting in the other corner. He's glowering at the floor too.

Mrs. Holden offers me a seat in front of her desk. I sit down. "Ms. Johnson, I'm afraid we can't have fighting going on in our school. Your sister attacked Jim, here, and gave him a black eye and bloody nose. Because of this, she will be suspended for the rest of the day."

"But what happened? She must have been provoked."

She holds up her hand. "As far as I can ascertain, Jim said something unkind to her and grabbed her sleeve. She turned around and punched him with her fist."

Jim speaks up, whining. "She kicked me in the nuts, too."

I cough to hide my impulse to laugh. "Well, it seems to me that she was defending herself. Jim's the one who should be punished, I would think."

"Oh, yes. He's being sent home too, with a stern warning. This had better not happen again. And Kali must learn to hold her temper. We just can't have physical violence in our school."

"I'm sure it won't happen again, Mrs. Holden. But I believe that Kali has a right to defend herself when attacked. These boys have been calling her names and making her life miserable. It has to stop."

"If they bother her again, please call me. I won't allow bullying in my school. I assure you I'll handle it and we won't need to resort to physical tactics."

"I will just do that. And I'm sure Kali won't cause any more trouble. Thank you for calling me." I stand up, glare at Jim, grab Kali's hand and head out the door.

In the outer office we pass a woman coming in, an angry frown on her face. She is well dressed in expensive slacks and cashmere sweater set. She pauses and looks at Kali. "Are you the girl who beat up my boy?"

Kali slides behind me. I look the woman squarely in the eyes. "Your son has been harassing her since school started. He got what he deserved. We are generally not violent, but we won't be bullied." I can feel my face heating up and my temperature rising.

She looks down her nose at me. "You're those 'wild girls,' aren't you? Well, this had better not happen again, or you will have a problem on your hands. You need to learn how to behave in civilization."

I feel the heat rising in my face. Furious, I snarl, "No, you're the one who'll have a problem. Teach your boy some manners."

I whirl and walk out of the room with Kali in tow.

At home, I ask her what Jim had done. "Called me 'dummy, 'and 'wild girl.' Grabbed my sleeve and ripped it and wouldn't let go, so I punched him."

So, we have a talk about violence and fighting. "Kali, you can't go around punching people. You should have gone to your teacher. You have every right to defend yourself, but violence only leads to more violence. It's much better to talk yourself out of the situation. You can make a joke out of it, maybe. Say something like, "I may be wild, but I'm smarter than you," and walk away. If they pick on you again, let me know, and I'll talk to the principal."

Her eyes spark, but she promises not to do it again unless she "has" to. That's good enough for me.

I call Lucy, and ask for her version of what happened. She breathlessly tells me it was all Jim's fault. She's glad Kali socked him. He's a bully and none of the girls like him. So, the girls are all on her side. This reassures me.

When I tell Paul what happened that evening, he's angry too. But he's more laid back about it. "That stinks, Judith. But these things happen and I think Kali handled it really well. Knowing boy bullies like I do, I suspect he'll be too humiliated by being beaten up by a girl to give her any more guff. If it happens again, then maybe we'll have to have a joint meeting with the principal and his parents. Don't you think? Kali seems to be okay now. And I'm actually proud of her for popping the guy. I'd love to have seen his face."

So, I follow his lead and let the issue drop for the time. We'll see how it goes.

Kali misses half a day of school, but after that things seem to have smoothed out. She promises to tell me if the bullying starts up again. Jim seems to avoid her, which is good. She is adapting to being around others her own age.

Meanwhile, Sharon is determined to take over our wedding. She insists that I have at least one bridesmaid as well as a maid of honor. So, I ask Beth to be my bridesmaid. She's thrilled and says, "yes, I'd love to," almost before I have the words out of my mouth. Kali will be my maid of honor. She, too, is very excited and practically elevates off the floor when I ask her, jumping up and down, clapping her hands and yelling, " Yaaayyyy!"

We pick out material for their dresses, pastel blue for Kali and darker blue for Beth, and patterns, and Sharon sets to work sewing them. I protest that it's too much work for her, but she is adamant that she wants to do it. "I always dreamed of having a wonderful wedding for a daughter I didn't get to have. Please let me do this, Judith. I love it and it makes me happy."

"That's really generous of you, Sharon. But don't forget that we're keeping it simple."

"Oh, I know. But that doesn't mean it can't be nice. It'll be beautiful, you'll see. By the way, don't forget that we're going to the bakery tomorrow to pick out the cake. And we'll have the reception in the hall afterwards, and I'm thinking we'll have it catered by Bayside Cafe. What do you think?"

I'm feeling pressured and frustrated. "I think it's getting too elaborate. And expensive." Paul and I are splitting the expenses so he needs to be in on this too.

"The wedding's at eleven and we just want a quick reception afterwards so we have time to head out on our trip. Can't we just have sandwiches and cake?"

Paul and I plan to drive up the coast for four days for our honeymoon, staying at different places. Then we need to return so I can start work at Cheryl's.

However, the crestfallen expression on Sharon's face gives me pause.

She persists, "But Judith, we can't just have sandwiches. We have to have some decent food at least, it'll be lunchtime. And wine and coffee and punch. I can make a big batch of those wonderful hors d'oeuvres that we made for the party." She's getting excited again. "Oh, and we need music. Do you think we should hire a Deejay? It'd be fun."

Now I'm really getting uptight, pressured and frustrated. Fighting to remain calm and reasonable, I put my foot down. "I think a Deejay would be too expensive. Why can't people just sit around and talk? I didn't realize that getting married was so complicated. I just thought coffee and cake was plenty." My voice is rising. "You're making me crazy, Sharon. Can't we just calm down? I don't want us to get all stressed out." I take a deep breath and try to relax.

She sighs and looks sad, her lips tightening. Regrouping, she says, quietly, "I just want my baby's wedding to be special, and to make it beautiful for the two of you. Can't you understand that?"

I feel mean, depriving her of her special occasion. Only, it's supposed to be our special occasion, isn't it? Nevertheless, I cave. "I'm sorry, Sharon. I know it means a lot to you too. I'll follow your lead. I've never been to a wedding before, let alone planned one. I really appreciate all your help. But please, no Deejay. And let's keep the lunch simple. Just sandwiches, and salad? Can't the Altar Society ladies do it? No fancy dishes. I'll help you make the hors d'ouvres. And can't we make our own wedding cake?"

Her eyes grow big and she's excited again. "Oh, Doug and I want to give you and Paul a beautiful cake for a wedding present. Can't we at least do that much?"

"If you really want to do that, we'll appreciate it, I'm sure. But please keep the rest simple. I'm really not a fussy type of girl. Okay?"

She gives me a radiant smile. "Oh, sure. I realize that. You won't be sorry. It'll be lovely, you'll see. I'm sure the Altar Society ladies can do a nice luncheon for us. And we can still make my party treats. And we'll just use some canned music on Paul's portable player for the reception. Would that be all right?"

"That sounds fine. Thanks, Sharon."

"We'll also need a photographer. Perhaps Paul could handle that?"

"That's a good idea. He needs to be more involved. He's asked Peter to be his best man and Bob to be his groomsman."

"Are you sure you don't have any family to invite? Relatives of your grandmother, perhaps? Or your parents?"

"None that I know of. My father's family disowned him when he married my mother. They called her a "dirty Indian." I don't want anything to do with them. Grandma was an only child, as was Mamma, so it's a dead end there. I don't know about my grandfather's side of the family. There's the gang from the cafe I would like to invite. And Cheryl and Aaron and Lucy's family. I think a minute. "You know, there is someone else I would like to invite. I'm related to him in a way. We come from the same tribe. I'd like to invite Virgil and his wife. Would that be appropriate, do you think?"

She hesitates, then, "Your tribal roots are important to you. Yes, I think that would be very appropriate."

So, I send an invitation to Virgil, and he calls to say that he'll come. "Sure, we'd be glad to come to your wedding, Judith. It'd be an honor."

Tears come to my eyes. I've been wanting to dig into my tribal connections to honor the memory of my Gramma and mother. I need to fill in the blanks of my heritage.

25

— CHAPTER —

Kali's Triumph

Paul and I have been busy. We've searched for a house big enough for the three of us, and finally found a small, two-bedroom rental that seems just right. It only has one bathroom, but that's not a problem. After living with an outhouse for so many years, an indoor bathroom is a luxury to me. The kitchen is small but well laid out and cheerful, with a stove and refrigerator. We may want to paint the bedrooms and living room and the landlord is okay with that. It has a fenced yard for the pets. And it has a garage, which makes Paul happy. We pay first and last month's rent and Paul moves his things into it.

Kali and I don't have much to move, so will do it a little at a time before the wedding. I'm thinking, maybe we can go back to our wilderness cabin some day and haul out Gramma's rocking chair and a few other things, like Mamma's teapot, and her favorite cast iron skillet. I take some of the items we won't need right away—warmer winter clothes, boots, bedding, into our new home and linger as I imagine our lives here. I feel an enormous sense of joy and gratitude.

Together, Paul and I spend our spare time shopping for things we'll need—a bed and dresser for Kali, a table and chairs for the dining area. We share similar taste in furnishings, comfort and sturdiness our top requirements, plus good looks. Second hand stores are a magnet for me. Gradually, our home takes shape and I am getting anxious to move in. I take Kali to the paint store so she can pick out the color she wants in her room. She's excited and spends at least forty minutes picking out a soft, mossy shade of green. Paul and I spend several nights painting our bedroom and living room walls in clean, warm white, and soft grey colors, then tackle her room. We turn the music on full blast and have a ball. It's often midnight before I get home to bed, reluctantly leaving Paul behind to sack out in our soon-to-be home.

We finish our marriage consultations with Father Phillips. I really like this kindly priest. He would never send his flock to hide in the wilderness, like Pastor Roberts did.

Paul seems to be in a fog about the wedding. When I bring up the many details to be decided, his eyes glaze over. Food, drinks, colors, dress—these are too many petty decisions. He'd be happy to leave it all up to his mother. However, he has engaged a photographer, so that's one thing off the list.

I tell him about my disagreement with Sharon over the music and food. He agrees with me that a Deejay is too much. When I fret about how the guest list has grown beyond what I anticipated, he does his best to soothe me. He puts his arms around me, rests his chin on my head. "Honey, this is the event of a lifetime for us and for Mom. She is so thrilled to be included. I think she's remembering the girl babies she lost and this kind of eases that pain." He stands back. "And you really don't want to have to handle all these arrangements, do you? She'll help us make it special so we can just relax and enjoy it. And don't worry about it getting out of hand. I'll have a chat with her. Maybe I can calm her down."

I felt better about it after that, and Paul did talk to his mother and asked her to tone it down a bit. After that, Sharon consulted with me before she went through with any new ideas she had for the occasion—"Shall we ask Lucy to be a flower girl? And her little sister? No?

"Maybe just Lucy." *We're keeping it simple, remember?*

"Okay, um how about tuxes for the guys? Still no? Okay. We'll go with dark suits. Oh—and I'll have to make a dress for Lucy too. That'll be fun." And so it went.

During all the excitement and planning, I'm still working at the cafe. I have handed in my notice that I'm leaving after the wedding. I could tell my boss was unhappy, but he accepted it and told me that he was sorry to lose me, but hoped I'd enjoy my future employment.

Ce is looking forward to coming to the wedding with her boyfriend. My boss and some of the rest of the staff will be there too. There's a lot of joking between the staff and me about what married life will be like. "Wait'll he starts explaining to you stuff you already know." "You'll be sorry when you have to pull his stinky socks out of the laundry." And so on.

Our friends surprise us with a wedding shower the weekend before the big event. Paul and I arrive at his parents' house from running errands, and I'm thinking of helping Sharon with dinner. We notice a couple of cars parked in front of the shed. Paul says, "Wonder who that could be?"

When we walk in I'm shocked by people shouting, "Surprise." It's Beth, Robert, Grace and Jack, the whole forest service gang, along with Cheryl and Aaron and Al and Gerry Lucas, and Cedar and my cafe work friends. There are balloons and a big sign that says, "Congratulations!" hanging on the wall. There's a stack of presents on a side table, and the air is redolent with the fragrance of pot luck dishes. I almost burst into tears. Now I know we are truly part of the community. Paul puts his arm around my shoulders. I sniff, "Did you know about this?"

He grins at me. "Gotcha, didn't we?" He indicates the group with a sweep of his hand, and puts his arm around me. "They all wanted to do this so I went along with it. I hope you like it?"

I lean against him. "I'm flabbergasted. Thank you so much."

Everybody starts talking at once and soon we're feasting on the delicious dishes that have been laid out. We spend the evening opening the presents, with Sharon keeping tabs on who gave what. There are many items we really need—a crock pot, table linens, towels, sheet sets, even dishtowels and pot holders. There are so many things needed to set up a new household. This will be a big help.

People start leaving around ten o'clock, and we are inundated with hugs and well wishes as they head out the door. I've never felt so much a part of an extended family as I do now. As I survey the pile of gifts I can't keep back the tears. It's wonderful to feel so accepted and loved. Paul holds me close until I calm down. "Gee, if I'd known it would make you cry, I'd never have gone along with this," he teases.

"These are happy tears, I'll have you know." I give him a quick kiss and push him away, "Now let's help your Mom clean up this mess. There's dishes and wrapping paper all over the place."

He rolls his eyes. "Okay. But only if you stop crying."

The Monday before our wedding, Kali comes home from school, plops her backpack on the dining room table, and walks with her head down into the kitchen. Sharon and I are busy making snacks for the wedding. With my hands full of phyllo dough, I smile at Kali and say, "Hi, Kali. Why the long face? How was school today?"

She leans her elbow on the counter, her chin resting in her hand. "Okay, I guess. But teacher wants us all to talk in front of the whole class. I'm scared. I don't know how."

"What kind of talk?"

"Has to be three minutes. About pets or something we like."

"That's a long time for you to talk. Maybe I can come up with an idea for you. You know a lot about animals. Probably more than any of the other kids. Why don't you have a glass of milk and a snack and start on your other homework? When I'm done here we'll see what we can figure out."

As I work, I'm thinking. What could Kali possibly do to impress her class? She's getting better and better at expressing herself verbally, but she's never had to stand up in front of a room full of people and talk. She's naturally shy. This will be really hard for her. On the other hand, it may be a chance to be seen as something other than an oddity. It will be a challenge. As I mull it over, the perfect idea pops into my mind.

"Kali, I'm done in the kitchen now. I have an idea for what you can do. Wanna go to the library with me?

She looks up from her book, eyebrows raised, eyes big. "Really? Sure. What idea?"

"I'll show you when we get there."

At the library, I ask the librarian where we might find illustrated bird books. She takes us to the small section where there are a number of large nature books. We pick out one that has beautiful pictures of Northwest birds. Kali's eyes light up and she flashes a big smile. We find a place in a corner with a table and I explain to her, "You can talk about the birds you know, and what kinds of food they like, and show the pictures. Many of these are birds we've seen in the Kalmiopsis. You can mimic their calls as you hold up the pictures. That way, you won't have to talk so much. I'm sure the other students will be impressed by your bird calls. Don't you think?"

She nods emphatically, grinning. "Good idea." She clasps the book to her chest. "Let's check it out."

"First, let's see if we can get photocopies of the birds you want to display. That'd be easier than holding up the book."

"Okay. Good idea."

We ask the librarian to make enlarged copies of ten of the most familiar birds. At five cents a page it's a bargain. Then we take the pages and check out the book. She suggests that we could use poster board to support the pictures. I've never heard of that. She tells us we can get it at the drug store. "Wow! That's good to know. Thanks so much."

On the way home, we pick up three sheets of it.

We cut up the poster board and glue the pictures to it. Since the copies are in black and white, Kali colors the birds to show their natural colors. Then she practices her spiel in front of Sharon and me several times. She holds up a picture, "I love birds. This is the eagle. It sounds like ..." and then she produces an exact replica of the eagle's warbled squeal. It eats ... "This is Golden Crowned Sparrow, sounds like..." and imitates the sparrow's high-pitched whistle. "This is the Osprey ..." loud, piercing scream. "This is the Thrush ..." the thrush's warbling song fills the air, then the tiny "chit-chit-chit" of the hummingbird. She manages to produce the sounds of ten of our local birds. She's even mastered the cries of the seagulls. Pointing to each bird in turn, she describes what each bird likes to eat and where they live. It's brilliant.

Sharon loves it, clapping loudly. "Oh, Kali, that's fantastic. You'll be great. Your class and teacher will be so impressed."

That Friday, I keep busy with wedding preparations, my mind split between the wedding and Kali's presentation. I'm so worried it won't be as well accepted as it was by Sharon and me.

When Kali comes home, she's beaming. She runs up the driveway and pops into the house. As she plops her bookbag on the table, I ask, "Well, how did it go, Kali? Did the teacher like your presentation? Did the other kids?"

She waves her hands. "It was g–great. Everybody excited when I did bird calls. Mrs. Ray said "wonderful." Kids all c–clapped."

Sharon's standing nearby at the kitchen sink. She claps her hands above her head in a winner gesture. "Woo-woo, Kali. You rule!"

"Yay," I yell. I grab her and lift her off her feet, giving her a big hug. "Good job, Kali. I knew you could do it."

She hugs me back. "Thanks for the idea, Judy. Hungry. What's to eat?"

She snacks on peanut butter and toast with jam and milk, and then runs out to see her cats.

I look at Sharon. I could almost cry. "I'm so proud of her I could pop."

She laughs. "So could I."

Filled with relief for Kali's sake, now I can concentrate on the wedding. It's onward to the rehearsal this evening. Then a get-together at the house where I'll meet Paul's cousins and aunts and uncles. My stomach quakes at the thought. It will be a long night.

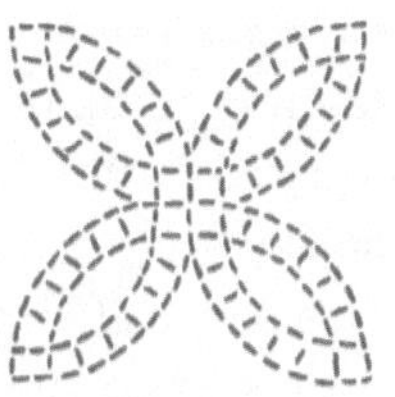

26
CHAPTER

The Wedding

I wake up in the morning before dawn with a flurry of butterflies in my stomach. The rehearsal really brought home to me the fact that I'm getting married. I slept sporadically last night. My brain just couldn't rest. Were the flowers in place? I don't like being the center of attention. Can I keep my cool through the service? Is everything done that needs to be done? Will the weather hold? Am I really going through with this?

This will be a long day. I bolt down a little breakfast and head out to the woods behind the house before the rest of the household is up. I need some time alone with my thoughts. I breathe in the woodsy smells, cedar and fir and earth and moss. To me it's the smell of *green*, of *home*. I think about the step I'm about to take, wishing my family could be with me. I hope they are aware of what I'm doing and approve. I sit on the soft moss and listen to the trees whisper around me. Gradually, peace settles in my soul. I say a prayer, asking God to bless us and help me to be a good wife. Finally, calmed in mind and spirit, I head back to the house.

The rest of the family is up, and after greeting them, I spend the rest of the morning getting dressed and fussing with my hair. Sharon flits about, helping Kali and me get into our finery. Beth comes over at eight thirty and gets into her bridesmaid dress. She helps me to put on a little makeup—a little eyeliner and lipstick and a quick powder of my nose. That's all I'll endure.

Beth and Kali look beautiful in their simple blue dresses. We work with Kali's hair too, and, with Sharon's help, place a pretty circlet of violets and daisies on her hair. Her eyes are sparkling and she's practically dancing on her toes, bouncing around us with impatience as we primp. "Isn't it time to go?"

"Just another half hour, Kali. I don't want Paul to see me until we're ready to walk down the aisle."

The girls watch as I place the finger-tip veil with its circlet of tiny white roses on my head. I look in the mirror. Today I feel truly beautiful. They all "ooh" and "ah" as they look on. My heart is so full.

There's one more finishing touch I need. I reach into the drawer where I have my few treasures. Taking out my mother's locket, I open it and look at my parents. My eyes tear up. They will be with me today. I place the chain around my neck. It's perfect with my dress.

Sharon, wearing a pretty, lacy peachy colored dress, sniffs. "Oh, Judith, that's lovely. And you make such a beautiful bride."

I turn and give her a hug. "We'd never have made it to this day without you, Sharon. I can't thank you enough. I love you."

She pulls me closer. "I love you too. You're going to make Paul a wonderful wife." She checks her watch. "I think we'd better get on our way. Don't want to be late."

We gather in the living room. Doug's looking handsome in a dark suit. It's the first time I've seen him dressed so formally.

When I had asked him to walk me down the aisle his eyes misted up, and he said, "Of course, I'd love to do that, Judith." He gave me an awkward hug. He's not prone to showing a lot of emotion, but I could see that he was moved by my gesture. I've learned to read his stoic features, and I've come to love this man like a father. He's been nothing but kind to us from the day we entered his home.

Finally, we all assemble and head out in two cars. I won't be driving this morning. I'm trembling all the way to the church.

Sharon is escorted to her seat. She has asked the church musicians, an organist and a guitarist, to play Pachelbel's "Cannon" for the entry. I had never heard it before the rehearsal the night before. It's so beautiful. When the organ softly begins to play, I can't keep the tears from my eyes. Beth and Kali head slowly down the aisle. Then Doug offers me his arm with a big smile and we head in. He pats my hand and comes to attention, facing straight ahead. I look up and see Paul, standing there, strong and tall, with a big smile on his face. He looks so handsome in a dark suit, I barely notice the groomsmen behind him. My heart is beating so fast I feel like I'm vibrating. As we proceed slowly down the aisle, my smile feels rigid as I work to keep it from trembling. My small bouquet is quivering in my hand. Paul steps out to meet me and I see the emotion in his face, his eyes glistening. I am suffused by love and yearning to be with him for the rest of my life. As we face the priest, I know that I've made the right choice. I'm in a daze as the ceremony goes by like a wonderful dream. We repeat our vows, and exchange the simple, matching gold rings that we had picked out together. When the priest says, "You may kiss the bride," Paul gives me a big kiss and the congregation claps. We head down the aisle as Mr. and Mrs. Paul O'Brien.

The photographer is all over the place, taking pictures of the wedding party and, once assembled, the receiving line.

As we stand and greet the guests in line after the ceremony, I'm pleased to greet Virgil and meet his wife, Jennie. (I later find out that Jennie was named after Jennie Clinton, the last survivor of the Modoc War.) I feel like a little bit of my Gramma is here to witness the biggest event in my life.

As the party proceeds, with food served buffet style, I am so grateful to Sharon for all her work and planning. It turns out that everyone has a wonderful time, and there is much joy and laughter. The chatter gets ever louder as the wine flows, and over the clatter of the dishes, we hear the tinkling of a knife against a wine glass. The best man, Peter, stands up to give a toast.

As he rambles on, talking about what a great guy Paul is, all I can think of is that I am ready to get out of here. Then I tune in to what he's saying. "We were all thinking that Paul was destined to be a permanent bachelor until he took a trip into the Kalmiopsis and fell right into the arms of a beautiful woman. I suspect he thoroughly enjoyed being cared for by her and her sister. He'd probably be there today if he hadn't been forced by circumstances to leave." Pause for a laugh— "Anyway, we're really glad Judith found him and that he found her. May they live happily ever after. Let's drink a toast to the bride and groom."

Paul puts his arm around me and gives me a smooch. I can feel my face heat up with embarrassment. There was a toast by Doug, and a couple more of Paul's friends. Finally, we cut the cake and it's distributed to the guests. After that, it's time to go.

We embrace Paul's parents and Kali. Kali will stay with Sharon and Doug for the duration of our honeymoon, then we'll all be back in our little house. Kali clings to me for a few seconds.

"Love you, Judy."

"I love you too, Sweetie. We'll be back before you know it. Okay?"

She nods, gives me a tremulous smile. Sharon puts her arm around her. "Don't worry, Judith. We'll have a good time while you two are away."

I've been told to toss my bouquet over my shoulder, so that's what I do. Beth catches it, leaping in front of the other young women, to my glee. She'll be the next bride.

Paul and I hop into his truck, which has been tricked out with "Just Married" printed along the sides, and tin cans tied to the rear bumper. We roar off and leave the party behind. We drive up to our new home and change clothes quickly, then switch to my car, which contains our luggage, and proceed up the highway. Our first night's stop is in Yachats. We stay at a place right on the water, where we can hear the waves crashing into the rocky shore. Once inside our room, we set down our luggage and, finally alone, are in each other's arms.

Paul rasps, "I've waited so long for this."

"Me too. You don't know how many times I've dreamed of our first night together." We just stand and hold each other for a long time.

He whispers in my ear, "Are you nervous?"

"Yes." Actually, I'm quivering.

"Well, we have all the time in the world. I promise to be gentle with you, Judith. I love you so much." He steps back. "It's still early. Would you like to take a walk along the shoreline?"

I gulp. "I'd like that."

We step out for a stroll along the rocky waterline, into our new world, together. Paul, pauses and smiles down at me. "Are you tired? Wanna go for a run?"

"Let's. A short one."

We take off, running along the path that follows the shoreline. After what seems like a mile or so, we slow down and plop down on the turf, watching the waves. My nerves have calmed down as a feeling of anticipation builds up inside me. He pulls me into his arms and we share a passionate kiss. Finally, I push him away. "Let's go back." As we head back to our unit, I know I'm ready to embrace the passion and love that I've been waiting for my whole life.

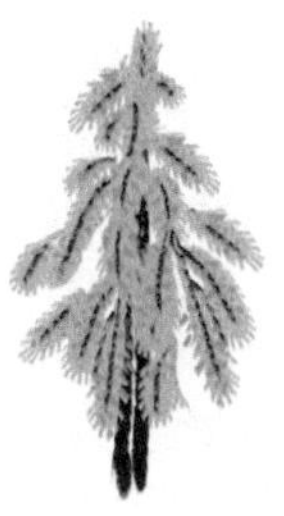

EPILOGUE

In the six years since our wedding we've purchased our own small spread in a sweet valley north of town. After working for Cheryl for three years, and learning all I could about goat dairying, I sold Gramma's place in Klamath Falls and we purchased our own property here. Cheryl and I parted on good terms, as she found a young man to take my place. We've formed a partnership, marketing our cheeses and milk together.

Our low, ranch style house sits on a hillside, overlooking the lush, green bottomland that spreads out below. We have twelve milking goats, one Billy, and three little kids, plus our goats from the Kalmiopsis. The eldest, Mabel, along with our beloved Amigo, is living in happy retirement with the rest of our herd. She's too old to breed and I can't just put her down. I think she's a calming influence on the rest of the herd. It hurt when old Fret passed away a couple of years ago. We buried him in our pet cemetery, in a distant corner of the back yard. We had a little ceremony, to calm our mourning Kali, and said a prayer as we put him in the ground. It took Kali a long time to get over her sadness. But our new, young, mixed-breed mutt, Blackie (Kali's choice), watches over the herd, along with Sandy, Paul's dog. Together, they shepherd them in for the milking. We've added a young pup, a black and white shepherd mix of unknown origin, named Streak, because she runs so fast, to our menagerie and are training her to help with the goats. Sandy mentors her and she joyfully follows her lead, and loves to play with the children.

Kali was delighted to welcome our two children, John Douglas, (named after our fathers), age four, and Sharon Fern, (after our mothers), age two and a half. Kali was a big help in caring for the children until she went off to college. She was a straight A student in high school, and has many friends. We had a bit of a rough patch when she got into her teens, as she didn't like some of my restrictions on her and was sometimes rebellious. She hung out with her girlfriends and went through crushes on boys, which she did not want to discuss with me. Probably just as well, as I hadn't had that experience living out in the wild.

Her love of animals never left her, and over the years she nursed a series of wounded creatures back to health—birds, squirrels, even a young fox once. She'd find a bird with a broken wing or injury and tenderly nurse it back to health. The same applied to any wild creature she came across that needed help. Occasionally one would die, and we had a small burial plot in the back yard where she would sadly bury it. She was a great help in the delivery of our baby goats, and tended the dogs' sore paws, and cared for our various cats. If any of our nannies developed a problem she was the first to notice.

By the time Kali was a junior, she really got serious about her studies, and ran for class president. After that she was voted prom queen, and then, her senior year, was the valedictorian of her class. She spoke clearly, slowly, congratulating her fellow classmates, talking about what was ahead for them. In her closing, she thanked her teachers and Sharon and Doug. Then she brought me to tears when she said, "My biggest debt of gratitude goes to my sister, Judith. She took care of me my whole life, from the time I was a baby. She gave me the love of a mother as well as a sister, helped me cope with years in the wilderness, and taught me how to be and how to live. I will be forever grateful to her, and love her." She pointed to me and said, "Stand up Judith. My accomplishments are your accomplishments." Everyone turned to look at me. I was so embarrassed and yet so proud. They all applauded loudly, cheering. I stood up, my face burning, and bobbed my head, and sat back down.

I was so proud of her, and could barely see through my tears, and felt such a heart full of love. She had come from not speaking at all to actually speaking in front of the whole school.

My baby sister is making up for her years of silence. She's still not a big talker but she speaks normally now, and often makes a crack out of the blue that makes us laugh. She's at Oregon State and wants to be a veterinarian. She'll be a great one. Kali was homesick at first but has made friends and seems quite happily settled now. I call her every week to keep in touch, and she sounds cheerful. I miss her terribly. I can't wait to see her during Christmas break.

Sharon and Doug are doting grandparents, and are always happy to have the kids at their house for a sleep-over. It gives Paul and me a chance to have some "us" time occasionally. Sharon was an invaluable help when the babies were born and my source of information on everything from nursing to teething. Sharon casually gives us lots of advice on how to raise them, ("You shouldn't let them sleep with you." "There's stuff you can buy to put on his thumb to keep him from sucking it," etc.,) and we always listen, sometimes even following her suggestions.

As for me, I have renewed my ties to the Modoc tribe, and love attending their gatherings every year. I've learned a lot more about our native lore and natural resources. Virgil and his family have become good friends. My mother and grandmother had registered me with the Klamath tribe when I was born, and I finally managed to get Kali registered too. That way, she could get grants for her college tuition to add to her scholarship winnings.

I planted my little sapling, which, I've learned is a weeping spruce, in a quiet corner of our backyard. It's nearly fifteen feet tall now. I've placed a little concrete bench beneath it. If I'm troubled by anything, or sad or anxious, I go and sit there and it calms my spirit, just as its mother tree did in the Kalmiopsis. I will always be connected to that place.

Paul and I made one last trip into the Kalmiopsis to my cabin. We took in a pack mule and Amigo with us and brought out Gramma's rocker, plus a little bench that my father had made, and Mama's teapot, her favorite cast iron skillet, and a rag rug and quilt, plus a shawl that my grandmother had knitted. We made love in my parents' bed, and I believe that's when Sharon Fern was conceived. It seems fitting to me that we have another connection with that place. And I'm happy to have some family history in my house.

My love for Paul gets deeper every day as we settle into our life here. We have our differences, but we talk them out. We have a pact to never go to bed angry. He has opinions about how I could manage the business better. I don't always take kindly to what I see as interference. His suggestions usually start with, "You oughta ..." Or, "Maybe you should ..." Sometimes I agree, sometimes I don't. When I need his advice, he always has good ideas. He's willing to pitch in with whatever needs doing. He's a great Dad and attentive to the kids. We enjoy fishing and hiking when we can get away, and every year we plant a big garden together. He still works for the Forest Service, and we have a busy social life between our church friends and our work friends. And we've taken up square dancing at the local grange, twice a month. It's great exercise and fun with a group of sociable people. However, I find that my solitary life in the wilderness has left me with a permanent feeling of unease when it comes to large social gatherings. I'm happiest when home alone with my family and occasional visits with friends.

I try to get into the public library once every week or two, to check out more books. I am so far behind in my knowledge of the world and literature. I love reading and spend whatever spare time I can find with my nose in books. I'll never run out of things to learn.

I'm training one of Lucy's younger sisters, Anne, to help with the goats. In the future, I'm hoping I can lead excursions into the forests and up the streams and rivers in our part of the state to teach people how to forage for natural foods. I'm planning that Annie can take over for me when I'm away for a day or two.

Little Johnny and Sharie love the goats too. They follow me out to the barn and "help" with feeding the babies and get underfoot during the milking. I love having them with me and they have a great relationship with the animals, especially with the little kids. The children can be distracting but I have a clean pen where I can put them if they get too out of hand. They enjoy playing with their toys in there.

As I stand on my hillside and look out over my little kingdom, I realize that I have the best of all worlds. I'm surrounded by nature, but I'm no longer alone. I have a family I adore and will be there for me, no matter what. My new-found faith has brought me peace and comfort. I think my parents would be happy for Kali and me. I am content.

- THE END -

ABOUT THE AUTHOR

Theresa Verboort was born in Coos Bay, Oregon, and grew up in the southwestern coast during the fifties. She worked in forest fire lookouts in the summers to earn her way through college to achieve a bachelor of arts in English. Her first novel, *The Communing Tree*, inspired by the Kalmiopsis Wilderness of Oregon, won the prestigious WILLA Literary Award for best young adult fiction of 2019. *A Sapling Grows* continues the story.

———

If you would like to receive news about A Sapling Grows and blog post updates from the author, please subscribe to Theresa's mailing list at www.theresavwrites.com

www.ingramcontent.com/pod-product-compliance
Lightning Source LLC
Chambersburg PA
CBHW020109310726
48970CB00002B/542